The
THIRD
DAUGHTER

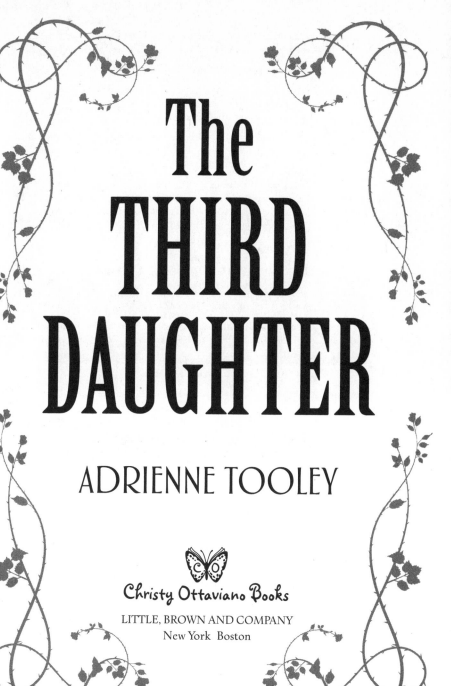

The
THIRD
DAUGHTER

ADRIENNE TOOLEY

Christy Ottaviano Books

LITTLE, BROWN AND COMPANY
New York Boston

Cover art copyright © 2023 by Gemma O'Brien. Cover design by Karina Granda. Cover copyright © 2023 by Hachette Book Group, Inc. Interior design by Michelle Gengaro.

Christy Ottaviano Books
Hachette Book Group
1290 Avenue of the Americas, New York, NY 10104
Visit us at LBYR.com

First Edition: July 2023

Christy Ottaviano Books is an imprint of Little, Brown and Company. The Christy Ottaviano Books name and logo are trademarks of Hachette Book Group, Inc.

The publisher is not responsible for websites (or their content) that are not owned by the publisher.

Little, Brown and Company books may be purchased in bulk for business, educational, or promotional use. For information, please contact your local bookseller or Hachette Book Group Special Markets Department at special.markets@hbgusa.com.

Library of Congress Cataloging-in-Publication Data
Names: Tooley, Adrienne, author.
Title: The third daughter / Adrienne Tooley.
Description: First edition. | New York : Little, Brown and Company, 2023. | Audience: Ages 14–18. | Summary: When Elodie and Sabine mistakenly put Velle's young queen, and Elodie's sister, in a coma, they must find a way to wake her before Elodie's siblings learn the truth and Sabine loses her magic—and herself—to the darkness that threatens her if she cannot find an outlet for her sadness.
Identifiers: LCCN 2022030347 | ISBN 9780316465694 (hardcover) | ISBN 9780316465854 (ebook)
Subjects: CYAC: Magic—Fiction. | Birth order—Fiction. | Sadness—Fiction. | Lesbians—Fiction. | Fantasy. | LCGFT: Fantasy fiction. | Lesbian fiction. | Romance fiction. | Novels.
Classification: LCC PZ7.1.T6264 Th 2023 | DDC [E]—dc23
LC record available at https://lccn.loc.gov/2022030347

ISBNs: 978-0-316-46569-4 (hardcover), 978-0-316-46585-4 (ebook)

Printed in the United States of America

LSC-C

Printing 1, 2023

To those who stagger beneath the weight of
expectations and emotions,
who worry they're too much, or not enough.
This one's for you.

PART ONE

*Before the New Maiden ushered in the light, She promised
her Favoreds She would return. "You will know me," She
said, "as a third daughter's third daughter. My spirit will
live on in the body of another."*

*"Maiden," asked Petra, who had been Her friend even
before She revived the Lower Banks, "why must You go?"*

*"I have done what I needed to do." The New Maiden touched
Her best friend's cheek. "Our time, though brief, was bright."*

*"Maiden." Mol gripped their sword with white knuckles.
"When will You return?"*

*"When the world needs me," She answered, tenderly
removing Her follower's hand from their weapon, "though I
know not when that time will come."*

*"Maiden," said Sebastien, who stood day and night by
Her side, "why will the world require Your homecoming?"*

*"I see the future," the New Maiden said, turning toward
Her most devoted disciple, "and it is bleak. I will return to
cleanse the world. To heal my people. To revive my word."*

—Book of the New Maiden,
verse 333

1

O n the final day of mourning, the wind shifted west, and the third daughter of a third daughter took the throne. Watching from above was the slighted eldest sister, clutching the balcony's divider with white knuckles as the Chaplain placed a crown atop the maiden-queen's head.

Elodie was pissed.

Her brother, Rob, placed a hand on her arm in warning. At sixteen, he was only thirteen months her junior and therefore much too perceptive of Elodie's moods. She smiled placidly, hoping to appease him, but she could feel his gaze burning a hole in her empty expression as she stared down at the Chaplain, who was leading a spirited rendition of "Prayer for the Virgin Maiden." The choice of hymn was a bit too on the nose for Elodie's liking.

The Queen of Velle had passed only three days prior, yet her crown was already perched atop the head of another. Elodie's youngest sister, Brianne, was merely thirteen years old—with bumbling, pitifully earnest energy that made the courtiers titter and her siblings roll their eyes. But Velle had been waiting nearly three hundred years for the New Maiden to return, and now She had: as Brianne Elisabet, the third daughter of third daughter Tera Warnou, the late Queen of Velle.

The Church of the New Maiden had practically fallen over themselves rewriting the laws of inheritance. Before the ink of Brianne's birth announcement had even dried, the entire country knew that one day she would take the throne and—according to prophecy—clean, revive, and heal the world.

Elodie thought that was quite a lofty promise, all things considered.

"That crown is too big for her head," Rob laughed goodnaturedly as he peered down at Brianne. The slight waif of a girl was dressed in a lavish gown of aubergine, cinched at the waist and fanning out like water falling over the edge of a cliff. The careful gold stitching glimmered in the afternoon light that poured through the church's northwest window.

"Not for long, the way people keep fawning over her," Elodie muttered, looking down at her own gown of gray, its subtle silver thread hardly a mark of distinction. In Velle, the queen's first daughter was supposed to inherit the crown, but Elodie's role as the heir apparent was short-lived. She'd been only four years old when she was cast aside for the prophesied Third Daughter. Now seventeen, Elodie ought to be used to their altered hierarchy. Yet moments like this one left her smarting.

"Be nice, El," Cleo piped up from her left. The middle Warnou sister was caught between loyalties. "She looks beautiful." Tears of joy glimmered in the fifteen-year-old's eyes as she stared down at

Brianne, yet her body was still turned decidedly toward Elodie, as a silent but stalwart supporter.

"I'm never nice," Elodie snapped. "Only honest."

But the truth left a sour taste on her tongue. That honesty— a trait that should have confirmed her place beside Brianne as Queen's Regent—had instead relegated Elodie to the balcony during the most important political event of her lifetime.

The Chaplain banged his scepter against the stone floor three times as the assembly completed their hymn.

"All hail the queen," he called, his voice sharp as a wasp's sting. His beard was threaded with silver, his hair carefully combed. His attendants were draped in long white robes, their sashes the same aubergine as Brianne's dress, a reminder that the new queen was permitted to don Her holy colors.

But then, she wasn't *just* the queen.

"Long live the New Maiden," the crowd answered back.

Elodie held her tongue. As though the Chaplain could hear her silence, he cast a glance upward to the balcony where the royal family sat. His icy blue eyes snagged hers like knees against gravel. His expression was triumphant as he curled his long-nailed fingers protectively around Brianne's shoulder.

I win, his eyes seemed to say. As though the crown resting atop the head of his daughter wasn't proof enough of his victory.

"I just can't decide," Brianne had admitted to Elodie the afternoon before, as she stirred sugar into her tea. The sisters had taken lunch in the queen's chambers. "You're so clever, of course," Brianne continued, the knot in Elodie's stomach tightening with every clink of her sister's spoon, "but my father said—"

Elodie had held up a hand. "Bri, your father is the head of the Church. What he says stands to serve only his allegiances, not ours."

Brianne had frowned. "But isn't everyone's allegiance to the New Maiden? The crown only exists to serve the Church."

Elodie had gritted her teeth. Of course her sister would think that. Brianne had been educated by the clergy folk, immersed in the Church of the New Maiden's word since birth. She had not been given the chance to develop the nuance required to rule a country. Velle demanded an unbiased regent, someone grounded who could see beyond prophecies and false loyalties.

After watching the Church indoctrinate her youngest daughter, Queen Tera had committed herself to untangling the interests of Church and crown. It was an effort Brianne and her father had not been privy to.

An effort that would disappear like hot breath on cold glass now that Elodie's dearly departed mother lay buried in the ground—unless her eldest daughter was chosen as Queen's Regent and finished what her mother had begun.

"Your father is lying to you, Brianne," Elodie had said, frustration loosening her tongue. "You're a pretty pawn in his game and nothing more." It wasn't until her sister's face fell that Elodie realized her mistake.

The crowd rose to their feet as Brianne led the procession down the aisle, the train of her dress slithering across the marble as fluidly as a serpent. The Chaplain followed close behind, his gaze fixed on the church's front doors, flung open to let in the autumn breeze.

None of the fresh, crisp air reached Elodie up in the balcony. Instead, she suffocated on the sympathetic glances thrown her way.

The coronation's guest list was incredibly exclusive—the audience included dignitaries from the Six Republics, historians from the finest colleges on the neighboring continent of Ideshore, and political allies who had known Elodie since birth. All had expected her to stand beside Brianne during the coronation as Queen's Regent. To keep the crown under the control of a Warnou woman until the Third Daughter came of age.

"El." Rob elbowed his sister sharply, nodding toward the narrow staircase that led to the ground floor of the church. "You're holding up the line."

Elodie got slowly to her feet, relishing the feeling of making people wait. She'd been kept waiting since the moment the doctor delivered the news that Queen Tera had perished in her sleep. One minute, grief rippled through the queen's chambers. The next, a burning question: Who would rule in her stead?

Brianne would wear the crown, of course. But as to who would be the voice in her ear—it took mere moments for the competition between Elodie and the Chaplain to spark.

Our mother spent her life preparing me to help you rule, Elodie remembered insisting, before the tears had even dried on her cheeks. *I was born for this.*

I'm your father, countered the Chaplain. *Even before I gave you life, I spoke for you. I have been the New Maiden's voice longer than your time on this earth. I knew you then as I know you now.*

It was difficult to argue with divine right. Still, Elodie had tried.

Rob nudged her forward and she stumbled, the toe of her satin slipper skidding against a knot in the wood floor. Elodie cursed, her already foul mood darkening further. "I'm going to bed," she announced, once she'd reached the bottom of the stairs.

"No, you're not," her brother said incredulously, joining her on the main floor. "I let you brush my hair for this."

Elodie reached up to ruffle his dark curls. "Not that anyone can tell."

"You have to come, Elodie," Cleo whined, sidling up to her sister. "Brianne will be devastated if you're not there. She's been so nervous she's cried every night this week."

So have I, Elodie thought selfishly, but Cleo's brown eyes were so infuriatingly hopeful that she couldn't bring herself to disappoint the one sister she actually liked. "Fine." She twisted a lock of Cleo's thick black hair around her finger and gave it a gentle tug. "One dance." Cleo clapped her hands excitedly, throwing her arms around Elodie. "And *one* lingonberry tart." Rob cleared his throat indelicately. "Okay, fine," Elodie conceded. "Two."

Cleo led Elodie out of the church and into the afternoon. Nut trees lined the winding path from the church to the north tower, their foliage glinting in the warm light of the golden hour; the masquerade ball would begin as soon as the sun set. For now, the dignitaries seemed distracted as they paused to bend a knee before Queen Tera's mausoleum. Elodie clenched her fist as the Chaplain dropped a flower in the doorway of his ex-lover's tomb, his face an irreproachable performance of pain. He was the picture of a brokenhearted widower, his hair and beard shorn short in mourning.

But Elodie saw right through him. Queen Tera, despite bearing four children by four different partners, had never married. Chaplain René had no more ownership over her mother's memory than anyone else.

The queen was the most combative monarch the Church of the New Maiden had been faced with for nearly a century. She had rolled her eyes at the clergy's requests for increased funds, had never bothered with mass herself but sent a proxy to attend in her stead. Her devotion to the New Maiden had been performative at best.

She'd had good reason to be cynical. As the youngest of three daughters, Elodie's mother had spent her life primed to one day parent the New Maiden. But Tera Warnou was always more interested in the power she could wield than the power she might bear. Her two older sisters had died young, leaving her the throne. Once the crown was on Tera's head, she'd turned away from the prophecy and toward Velle's future. She'd taught her eldest daughter to value country and crown above all.

No, Tera Warnou had never wanted to mother the New Maiden. She'd wanted to rule in her own right. But even once she'd claimed ultimate power, there was pressure from her country to bear children. Expectations from her people. From the Church. Elodie couldn't help but think the brunt of that force had come from the once-charming Chaplain, who was now simpering before the departed queen's grave.

Sensing a lapse in her older sister's attention, Cleo quickened her pace, nearly jerking Elodie's arm from its socket.

"I thought you were supposed to be the gentle one," Elodie said darkly, rubbing her shoulder.

"Not when there's dancing to be done." Cleo smiled sweetly.

Empires would fall for that smile. Cleo had inherited the dark, shiny hair, golden skin, and full lips of her father, a cartographer from the western Kingdom of Ralik. With her good looks came a tender temperament and purehearted charm.

Elodie and Cleo were just as different in personality as they were in appearance. Where Cleo was warm, Elodie was cold. Where Cleo was bright, Elodie was pale.

She'd often heard the castle guards, the Loyalists, whispering about her when they thought she was out of earshot. *Elodie, the colorless girl, as pale as the palace and just as impenetrable.*

So be it. Powerful women were always disreputable.

Begrudgingly, Elodie allowed herself to be led past the stables and the storerooms and into the north corridor, through the white marble hallway where the coronation's attendees were filtering back into their rooms to pick up their elaborate masks for the costume ball. Lord Tybert of the House of Hale donned a papier-mâché monstrosity boasting real peacock feathers that must have cost nearly half of his family's rapidly diminishing fortune. A lady emerged from the third stateroom with a mask made of pure gold, glimmering in the light of the candelabras that sat in every arched window lining the long hall.

"It's all so gaudy," Elodie muttered, loud enough that a man wearing a mask made of eucalyptus leaves turned to look over his shoulder to glare at her. She was used to the sharp, clean lines of her white palace, where she perfectly matched the decor. All these embellishments threw strange shadows against the wall, leaving glitter, feathers, and flecks of color in their wake.

"I think they all look nice." Cleo sounded wistful. "I wanted a mask of white feathers, but Chaplain René said that doves are too rare to be used so frivolously."

Elodie chewed on her bottom lip. "Why is the Chaplain telling you what you can and cannot wear?"

Cleo shrugged. "He's probably right."

"You should have asked me," Elodie said sharply. That Cleo

was obeying the Chaplain's orders as though he was her own father stung like the slap of a leather belt. "I would have trapped and plucked a dove for you myself."

"Maybe that's *why* she didn't ask you, El," Rob said, biting back a laugh.

"If you want something done, best a Warnou woman do it," Elodie said darkly, repeating her mother's favorite phrase.

It was still unfathomable to her that there would be no more afternoon teas in her mother's chambers, Elodie curled up on a cushion by the window while the queen sighed over paperwork, offering tidbits of political gossip and military strategy. Even after the prophesied Third Daughter was born, Queen Tera had kept her eldest daughter close.

With such a prophecy comes fear, Elodie recalled her mother's words. *The New Maiden will live in danger—from political rivals to warring religions, there will always be those who do not wish for her to grow old. She will spend most of her time protecting her own life. That means it is up to* you *to protect our country.*

Elodie had taken her mother's warning to heart. It was the reason she could identify every single political leader staying in the castle. Could recite the names of their partners and children; could recall their wartime allegiances; could even trace the routes each had traveled to get to Velle.

Her best friend, Tal, had often teased her for sneaking maps from the library and poring over them in the courtyard while he and Rob parried with swords. The son of the castle's blacksmith, Tal was obsessed with steel, always smuggling out some heavy, fearsome-looking weapon for the Warnou siblings to study. Elodie would dodge the blunt end of Tal's training rapier as he tried to

11

distract her, tripping him for good measure so Rob could get in the final blow.

Tal was kinesthetic—tactical and possessive. He learned by doing, and thus was always pacing, darting, poking, drumming, picking things up and examining them to determine where they fit. But despite his teasing, he never plucked the books from Elodie's hands, never tore the maps from between her fingers. Instead, he stood patiently beside her, waiting in the wings to execute Elodie's strategy.

They'd been a good team then, laughing in the afternoon sun, dreaming of what could be. It was no surprise when Tal had enlisted in the First Army. He needed to do, needed to fight, needed to enact. That had always been his destiny. But where Tal had embraced his future triumphantly, Elodie failed to meet hers.

As the Warnou siblings turned toward the ballroom, the swell of instruments tuning echoed through the corridor like the screech of a cat trying to drown out the warbling of birds.

"That viola string is flat," Rob said, almost idly. Despite being the son of the highest-ranking general in Velle's army, Elodie's brother had shown no interest in military tactics and instead had found solace in music. His lithe fingers flew across piano keys like skin against silk, and his compositions could be heard throughout the country, played in taverns and concert halls alike.

"Why don't you go up there and fix it for them?" Elodie teased. Rob blushed, the tips of his pale ears turning a soft pink, cementing Elodie's suspicion that he was harboring a crush on his friend Avery, the viola player. "At the very least, when the string section takes a break, you must ask them to dance."

"I don't dance," Rob grumbled, throwing Elodie an absolutely foul glare. "I would never subject them to my lumbering feet."

"I'll teach you," Cleo nearly shouted with glee. "Let me find Pru—she has my mask. Then I'll meet you on the floor!" She scurried to find the royal nursemaid with the sort of boundless energy that nearly made Elodie want to dance, too. Instead, she sighed deeply and rummaged through the left pocket of her gray satin gown, pulling out a small mask of black lace.

"She'll have me waltzing with her until midnight." Rob reached for the ribbons of his sister's mask, tying what Elodie knew would be a perfect bow to secure it tightly on her head. The mask was simple and slightly itchy, but Elodie only planned to attend the festivities long enough to be seen. "I hate you sometimes, you know," Rob grumbled.

"I know," Elodie agreed. "But you love me more."

"Maybe," Rob conceded as he put on his own eye mask of black leather. The music swelled, a tune bold and bright and beautiful. The Loyalist who was standing guard gave them a nod of recognition, reaching for the door. Elodie steeled herself, slapping on a false smile.

She would stay for one hour.

She would eat two lingonberry tarts.

And then, Elodie Warnou—whose mother was dead, who had been passed over for the position of Queen's Regent, who would go down in the history books as a mere footnote—was going to bed.

2

The evenings were the hardest.

When sunlight streamed through the grimy window of her family's apartment, Sabine could almost pretend it was light at the end of the tunnel, that the swirling sadness that held a hand to her throat didn't run through her blood, didn't threaten to topple over her optimism and take root in her heart. But at night the main room was full of shadows. From where she lay on her straw-stuffed pallet, the flickering flame in the hearth cast strange ghosts across the walls. Sabine pulled a patchwork quilt over her head. The darkness was now even more complete, but at least the ghosts were gone.

They're never really *gone*, whispered that cold voice, the one that crept in only during the worst of it. A flat, punishing voice that turned her blood to ice. Sabine shivered. She ought to be used to it by now. She'd done this enough in her seventeen years—bottled up her emotions so viciously, let herself dwell in the sadness inside of her until the voice took over, uttering all the things she was too frightened to say herself.

The floorboards creaked as footsteps shuffled about the small room. Although the sounds were muffled by the quilt flung over her head, Sabine could still make out the cadence of the steps: steady and slow. When her sister, Katrynn, moved, she glided, a stone skipping on the water's surface. When her brother, Artur, walked, he clomped like the Loyalists' horses thundering across the cobblestones. This must be her mother, then. Beneath the blanket, Sabine groaned.

"Sabine?" The footsteps stopped. The quilt was flung away from her face, the light of a candle dancing behind her closed eyelids. "It's nearly time, Bet." Despite the lighthearted use of her childhood nickname, her mother's voice was sharp. Stern. Her eyes lingered on the dark, prominent veins on Sabine's hands. They were black, like pitch. "You've waited long enough."

"No," Sabine moaned, even though she'd known this was coming. They'd planned for it, after all. But the planning was easier than the doing. The doing hurt. "I don't want to."

"I know, babe," her mother sighed, pressing a hand to her daughter's sweaty brow. "But sadness is like a splinter. You've got to root around inside to find it. Hell to extract, but it's the only way you'll be able to properly heal. Besides," she said, "tonight's the ball. There's too much coin to be had. They'll be coming from all four corners of the world now that the New Maiden is crowned."

The coronation had attracted people from Velle's many territories and neighboring countries to the center of the city. They'd docked their posh ships in the harbor, noses up as they took in the foul atmosphere of their surroundings. But with their strange dresses, superior airs, and funny-looking horses also came their coin.

The exchange rate between crooners and kelbers was exceptionally high at the moment. Sabine's family only needed to bully a handful of drunken lords from Wilton into overpaying for sleeping draughts, and the family could turn one quarter's rent into a year's. The fools from the Outer Banks still used real gold in their currency. Sabine knew this. It was all part of the plan.

But the plan had been concocted right after a brewing, when Sabine's mind was clear and her emotions under control. Now, though, after weeks of holding all her feelings in, nothing sounded worse than being enveloped by a throng of excitable people. Having to smile, lie, and flirt her way into coins when all she wanted was to stay wrapped up in this blanket by the dying embers of the fire.

"Katrynn and Artur are already there," her mother reminded her. "My cursed knee has flared up again, so I can't go in your stead. They need you."

And your magic, came that voice, reminding Sabine where her value truly lay.

Both she and her mother looked back down at Sabine's dark veins. "You've never let it go this long, love," her mother said gently. "We've got to get it out before it consumes you."

And before anyone outside the family notices, the voice finished for her.

She never said it aloud, but Orla Anders was ashamed of her daughter's sadness. It was clear in the way she inhaled sharply each time Sabine's veins turned from blue to black. The pity that welled in her eyes when her daughter could not muster up the energy to join the rest of the family for supper. The way she would not let Sabine outside until all traces of sorrow had faded from her skin.

Sabine pulled the quilt back over her head. "I don't want to. I just want to stay here."

16

"No." The blanket was pulled completely off. "I'm sorry, Bet," her mother said, "but what's rule number one?"

"'No rest when there's money to be made,'" Sabine grumbled as she pushed herself up to a seated position. The family rules served mostly to trick her into doing things she didn't want to do. Her parents were brilliant that way. And Maiden knew they needed the money. The paint on the walls was peeling. The room stank of wet wool, condensation clinging to the window so it always appeared to be raining.

Satisfied, Sabine's mother got to her feet and rekindled the fire in the crooked, red-bricked hearth. Then she flung open the doors to her curio cabinet and rummaged around the top shelf, filled with bottles, vials, and vases made of amber, green, and blue glass. The cabinet's middle shelf was overflowing with bundles of dried herbs and pressed flower petals, twisted roots and crepe-paper-thin, iridescent beetle wings. The bottom shelf, which normally held her mother's finished brews—hangover cures, health tonics, potions to inspire love, and potions to stoke the fires of hate—was empty. All their wares had already been packed away safely by her siblings, ready to be sold at the midnight market.

There was only one thing missing: Sabine's tears.

Her mother placed a clear glass vial on the kitchen table, then carefully lifted a chair from the hook on the wall. "Sit," she commanded.

Sabine pushed herself to her feet and staggered forward. Her legs wobbled like she was at sea and her heart cried out, frantic as a hungry gull. She collapsed into the chair.

On the tabletop, her mother arranged bundles of herbs: lavender, nightshade, and chamomile. She placed quartz and moonstone

17

in a circle, lit a candle in the center, and then put her hands on Sabine's head.

"Let go," her mother whispered, soft at first. Hesitant.

Hold tighter, came the voice, louder. Insistent.

"Let go, let go, let go," her mother continued, steady, careful. An incantation. An urging. And blessedly, as it always did, her mother's command won.

Sabine went to war with herself. Her body ached, her heart roared, her ears rushed with the sound of blood and breaking glass, and all the while she fought with the voice shrieking within. And then came the pain. White-hot fire through her veins, her limbs jerking and swelling like her skeleton was stretching out her skin. Her eyes watered. Tears welled. Her mother snatched up the glass vial and held it at the ready.

As a child, Sabine had cried daily. Her feelings were so heavy it seemed the only way to make it from one day to the next. But the day Sabine turned ten, her sister, Katrynn, the eldest Anders child, had rolled her eyes at the sight of her sister's tears. "Stop crying, Bet," she had said. "No one likes a baby." Properly chastised and desperate for her sister's affection, Sabine obeyed. She clamped her wavering lips shut and fought back the swell of tears, her throat turning tight and sour. As she struggled, a darkness bloomed beneath her white skin, turning her blue veins black.

Katrynn had shrieked, hands clapped over her mouth. Their mother, half observing from the hearth, had gone very white. "Stop that, Sabine," her mother had commanded. "Cry."

But in her head, ten-year-old Sabine heard another voice. A very faint, gentle: *Don't.*

In the end, her mother's urging won. Sabine wept.

The first time, those precious tears—their potency unknown—had fallen to the floorboards. Now that they knew the value, her mother carefully collected every last drop.

The power of Sabine's tears had been uncovered slowly. To avoid the darkness, Sabine had wept frequently at her mother's insistence. But soon she grew weary of the headaches and chafed skin on her nose, the sour lump in her throat, and the feeling of emptiness it left her with. And so she began to bottle her feelings up, carefully crafting her smiles and hiding her hands beneath Katrynn's too-big coats.

But when the whisper in her ear grew too cruel, too honest for her to bear, Sabine's strength slipped. Sitting at the table while her mother brewed, Sabine began to cry over a bundle of dried herbs. To her fascination and horror, the sage sprang back to life, as green and fragrant as though it had been freshly picked. When her mother reached for the ingredient, she paused, taking in her daughter's tearstained face.

Sabine braced herself for a scolding, but her mother softened. "What happened here?" she had asked. "And can you do it again?"

Tonight, Sabine wept until the vial was full, until the knot in her chest unraveled and the shrieking in her head stuttered, then silenced. She took a deep breath. The air was fresh and bright in her lungs. The ghosts on the walls had settled back into shadows. The darkness retreated from her veins. Sabine was herself again. Right on schedule.

Her mother sealed the one precious vial with a soft squish of wax. "All right, Bet?"

Sabine nodded. Forced a smile. It still surprised her how much the magic hurt. But she'd never shared the full extent of the pain. Her mother wouldn't let her brew if she knew her daughter was suffering. She would stop scooping spoonfuls of mushy fish onto her own plate so they would have one fewer mouth to feed. Orla would slowly disappear, from flesh to bone, would give up her world, if she knew the way Sabine's head shouted at her to surrender to the darkness.

But their family needed the money. Which meant the only thing Sabine could afford was to sacrifice. That started with keeping her mouth shut. With letting the dark cloud swirl around her head like the halo of light painted above the New Maiden and Her Favoreds on the ceiling of the padlocked chapel by the docks. With reminding herself that all these feelings were valuable, even when they felt anything but.

Emotion was the root of magic, after all. There were legends of folk so joyful their laughter could call forth the sun amidst the rain. Particularly sour sea captains were said to use their anger to sink enemy ships. The New Maiden Herself was said to possess a calmness so gentle that a mere smile could turn a bear as docile as a house cat.

Sabine's sadness amplified the effects of her mother's potions tenfold. Healing salves tinged with her tears repaired wounds in seconds. Digestifs flavored with her salt armed the drinker with an iron stomach. Once, a good-fortune potion containing her sadness resulted in the customer inheriting a sprawling estate in the Third Republic. Sabine's magic set the family's wares apart. It kept them all in hearth and home.

But her power was inconsistent. Not every tear would do. It was only when she held her sadness inside the way she had done to obey Katrynn, bottled it up until the darkness pooled in her veins, until that slithering voice threatened to take over, that her magic truly worked. This meant she needed to time her outpouring. Save it for the markets that mattered most. She could not waste a single tear on a heartbreak or a sad, longing song. She had to be steely, like a Loyalist's sword.

It was why she'd hung on until tonight. Fresh tears would garner the most coin. The longer they sat encased in glass, the less potent they became. And if that meant she had to dwell in the darkness for a bit longer than usual, well, Sabine would do anything to ensure her family could keep a roof over their heads. They'd spent so long scraping by. But tonight the Anders family would sell at the midnight market during the largest celebration of Sabine's lifetime. They'd been planning their pitches for weeks. Nothing would deter her; nothing would go wrong. Not tonight.

Are you certain? asked the voice, the one that should have disappeared after the final tear fell. The one she'd always been able to silence after her ritual.

"Be safe, love." Her mother planted a kiss on Sabine's cheek as she handed over the vial of tears. She didn't seem to notice the goose bumps that had popped up on her daughter's forearms.

Sabine shivered, pocketing the vial. Her heart hammered as she examined the veins peering through her pale skin. By now they should have faded from black to blue. Yet a thin, dark line still ran across her right hand, from middle finger to wrist. Something wasn't right. But there was no time to dwell. Her siblings were expecting her. Hands shoved deep into her pockets, Sabine bade Orla farewell and hurried out into the night.

3

The ballroom had been turned into a veritable menagerie. A
tiger sat in the center of the room. Peacocks roamed the perimeter, towering brown bears roared in gilded cages affixed to
each of the four corners, and a flock of doves circled near the ceiling, flapping precariously close to the crystal chandeliers.

The hall's ordinarily white marble walls were draped with purple tapestries threaded with gold. The pale floors were covered with
a lush, padded rug that made Elodie feel as though she was sinking into snow. Just as the Chaplain had usurped Elodie's place as
Queen's Regent, the Church had overtaken the celebration hall,
trading in its usual casual elegance for the rich, garish colors of the
New Maiden.

A small stage had been constructed for the orchestra, and the long
tables from the great hall had been brought in to line the walls. One
table was set with golden goblets, golden cutlery, and golden napkins
folded to look like swans. That was the queen's table, her place marked
with a glimmering placard. The seat beside Brianne's was reserved

for the Chaplain, the rest of the table for the other officials of the Church. There were no chairs intended for any of Brianne's siblings.

Elodie turned her attention to the other tables, all dripping with the finest imports—dewy fruits, fresh-baked bread, towering cakes, and platters of roasted meats, aged cheeses, and smoked fish. Elodie dropped Rob's arm and shot directly toward the buffet, filling her plate with everything she could manage, using the potatoes to hold the meat in place so she could balance the fruit on top and prevent any contamination of the gravy. When her plate ran out of room, Elodie tucked several pastries into the folds of her skirt for safekeeping.

"Cakes in your pocket, El?" The voice to her right was so comfortingly familiar it made her want to weep. "And here I thought this place taught you some manners."

Elodie turned toward the tall man in a mask with a long beak. "Father." That one word threatened to release the stockpile of emotion she had spent this entire wretched day trying to tamp down. If her plate hadn't been so full, she would have thrown her arms around him. "I didn't know you were coming."

"I always planned to attend the coronation of Velle's next queen," her father said. "Of course, I expected it to be under slightly different circumstances."

Her mother's absence loomed large between them, a wound so fresh it wept. Elodie swallowed the lump rising in her throat. "Me too."

Elodie's father, Duke Antony Wilde, had been her mother's childhood best friend. The entire country assumed that one day they would marry. But marriage was not something that Tera Warnou had ever desired. She cared deeply and tenderly for many different partners. Elodie's father's only claim to the queen was that he had loved her first.

They'd stayed friends even after Elodie's mother had moved on to other lovers. But the news of Tera's death had hit Antony hard. Elodie could see the sag in his usually upright shoulders. She suspected that behind his mask she'd find hollow eyes and a weary frown.

"Well, your appetite hasn't suffered, I see," her father teased, gesturing to her loaded plate. "I heard the fruit was imported from Ethliglenn."

Elodie frowned down at her plate. Ethliglenn was a small, relatively unimportant ally tucked into a corner of the western highlands. "Why their contingent earned an invitation to the coronation, I do not know." She pinched a round, red berry between her fingers until it bled pulp. "Although I imagine the Queen's Regent does."

She glared sourly across the room to where the Chaplain held out a chair for his pink-cheeked daughter. Brianne, who was talking animatedly, nearly missed the seat and went tumbling off the platform.

The duke followed his own daughter's gaze. "I'm sorry your father wasn't the queen's most conniving lover," he said blithely. "I didn't realize it was a competition until I'd already lost."

"Yeah," Elodie said darkly, still scowling at the high table, "thanks for nothing."

Duke Antony made a thoughtful noise. "Strange, isn't it?" He returned his attention to his daughter. "In another world, this coronation might have been yours."

Elodie's anger simmered. "I never really thought about it."

That was almost true. When Elodie was younger, she had harbored some jealousy toward Brianne, the object of endless attention and acclaim. But her time in the queen's chambers learning the ins and outs of the role had reframed Elodie's jealousy into something else: opportunity.

Still, she had whispered it once, in Tal's ear—a secret for a secret, shared in the servants' stairwell. It was where they went to escape their responsibilities, squishing together on the steps while a scullery girl balanced a laundry basket on her hip, or a stable boy stomped mud across the floor on his way to the east tower. There, the two of them could forget themselves for a moment—he could avoid the punishing heat of the blacksmith's forge, and she could evade her never-ending royal duties. "I would make a better queen," Elodie offered in exchange for Tal's wide-eyed "I don't want to become a murderer." Spoken into existence, then set free. Tal still enlisted in the army. Elodie remained at Castle Warnou, expecting to stand by her sister's side.

The duke smiled wryly. "I imagined it several times, when you were three and particularly demanding, calling for milk and sweets. I told Tera, 'There is a girl who will stop at nothing to get what she wants.'" His eyes were sad.

The lump had returned to Elodie's throat. "I'm sorry to have proved you wrong."

Her father's face fell. "You've done no such thing. You are my daughter, a fearsome, incredible woman. I believed in you then as I believe in you now. You can do whatever you set your mind to. Your mother knew it, too." He cleared his throat self-consciously. "Oh, now," he said quickly, flicking away tears. "I appear to have misplaced my handkerchief. I must go, before I make a fool of myself."

"Too late." Elodie smiled softly.

"Touché." Her father tugged the end of her curls. "Now try to have some fun. And if you don't have fun, at least try harder to pretend."

"Save a dance for me?" Elodie asked before he swept away.

"Anything for my favorite daughter."

"I'm your only daughter," she reminded him.

"Yes," her father said, shrugging, "but not the queen's."

"Bastard." Elodie didn't bother to lower her voice. Her father's eyes sparkled with mirth. Elodie gave him a gentle shove and he wandered off, still chuckling. She discarded her full plate on the nearest table, stomach roiling, as she continued to survey the crowd. Brianne was sitting alone, twirling a fork in her plump fingers and looking bored. Elodie supposed she ought to go and greet her, however resentful she might feel in this moment.

But she had taken no more than a single step before she was accosted by the Chaplain, accompanied by a pale boy with a shock of red hair.

"Hello." Elodie shot the Chaplain a quizzical look. "Who's this, then?" She scanned the room for Rob, who was leaning against the stage, gazing up at Avery with a lovesick grin. She willed her brother to glance her way. He did not.

"Elodie." The Chaplain's eyes glittered, setting her teeth on edge. "Have you met Edgar DeVos? His father is William DeVos."

The son of the recently unseated despot of Ethliglenn smiled up at Elodie from behind the papier-mâché mask of a snake's head. Green scales were stitched onto his ill-fitting suit, the pants short enough to reveal his pale ankles.

"Charmed, I'm sure," Elodie said, smoothing her skirt. She cast another desperate glance at Rob.

"Eye contact, Elodie," the Chaplain chastised, returning to his role as adviser rather than competitor. "You're being rude."

"To Edgar?" Elodie grimaced at the boy, who had yet to contribute. "I think he'll be all right. My condolences about your house," she added. The despot's estate had been destroyed by the revolutionaries' explosives.

"S'all right." The boy shrugged, his voice deeper than Elodie had expected. "We'll rebuild."

"Riveting." Elodie turned herself solely toward the Chaplain. "May I be excused? My sister looks as though she's about to fall asleep in her potatoes." She gestured toward the head table, where Brianne's eyelids were beginning to droop.

"She's pouting," the Chaplain said dismissively, adjusting the chain of the gold pendant he wore around his neck. "I won't allow her a glass of peich-nat."

"She is our divine ruler," Elodie said sardonically. "Surely she can have anything she wishes?"

"Not anything," the Chaplain said sourly. "Her instincts cannot be trusted. Why, only yesterday, she was considering *you* for the role of Queen's Regent." He laughed obnoxiously, Edgar joining in a moment too late. "But it's clear you no longer belong in Velle."

Elodie frowned, too hung up on the first half of his sentence for the second part to register. "I...what?"

"You leave with Edgar tomorrow for Ethliglenn."

Elodie blinked up at him. "Why would I do that?"

"Because your queen commands it." The corners of the Chaplain's lips quirked upward. "Velle requires a diplomatic rapport with the Sixth Republic. Who better to keep the crown informed than the wife of the newest Council-elect?"

Elodie burst out laughing. When no one else joined in, she sobered. "You don't mean me?" Edgar leered at her. She glared at the Chaplain. "What did you do?"

She couldn't leave home. Not when Brianne had wanted her to be Queen's Regent. Not when the Chaplain had gotten in her way. The only question now was *why*?

"*I* haven't done anything," he said lightly. "I merely advise our new queen. She is the one who makes the decisions. But if I *may* offer you some advice…" The Chaplain took a step forward. "Go quietly, while you have the opportunity. You cannot turn my daughter against me—you will *not* turn the New Maiden against me. I have made sacrifices for our lady above you would never understand. I will not let you dilute Brianne with your poisonous heart."

"Careful, Chaplain," Elodie said, her voice as cold as the ice sculpture of a swan that sat in the middle of the table, even as her blood blazed. "You know nothing about the contents of my heart."

"I know all, dearest Elodie." The Chaplain smiled through clenched teeth. "Do not challenge me to prove it."

A chill scurried down Elodie's spine. He had the same look in his eye that came before one of his visions where he shared the New Maiden's word on the pulpit during mass, then brought divine requests to the queen's chambers. Most recently, it had been to demand the redirection of funds from Harborside to the Fourth Republic for their faith and fealty. "It was Her will," the Chaplain insisted, but Her will seemed to favor some more than others, and Her favor was increasingly rerouted from Velle's people to the citizens of faraway lands.

The coronation was proof of that, with delegates from the Fourth and Fifth Republics making up nearly a quarter of the attendees. It appeared the newly minted Sixth Republic was next in line for Her will to be done.

"So it's settled." The Chaplain did not phrase it as a question. "You leave tomorrow."

"Not until I speak to the queen." Elodie's voice was sharp, but the Chaplain did not flinch.

He nodded his head reverently. "As you wish. I am right behind you."

Elodie scowled as she led the way toward the high table, feeling like a chaperoned child. As she passed the stage she yanked Rob away from ogling Avery, who was biting their lip with concentration as they played. "I need you."

"What are you—" But Rob's question died on his tongue as he took in Elodie's expression.

"They're shipping me off to Ethliglenn to marry"—Elodie cast a sparing glance over her shoulder at the snakeskin-clad Edgar—"*that*."

It took Rob no time at all to echo his sister's horror. "Absolutely not. You are not going to *Ethliglenn*."

"That's exactly what I'm going to tell the queen." It wasn't Brianne's idea to send her away, that much Elodie knew. And her sister wore the crown, which meant she could overrule her Regent should she so decree.

Elodie was going to demand she did.

Brianne's face lit up as her siblings approached. "Oh, good! Company!" She sat up straighter, her cheek red where it had rested on her palm. "Everyone at this table is horribly old, and Papa won't even let me have a glass of wine."

Elodie knew the best way to appeal to Brianne was through sympathy. But her patience, already worn thin from the coronation, had all but disappeared. "I will not go to Ethliglenn," she said instead.

Her sister blinked up at her quizzically. *"Where?"*

"The Sixth Republic." A shuffle behind her as Edgar and Chaplain René approached.

"I thought there were only five republics." Brianne frowned. "Interesting."

Elodie fought the urge to scream. While her sister was not kept abreast of all political machinations, surely this shift in power should have been important enough to be shared with the future queen.

"We talked about this, pet." The Chaplain's voice was soft and slippery as an asp. "It is *essential* to your cause that your sister takes her place there."

"My cause?" Brianne looked truly baffled. "I don't…"

The Chaplain placed a hand on his daughter's shoulder. "The *New Maiden's* cause." His fingers tightened, Brianne shifting uncomfortably. "Remember?"

"Oh, right"—Brianne nodded so vigorously her ringlet curls bounced—"of course." The Chaplain relaxed his grip. "Yes. Ellie, you must go to Ethliglenn."

Elodie blinked at her youngest sister. "Why?"

Brianne looked desperately up at her father. "I…"

"It does not do to question the New Maiden's word, Elodie," the Chaplain said gratingly. "Especially not tonight, of all nights."

"That isn't Her word," Elodie snapped, "it's yours. Look at Brianne, she doesn't know what you're talking about. She doesn't even know where Ethliglenn is on a map."

"It's near the top," Edgar added, unhelpfully.

Brianne chewed on her lip. "That wasn't very nice, Ellie."

"Well, it wasn't very nice to choose him over me as your Queen's Regent," Elodie said, cursing herself for the way her voice broke. "And now you're sending me away. So I'd say we're even, wouldn't you?"

The queen's eyes filled with tears. Her bottom lip wobbled. Elodie refused to fall for it. Every time Brianne cried, she found herself offering comfort. But what her sister had done this time was unforgivable.

"You've upset the queen," the Chaplain said sharply, tightening his grip on his daughter's shoulder. "Leave us."

"Gladly," Elodie grumbled, turning on her heel and dragging Rob along with her.

"What in the twelve hells was that?" Rob's eyes were wide, his eyebrows threatening to disappear beneath his curls as he caught up with her.

Elodie scowled. "Our country's downfall."

The orchestra was playing in earnest now. The music swelled and couples began to move toward the dance floor. The festivities would likely carry into the early hours of the morning, hardly giving Elodie enough time to pack her entire life into the contents of a few trunks.

"I can't imagine this place without you." Rob shook his head.

"According to the Chaplain, Velle will be better off without me and my poisonous heart." She glowered, the words still stinging. "But he's the one funneling Velle's funds outside the country. I wish I could poison *him*."

"Elodie," Rob screeched, looking scandalized. "You can't go around saying things like that in public." He gestured vaguely at the several hundred people in the room, none of whom were paying a whit of attention to the two of them. "Anyway, that would only allow another member of the clergy to step in and guide Brianne. It's not as though the regency would transfer to you."

"It wouldn't?"

Rob chuckled. "You sound far too disappointed."

"He talked Brianne out of selecting me. He's up to something, Rob, I know it."

"A father trying to support his daughter?" Rob raised an eyebrow. "How sinister."

Elodie smacked him. "You're far too trusting. Where's Cleo when I need her?" The middle Warnou sister was notoriously discerning. Food, compliments, and commands were all met with the sincerest scrutiny.

"I know you're disappointed, but maybe Ethliglenn won't be so terrible."

Elodie did not deign to dignify that with a response. Instead, she stewed. Rob was right. Were the Chaplain to be eliminated, another clergy folk would step in to take his place. His death wouldn't alter the transfer of power. Elodie paused as her brain snagged on the relevant word. *His* death.

For one terrible, monstrous moment, Elodie considered whose death *would* alter the line of inheritance.

Up at the high table, Brianne emitted a shrill, hesitant laugh in the direction of a delegate from the Fifth Republic. She looked small, as though her purple dress might swallow her whole. Just as the clergy would wrap themselves around her and bury her in their agenda, in their interpretation of Her word.

It frightened Elodie, the damage that the Church might inflict on Velle in the four years before Brianne came of age at seventeen. By then, the entire country might suffer like those citizens in Harborside, with their gambling dens and crumbling homes. Even their chapel had fallen into disrepair once the Chaplain had deemed them "nonbelievers unworthy of Her grace."

Brianne was so earnest, and so unprepared for power. The clergy would manipulate her every chance they received. If only she could be encased in glass, perfectly preserved so that her father and the clergy could not touch her until she was free to rule of her own accord.

But if such a possibility existed, Elodie wouldn't find it here, amidst the finery and perfumed flowers. It wasn't until she caught sight of a guest sipping from a brown tonic bottle instead of a crystal goblet that Elodie remembered what must be happening in the city center below.

While the upper class toasted Velle's newest queen in the marble palace, the citizens of Velle gathered at the midnight market, a host of oddities, art, and antiques. Stalls would be lined with potions and powders, tapestries and dyes and brightly colored spices. If ever there was a place to locate a person who knew how to speed up time—a person who knew how to protect and preserve the goodness of her sister—it was the midnight market.

"You all right, El?" Rob nudged her side softly. "You look a little pale."

"I promised my father a waltz." Elodie grimaced playfully. "I'm trying to mentally prepare."

But Elodie had no intention of dancing. Instead, she wrapped herself up in the Chaplain's insults like a shawl to keep warm. If he was so sure that she had a poisonous heart, then Elodie would prove him right. She would make her thorns sharp enough to draw blood. Elodie would find a way to use that poison to reclaim what was rightfully hers.

4

An unfamiliar weight settled upon Sabine's shoulders as she hurried down Harborside's main thoroughfare, if one could call the dimly lit cobblestone path that stank of rotting fish and salt licks a thoroughfare. The heel of Sabine's boot crushed a bone with a sickening crunch. She shivered.

Her earlier desire to stay indoors hadn't merely been motivated by the exhaustion that always accompanied her sadness. Harborside was filled with shadows even in the daylight. At night, it was downright feral. Gamblers, assailants, and ghosts prowled the cramped alleyways, searching for the most exciting game, the prettiest girl, and the strongest ale.

A flash of red uniform sent Sabine skittering into the shadows of a stone building. Despite the crown's propaganda, an increase in Loyalist patrol was *not* a good thing for the eastern part of the city. The queen's militia didn't seem to include Harborside's residents in the list of Velle's citizens they'd sworn to protect and serve. At least when a club owner beat a person senseless, he left a ledger in his wake, offering proof of funds owed. When Loyalists targeted a Harborside resident, they didn't appear to need a reason.

Once the footsteps had passed, Sabine exhaled sharply, then forged ahead. She walked until the alleyways no longer stank of fish but of rotting produce, until the angry voices that floated through open windows changed their accusations from *cheater* to *liar*. The breeze off the water had all but disappeared; the air was thick as smoke and just as heavy. The city center held neither ghosts nor shadows, only endless waves of people. Bodies were everywhere, sticky, sweet-smelling, and sharp-elbowed. Sabine fell into the crowd's momentum, allowing herself to be pushed forward through the iron gate and under the stone arch that led to Velle's marketplace.

The queue to enter the masquerade snaked up and down the square, bursting with guests dripping in finery—feathers and glitter and lace and gold, so much gold. As the line inched forward, the partygoers were forced to take stock of all the market's vendors.

Every stall was occupied, dripping with ribbons as silky as spiders' webs and glowing with lanterns of silver and gold. Bottles of blue sand from the edge of the Seventh Sea lined one stall, while flowers with petals as long and soft as swan feathers burst to life at the next.

Rather than join the queue, Sabine slipped through the back of the stalls, a hand clutching the precious ware in her pocket. It didn't take long before she caught the dulcet tones of her younger brother, Artur, bellowing into the night.

"A toast to the new queen," he shouted, as Sabine approached the stall from behind. "And a tonic to revive you before you've drunk yourself to death."

The table was tastefully decorated in a minimalistic style, the potions laid out on lush velvet fabric Sabine didn't recognize. The bottles and vials sparkled in the light of the star-shaped lanterns strung up between the stalls.

"How'd you manage this, then?" Sabine sidled in next to her older sister, who didn't even bat an eyelash. "It looks expensive."

Katrynn shot Sabine a smile. "I never kiss and tell, dear sister."

Sabine chuckled, despite herself. Katrynn was a whirlwind of a girl—she laughed with reckless abandon and never seemed to sag beneath life's enormous weight the way Sabine did. The family did not live in fear that *Katrynn* would ever succumb to her sadness. *Katrynn* was never subject to a thorough inspection before being sent outside to run an errand. Her sister's effortlessness made Sabine feel impossibly inferior.

"Bet!" Artur ran toward her, grinning wildly. His breath smelled of peich-nat, the fruity, lightly carbonated wine made from the nut trees that littered the country.

"You stink," she laughed, tousling her brother's blond hair.

"And you're sober." He extracted a flask from his vest pocket. "More where this came from."

Sabine wrinkled her nose. "You know I can't stand that stuff."

Katrynn took a swig in her sister's stead. "You've got it, then?" She held out her palm expectantly. Sabine extracted the vial, careful to offer it with her left hand so as not to reveal the darkness in the veins of her right. "Brilliant." Her sister tugged the wax free and gave it a sniff.

"Don't *smell* my tears!" Sabine blanched.

"Smells like money, Bet." Katrynn grinned. "Now we can put out the good stuff." With the vial still in hand, she knelt behind the stall and rummaged through the crate before locating a hand-painted sign: 20 KELBERS FOR A DROP OF PURE MAGIC IN ANY ELIXIR. INCREASES EFFICACY TENFOLD!

"Twenty kelbers for a single tear?" Artur scoffed. "No one's going to pay that."

"They will once they see how good a time you have with your potion." Katrynn handed over a worn brown hat and a coat with patches on the elbow. "You're our next customer."

"Why do I always have to buy?" Artur grumbled, but he did as he was told, swapping his vest for the costume. Sabine noticed he did not part with the flask. "I'll make a lap."

As Artur wandered away, Katrynn looped an arm through Sabine's. "Good to have you back." Her voice was light, but her closeness told another story.

"You were worried about me?" Sabine's chest tightened. So often it felt as though her family's focus was only on what she could produce. She put a hand on top of her sister's. The black vein flashed in the lantern light. *Who do you think you're fooling?* She shoved her hand back into the depths of her skirt pocket.

Katrynn bit her lip. "It was different, this time. You didn't move for days."

"Of course I did." But Sabine frowned. She could only remember the exhaustion. The way her mind, body, and bones were so heavy she thought she might fall through the floor.

That gap in her memory frightened her. Yet she couldn't dwell. Her family's debt was adding up faster than she could bottle her emotions. Rent collection was nearly upon them. And while pickpocketing and swindling sailors out of their salaries were reliable grifts, they were small potatoes. The thick tally marks on her father's ledger told a much more sinister story. The family needed her sadness to survive.

"What's this, then?" Artur's voice was falsetto sweet, his nose close to the bottles as he examined the brews. None of the bottles were labeled. Each was recognizable by its distinct color and packaging. Tonics and teas went in bottles, salves went in jars, and the really potent stuff, the specialty brews that demanded a drop of Sabine's sadness, were sold only by the vial.

Katrynn's fingers closed around a medium-sized bottle that held a bubbling, earthy brown liquid. "Hangover tonic," she said snidely. "Based on the state of your breath, you'll need it."

Artur laughed, bright and open. "It's not a crime to celebrate our good fortune," he said, throwing back his head and letting out a crow: "To Velle's maiden-queen." The crowd echoed his cheer back.

The noise from the queuing partygoers rumbled like a clap of thunder as vivid green sparks shot above the castle walls, the fire cascading down to the cobblestones like the winter's first snow. A roar of appreciation echoed through the castle passage, the throngs of people dressed as jungle cats and plumed peacocks hooting and hollering as the line inched forward, toward the raucous party thrown for the newly crowned queen.

"Seems like quite a lot of fuss for a thirteen-year-old," Sabine grumbled. The royal family's goodwill never made it as far as Harborside, so it mattered very little to her who occupied the throne. The Loyalists still patrolled, the Church still demanded their tithes, taxes were still owed, and those near the docks were left to scrabble and scramble to survive.

A dark-haired man who had been lured by Artur's shouting stopped examining a vitality elixir. "You're not a believer, then?"

"In the monarchy?" Sabine raised an eyebrow. "Not particularly."

"In the prophecy," the man corrected her. "The scripture says the New Maiden will heal the world and save us all from destruction."

Sabine fought the urge to roll her eyes. Once, she had been thrilled by the prospect of the New Maiden's return. When she was young, she'd count the babies born to the families who lived in her district. Harborside was teeming with children. Surely, she told herself, the odds were in her neighborhood's favor to host the New Maiden when She finally came.

But then Brianne Elisabet Warnou was born.

It was strange that the New Maiden had returned as a princess. All the stories Sabine had been told about the New Maiden's exploits spoke of Her calloused hands, Her hard work, Her suffering. But none of that emanated from the castle on the hill, where smoke always pumped from their hundreds of chimneys, and perfectly good food was left for the birds while half the city starved.

The new queen's ascent only confirmed a truth Sabine had always known: Girls from Harborside did not fulfill prophecies.

"That's...nice," Sabine finally managed, swallowing the lump in her throat. "That one's twelve kelbers. Thirty-two if you'd like a drop of magic."

The man eyed her suspiciously. "I've no need for any of that," he said carefully, placing the bottle back where it belonged. "Velle has fine minds of science now. You can retire your cauldron and purchase pills from the dispensary like the rest of us."

Sabine frowned. If her magic wasn't enough to incentivize buyers, she didn't know how her family was going to survive. Her sister didn't seem to share the sentiment. Katrynn merely rolled her eyes. "Be gone with you, then. You're blocking our wares." She waved the man away, dropping her irritated expression the moment he was gone. "This isn't working."

Sabine glanced at the coin purse, limp as a head of rotting cabbage. There couldn't be more than a single coin inside. Even though she wanted nothing more than to pack up their wares and go home, fall onto her thin pallet and sleep until morning, their work was not done. "Should we run the Agitator?"

Artur's eyes lit up.

"I hate that one," Katrynn groaned as Sabine pocketed a tin of herbal salve.

"Two out of three, the house always rules," Artur said, doing an odd little jig. "Now, let me find my mark." He scanned the crowd, dripping in finery and donning outlandish masks. But he passed all of them by. It couldn't be too obvious a ruse. Anyone threaded with that much gold had sewn all their coins to their garter belt to prevent becoming the victim of a grift.

Sabine witnessed the moment her brother found his mark. His eyes followed a ghost of a girl, her elaborately braided hair nearly as white as her skin. She was almost colorless, save for the pink of her cheek and lip paint. She wore a pinched expression on an otherwise lovely face.

The moment of impact happened so quickly that if Sabine hadn't known to look, she would have missed it. Artur collided bodily with the girl, who went flying across the cobblestones, landing in a heap right in front of the Anders' stall. The girl cried out, searching wildly about for whoever had knocked her off-balance, but Artur, ever the professional, was nowhere to be found.

"Flying fish!" Sabine rushed forward, offering the girl a hand up, but the girl shook her head, showing Sabine her palms. Blood bloomed red from the scrapes she'd gained upon her spill. "Are you all right?"

"I'm fine," the girl snapped, her voice surprisingly musical for someone so colorless. She wiped her hands on the bodice of her gray dress. Then she held out her palms, looking helpless.

"Here." Sabine pulled the tin of salve from her pocket. "This might sting a bit." Carefully, she scooped out some of the ointment and began to apply it in small circles.

As expected, the girl hissed with pain. "What is that?"

"My own concoction. I'm an apothecary." Sabine offered her a small smile. "Not that I'm trying to sell you anything, mind. First salve is on the house." She laughed. "Unless you're in the market for anything...?" She let the question linger between them as she scanned the crowd for Artur.

The girl studied her curiously. "Depends on what you've got."

Sabine bit back a smile. All was going according to plan. Step one, be a savior. Step two, become a vendor.

"Home brews, mostly," she said, glancing at the stall before them. "Tonics, teas, draughts. Hangover cures, sleeping potions, energy boost—"

"Go back," the girl interrupted, eyes bright.

"Sleeping potions?" Sabine raised an eyebrow. The stranger before her looked incredibly well-rested, like she slept on a proper mattress, not a bedroll on uneven stones. "Are you an insomniac?"

"Yes. Well, no..." The girl grimaced as Sabine started work on her other palm. "I'm looking for something"—she considered—"stronger than a single night's sleep."

Sabine frowned, suddenly wary. "Stronger than sleep is death," she said carefully.

The girl jerked away, looking horrified. "No! Lady above and among us, that is not what I meant." She shook her shiny palms, then tried again. "What if I wanted to sleep for a long time? So long that when I woke up, the world was different. *I* was different."

Sabine's chest tightened. She could relate to that far more than she cared to admit.

"Henbane," she said quickly.

The girl looked at her oddly. "Is that your name?"

"No." Sabine let out a self-deprecating chuckle. "It's your ingredient."

She guided the girl toward her family's stall, where Katrynn was carefully adding a single one of Sabine's tears to a brown bottle for a redheaded girl about her age. Sabine reached for a green glass vial. "Drops of henbane, mandrake, and datura with a base of lavender and chamomile," she told the girl.

The potion was an anesthetic, meant to put the drinker into a trancelike state until a procedure such as surgery or a tooth extraction could be completed. "This might do the trick. Smelling salts should reverse the effects, if necessary."

"That's perfect." The girl looked up at Sabine, cheeks flushed. Her eyelashes were wickedly long and black as spider legs. Sabine wanted to pluck one and keep it in a minuscule jar by her bed. *What an odd thing to want*, came the voice, sending fog swirling through her head. *She can sense how broken you are. How curious. How bizarre.*

"You are. I mean…" Sabine stammered, fumbling with the vial and nearly dropping it. "Flying fish!" she swore, scrambling to stop the vial before it rolled off the table. "I'm—"

Mercifully, Katrynn interrupted her babbling. "Can you take this, please?" She handed over the vial of tears and its wax seal. "Try not to drop it." She winked, before turning back to her customer.

Sabine hardly dared to look back up at the girl. Her neck burned with embarrassment. But the girl didn't seem to notice.

"How long?" The girl's eyes were gray, but her gaze wasn't dull. There was a sharpness there, an edge that Sabine felt could slice through the very heart of her. "Will the potion last, I mean?"

Sabine's heart sank. The brew in the vial would offer less than a day of dreamless slumber. Not nearly long enough to give the girl what she wanted. But her ask was so familiar, so pointedly intimate, that Sabine could not help but give the girl all the assistance she could.

So instead of replacing the cap on the vial of tears, Sabine uncorked the vial of henbane. She let three precious tears plink into the potion, extending its power thirtyfold.

"This will last long enough to matter," Sabine confirmed, capping both vials and setting them down on the table. "That'll be ten kelbers."

The girl dug through her pockets, looking for her coin purse. "Damn." The colorless girl frowned as she came up with a handful of crumbs and a single silver coin. "Will this do?"

Sabine nodded, unable to bring herself to break the girl's gaze. She tapped the table for the vial of henbane. Her fingers closed around the smooth glass, and she shivered as her skin met the customer's in the handoff. "I hope this brings you peace."

The girl blinked at her in surprise. "Thank you." Her voice was soft and sincere. She offered Sabine an impressive curtsy before tucking the vial in the pocket of her silver dress. Sabine noted the wax cap. That precious wax, which cost seven coppers from Arsinoe, the old woman who kept bees in her basement. The wax her mother only ever used to seal Sabine's tears.

Sabine glanced down at the table where the henbane lay in wait. She had offered the girl the wrong vial. Had given her magic instead.

"Wait," Sabine shouted, desperately, as the colorless girl slipped away into the chaotic crowd. "Come back."

She ran out from behind the stall, chasing that gray dress and white hair. But just as suddenly as she'd appeared, the girl was gone, taking Sabine's entire store of tears with her.

5

Elodie kept her cloak pressed to her nose as she traveled back the way she'd come, through the endless maze of the midnight market and the elaborately dressed partygoers waiting to enter the castle's golden gates. She hated how the city smelled, all sewage and violence and restless energy. Nothing like the bright, fresh scent of peppermint oil that permeated her rooms at home.

It had been years since the last time she, Rob, and Tal had snuck out from the safety of the castle to the chaotic force of the midnight market, passing a bottle of peich-nat between them, spending too much time at the stall of enchanted spyglasses, which offered glimpses onto the shores of countries far beyond Velle's borders.

Rob had always been drawn to the charcoal sketches for sale, renderings of people, places, and things both foreign and familiar. Elodie had run her fingers lazily across all manner of fabrics—velvet, crinoline, linen, silk—studying the curious cuts and muted colors of commoners' garments. Tal would stop before the spices, pinching his fingers in the little pouches to sample the bright, round flavors. He often left with something for his mother, and he never failed to tip the vendor handsomely. Tal always managed to part the crowds with a nod of his head, guiding Elodie forward with a careful hand on the small of her back.

Alone, Elodie found navigating the city square disorienting. There were too many bodies bumbling about. It was all sharp elbows, sticky streets, and boys who didn't even blink when they sent girls tumbling to the cobblestones. *Clumsy bastard.*

She was limping slightly, she'd lost her lingonberry tart, and her hands still stung from her tumble, despite the herbal salve that apothecary had spread across her skin. Still, Elodie could recognize a lucky break when she stumbled upon one.

She hadn't known, before she'd come face-to-face with the pretty brunette and her stinging salve, what she was going to do. She'd prowled the path between the endless stalls, colorful flames casting shadows on swords that swore to offer the final strike, decks of cards that claimed communication with the dead, and even a crow whose owner said it could retrieve anything that had been or would be lost.

Enticing as such oddities were, none would solve her plight. It wasn't until she was in front of the apothecary, bruised and bloody, that the answer had presented itself.

The word *sleep* had snagged in her mind like silk on a nail. Sleep had taken the crown away from her mother, but perhaps it could preserve Brianne's. Asleep, Brianne could not rule. Which meant that until she awoke, the crown would pass on to the next Warnou woman in line: Elodie.

As the first daughter, you have an obligation to Velle, Elodie's mother had reminded her, one rainy afternoon a month before her passing. Elodie's head had been leaning against the windowpane, one finger tracing the crack of lightning that pulsed in the distance.

This country is enduring, but fragile. It would not withstand the rule of anyone other than a Warnou woman.

Elodie had nodded sleepily, lulled into complacency by the warm rumble of thunder. She hadn't known, then, what it was her mother feared. But after staring into Chaplain René's cold, merciless eyes this afternoon, Elodie finally understood: Brianne wore the crown but she wasn't truly queen. The Third Daughter wouldn't be free to rule without an adviser for another four years. Which meant that until Brianne came of age, the Church held Velle and the New Maiden in its icy grip.

Her mother's final words on that not-so-distant afternoon thundered in Elodie's head: *One day, you may need to make a choice others cannot fathom. And if you are forced to choose*, Queen Tera had said, her expression impenetrable, *I hope you remember that sometimes it takes a monster to keep the beasts at bay.*

Elodie would seize the throne only until Brianne came of age, until her sister could make her own decisions. Her *own* plans.

Four years would fly by, Elodie reminded herself, as her chest tightened and the vial threatened to burn a hole in her pocket. It was only until Brianne turned seventeen—then she would wake her sister up and reinstate her on the throne. Four years was nothing. During Elodie's first four years she had been the heir apparent. That alternate reality was so far gone it seemed as though it had never truly existed.

This, too, would be over before she knew it. Elodie lowered her cloak once she reached the castle's south gate at the top of the hill. The iron behemoth was tightly shut, and the tower was heavily barred. Elodie rapped sharply on the door anyway.

"Visitors through the north gate," shouted an irritated voice, muffled through the thick door.

"In truth the Maiden, in honor the crown." Elodie offered her royal code in a high-pitched singsong. The top half of the door swung open to reveal Maxine, a broad-shouldered young woman whose dark hair was always coiled in a tight braid. She didn't even look up from the gigantic tome she was reading.

"What if I'd had a knife?" Elodie asked, slightly miffed at the lack of fanfare.

"You don't have a knife." Maxine snorted. She was only a few years older than Elodie and had been assigned to the castle guard after serving in the army's Second Division. Tal had pestered her incessantly about military training and her time served. He had even adopted her vernacular—her self-appointed "soldier-speak"—so desperate was he to make a good first impression when he arrived on the front lines. Secretly, Elodie blamed Maxine for her best friend's decision to enlist.

"You have blood on your dress," Maxine noted as she turned the page. "Wait, *do* you have a knife?" Her brown eyes finally met Elodie's.

Elodie tucked a stray lock of hair behind her ear. "Do you want to search me?" She grinned, waggling her eyebrows.

Maxine rolled her eyes. "Go back to the ball, Princess."

Elodie huffed, her bravado failing with the guard's dismissal. "You're no fun," she snapped. The Loyalist seemed immune to her flirtations—unlike the apothecary, whose cheeks bloomed a delightful red when Elodie had teased her.

"The crown doesn't pay me to be fun," Maxine chided as she opened the door and waved Elodie through. "They pay me to protect the queen."

"Oh, I know where your loyalties lie," Elodie muttered as she stalked past the guard, giving Maxine's braid a sharp yank. She'd seen Maxine in step with the Chaplain only the day before.

The Loyalist yelped, one hand going for her sword, but Elodie knew she wouldn't unsheathe it. Elodie was still a member of the royal family.

"Brat," Maxine snapped.

"Brute." Elodie flashed the guard a vulgar hand gesture before flouncing up the spiral staircase of the south tower. She hurried down the stone corridor and back out into the night, where glasses clinked and strains of the orchestra faded in and out as the ballroom doors were flung open and shut. Loud peals of laughter burst through the courtyard like fireworks.

Once she reached the edge of the gardens, Elodie removed the glass vial from her cloak pocket and examined its contents for the first time.

The liquid inside was surprisingly viscous. It swirled about its container slowly like a tiny whirlpool. All in all, it was rather innocuous, this potion that was going to rewrite history... if only temporarily.

More often than not, Queen Tera had once told her, *the littlest things make the biggest difference. Take you, for example, my darling girl*, she had offered, while Elodie sipped her afternoon tea. *You look unassuming, but inside that head of yours is enough knowledge to topple an empire. That is how you will win. By taking the world by surprise.*

Elodie maneuvered the vial down the front of her dress, using the underwire of her corset to hold the potion in place. Then she shrugged out of her cloak and balled it up, shoving it deep into one of the hedges. She retied the lace mask across her eyes and took a deep breath.

"You're not fooling me," whispered a voice in her ear. "I know who you are beneath that mask."

Elodie's heart stuttered, then sank at the accent. The vowels rolled high and consonants swept low, just like the hills and valleys of Ethliglenn. She tightened her hands into fists, hissing with pain as her nails dug into her already injured palms. She sighed. "Edgar, was it?"

"You don't sound happy to see me." Edgar looked wounded.

Elodie turned to face him, wincing at the way his shock of red hair hung like a cloud above the shiny head of a snake. The scales on his mask shimmered in the moonlight. A long, pink tongue flitted in and out of the serpent's mouth.

This was the man she was supposed to marry. Their union would make them Lord Edgar and Lady Elodie of Ethliglenn. The alliteration was practically obscene.

"Not particularly," Elodie snapped. "Why?"

Edgar tsked, looping an arm through Elodie's and beginning to parade her about like one of her mother's pet lions. "That's because we weren't afforded a proper courtship. But look at us now, promenading through the royal gardens. I do love the smell of honeysuckle in the evening." Edgar took a deep sniff. Elodie shuddered. From his fashion to his fidgets, everything about Edgar was exaggerated.

"I've had the servants working on your quarters for weeks now," Edgar told her. "I picked out all the furniture myself. I do hope you'll be comfortable. And that you'll be as agreeable as Chaplain René promised."

Elodie wrenched her arm away, flying backward into a hedge. While their impending union had come as a surprise to her, Edgar, it seemed, had been offered more time to prepare. "Chaplain René does not speak for me." She worked to extract a twig from her braids. "In fact, whatever he said, expect the opposite."

"So, you *do* love to cook, then?" Edgar's eyes lit up. "I was told you'd be most difficult in that regard."

"Except for that," Elodie said flatly. "I am too focused on strategy to season a stew."

Edgar began to chortle, a thick, phlegmy sound. "Strategy?" He managed, through deep breaths, "Oh, my dear wilted flower, no. There is no *strategy* to be found in Ethliglenn, thank the New Maiden. We will have a quiet, peaceful life in the new republic. Nothing less, nothing more."

Elodie stiffened. Nothing less than quiet. Nothing more than peaceful. Edgar was describing her worst nightmare.

She gave him a thin-lipped smile and began to worm her way out of his grasp. She had business to attend to. "If you'll excuse me."

Edgar tightened his hold on her arm. "And what if I won't?" His voice was low, the careful calm in combination with his viselike grip sending a shiver through Elodie's blood. That was the easygoing tone of a boy who had never faced a consequence. Had never understood *no*.

Elodie had the sudden urge to knee Edgar between the legs. It was a pity she was forced to showcase restraint when her betrothed had none. "That wasn't a question," she said instead, digging her fingernails into the soft flesh of his pale wrist. "You do not own me, Edgar."

The combination of pain and surprise caused Edgar to loosen his grip. Elodie yanked her arm free, backing away slowly.

"Not yet, I don't," Edgar said, his words sharp as knives, "but it's only a matter of time, dear." His cheeks flushed nearly as red as his hair.

Elodie tried to keep her expression neutral. Power was in the lack of reaction. But she felt no victory. No might. Only a fierce, unrelenting cold. She couldn't stop shivering.

"Everything all right here?" Elodie could have wept at the sound of Rob's voice. Yet even through her relief she couldn't help but notice Edgar stiffen. Now that another man was present, he suddenly had the wherewithal to look chagrined.

"Lover's spat." His attempt at a smile was more like a grimace.

Elodie refused to dignify that with a response. She turned on her heel and strode away, Rob trailing behind like the puppy dog he was.

"Whoa, El, slow down." Rob made to grab her wrist, but Elodie yanked her arm out of his grasp.

"Don't touch me," she snapped, and Rob looked properly chastised.

"I'm sorry." He looked pointedly at her dress. "You're bleeding." His concern turned to anger. "Did he hurt you?"

Elodie glanced down at the rusty lattice of blood crusted across her front. "Not in any lasting way. Scars fade, brother."

"But emotional trauma lasts a lifetime." He gave her a knowing look.

"Such well-adjusted children we are," she muttered, stalking back toward the ballroom. They had their mother to thank for that.

The scene inside was the same, save for a few hundred more people. The music had swelled to a preposterous volume, and the bodies on the dance floor seemed to spin faster and faster with each new verse. People were laughing louder, talking closer, clanking silverware, and spilling peich-nat on the marble floor. It was almost as dizzying as navigating the midnight market, but this time when Elodie's heart thundered in her chest, it beat against the vial tucked between her breasts.

She cast a glance up at the high table. Brianne's head drooped dangerously near her plate. Neither the Chaplain nor Prudence, Brianne's nursemaid, were anywhere to be found.

Elodie tsked. "Someone needs to get our queen to bed. Where's Pru?"

Rob rubbed his neck. "She's...erm, otherwise engaged. In a broom closet."

Elodie made a thoughtful noise. "I didn't think Pru had it in her." She was almost impressed. "Guess I'm up, then."

Rob frowned. "It's early yet. I can find someone else to take her."

"I was looking for an excuse to leave." Elodie shrugged a shoulder.

"But it's your last night." Rob ran his eyes across her rumpled appearance. "You can't go out like this."

Elodie shifted, her corset pressing the potion against her heart. Rob had a point. Tomorrow, life as Elodie knew it would end, one way or another. Either she'd manage to preserve her sister's crown and wrangle control from the Chaplain, or she'd be banished to Ethliglenn. Elodie refused to spend her final night in Velle beaten down and bruised. She would go out with fireworks and flames, a phoenix burnt to ashes.

"You're right."

Rob's lips quirked upward. "Say that again."

Elodie rolled her eyes. "I'll take our queen to bed, get myself changed, and be back before they reach the end of this song." She held out a pinky to swear it.

Rob's already wide eyes were somehow as big as two moons. "What are you scheming?"

Curse him and his infuriating ability to read her. Elodie smiled placidly. "Nothing, dear brother—just anticipating my eventual death from sheer boredom. Promise you'll never come to visit Ethliglenn, or you'll fall victim to the same fate." She gave him a long look. Reluctantly, Rob twined his pinky through hers.

Elodie winked as adrenaline coursed through her like the thrill of poison entering her veins. "I'll be back before you know it."

6

The tears that fell from Sabine's eyes were useless. They hadn't had time to settle, to swirl. It was salt water, nothing more. What a waste. Sabine hadn't cried for the sake of crying in years. Any time she'd felt the urge she'd turned to distractions—floor scrubbing, pickpocketing, anything that might hold her attention long enough to sweep her sadness back under the rug. To save it for later when it was truly valuable.

Now she'd wasted her emotions twice over, and of her own accord. There was no one else to blame this time. No clumsy brother who bumped the table, causing the contents of the vial to slosh and spill. No curious sister who swiped a finger across Sabine's tearstained cheeks and put the salt on her tongue, just to see what it tasted like.

No, these tears had been lost, this magic wasted, because of Sabine. The customer's request was so personal, so honest, that for the first time in her life, Sabine felt well and truly *seen*. But that attention had made her sloppy. She had let her family's only chance at survival slip away because a girl with gray eyes had deigned to smile at her.

"You're sure you didn't see which way she went?" Katrynn had set to pacing, her light steps as graceful as a dancer's. Her usually upturned mouth was pinched, her pink lips pale with tension. Despite the extra height she had on her older sister, Sabine felt small. Ashamed. Foolish.

Artur had settled on a different approach. "You idiot," he groaned, head slumped on the table. "Without magic, these bottles might as well be just colored water. We'll never make rent." He nudged the purse, which clinked sadly on the table, like a single coin clattering at the bottom of an empty wishing well.

"And we'll be out on the street," Sabine said softly. *Because of you*, that voice added, unhelpfully. She clenched her right hand into a fist, stuffing it deeper into her pocket. "We can keep trying, though," she continued hopefully. "A few more hours of Katrynn fluttering her eyelashes might help, some."

Katrynn scowled. "I'm more than just my looks, Bet." She flicked her hair over her shoulder, wisps emerging ephemerally from her long brown braid.

"I know," Sabine said quickly, shaking her head. "That wasn't what I meant, I just…" Katrynn could be so difficult sometimes. Sabine kept herself sad as a sacrifice. Surely her sister could stand to twirl her hair a little bit longer if it meant they'd end the night with some silver.

"Probably best to leave it, Sabine." Even half-drunk on peich-nat, Artur tried his best to keep the peace. "Without your tears we've got nothing more than warm lavender juice." He grimaced.

"I'm sorry," Sabine said, swallowing the lump in her throat. It felt as though she was apologizing for much more than a few words spoken in annoyance. "I'm so sorry. Forgive me?"

"I have to," Katrynn said darkly.

"Why'zat?" Artur snapped a loose thread from the sleeve of his shirt.

"Loyalists," she hissed. "Vendor in tow. We have to move, now."

"What do you...?" Sabine looked again at the stall's fine fabrics their family could never hope to afford to wear, let alone decorate with. "This isn't our stall," Sabine realized, far too late. Upon arriving at the midnight market, her siblings had done what they did best: swindled.

"Anders family rule number seven." Artur grinned. "Never pay for space when you can steal it." Her brother was suddenly full of energy. He was young enough that nothing ever seemed to fully stick to him. Not stain, nor spite, nor spirits.

"Better run for it," Sabine grumbled. "She looks mad." The vendor's face was tomato red; the paint that rimmed her eyes was smudged.

"And those Loyalist swords are sharp," Katrynn added. "Ask me how I know." Sabine hardly believed her sister had time to wink as the sweep of her arm sent their mother's potions tumbling into the waiting crate.

"You're awful," Sabine laughed, even as she pocketed their paltry earnings. Where a moment ago she'd been chastised, now it felt as though she was forgiven. Katrynn had that effect on people—making them feel like the most important person in the room. But sometimes her sister's charm slipped, and Sabine saw pity in Katrynn's eyes as Sabine squirmed on the straw pallet they shared, her sadness growing stronger—always stronger—with every passing day.

"Good thing I can run faster than you two," Katrynn shrieked before taking off at a sprint, the crate of potions clinking wildly beneath her arm as she bobbed and weaved through the throng of masked partygoers. "Love your mask," Sabine heard her sister gush to someone in the queue, even as she ran for cover. Katrynn never ceased to amaze.

Artur was close behind, much steadier on his feet than he had any right to be, with Sabine bringing up the rear, her skirt just a hair too long, causing her to stumble. *You've made quite the mess, Sabine, haven't you?*

Sabine moaned with frustration, the sound lost in the babble of the crowd. Never before had this voice followed her outside the four walls of her family's apartment. After an extraction, Sabine had always returned to her even-tempered self. It was usually refreshing, like a rebirth. A soft rain in the sweltering summer months. But this... this was a slow and painful death.

"It isn't my fault," she whispered, hoping her voice would drown out the one of her detractor as she struggled to catch her breath and keep pace with her siblings. *Isn't it?* came the sharp reply, so quick it was unnerving. *You'd better find a way out of this, or your mother will wish that you had been the child to die.*

Flying fish, what a foul thing to think. Her mother tried her best to hide that unknowable loss, but a baby born still and cold would leave a gaping hole in anyone's heart. The distance Sabine sometimes felt, the way her mother's eyes clouded over, watching a ghost—well, it was clear who Sabine got her sadness from.

"Bet!"

Sabine stopped running, searching wildly for the source of the sound as she struggled to catch her breath. They were outside the city's center now. The alleyways here were wider, the moss that clung to the side of the stone buildings greener. Above her head, a woman hung laundry and hummed a hymn.

"Sabine," her brother called again. A shock of blond hair popped out from behind a door covered in peeling purple paint. "In here." Artur was bent over double, panting. Katrynn was laughing.

"A church?" Sabine hovered at the threshold while her brother and sister stared at her from the foyer. "Are you sure?" Like all children, the Anders siblings had been raised on stories of the New Maiden. They'd attended mass regularly until the roof of their neighborhood chapel was destroyed by a storm off the harbor six seasons ago. While the citizens of Harborside had continued to pay their tithings, no repairs were made. It was cold and damp, the wood stinking of mold, the hymnals warped by the salty air.

"It was because their faith had wavered," the Chaplain decreed, before padlocking the church doors shut. "Harborsiders were not fit to worship." The neighborhood took that to heart and traded their chapel for gambling halls, turning virtue into vice.

"What better place for thieves to take shelter?" Artur said in singsong. "She can guide us to the light." He gestured to the painting of the New Maiden that hung above the alter. Her eyes were stoic, Her mouth tense.

It always surprised Sabine how young the New Maiden had been. As a child, Sabine would look up at the painting and see the features of someone older and wiser—an adult. Now, when she looked up at the New Maiden, she saw a girl no older than herself, trying Her best to look strong. But there was uncertainty, beneath it all—something Sabine recognized: A girl who was afraid Her best might never be enough.

"You really need to work on your bobbing and weaving, Sabine." Katrynn wiped a single tear of mirth from her eye and flicked it away. Sabine envied her sister's ease, the way she could enjoy and

58

express her emotions without a second thought. "You looked ridiculous, running for your life."

Sabine shot her sister a weak smile. She supposed she deserved Katrynn's ire, but that didn't make her teasing any easier to digest. She took a step down the aisle to avoid having to respond.

Moonlight pooled through the stained glass window, sparkling upon the stone floor. The pews were abandoned, absent of any patrons or devotees save for a single candle, a tall white taper, burning brightly amidst the silence.

Artur cleared his throat. "What are we going to do?" He nudged the bag hanging limply from Sabine's hand. It was almost as empty as her stomach. "Da's not back from sea until next quarter. I'm certain he'd prefer to have a home to return to."

Fear and frustration were written all over her brother's face. With her father working off his gambling debts on a merchant's ship, Artur had tried his best to assume responsibility for his family. But he was barely fifteen. Still unsteady. Still uncertain. Still desperate to have someone tell him what to do.

"Da wouldn't want you to worry," Katrynn said, brushing her thumb across Artur's cheekbone. "So don't."

"Yes, because telling me not to worry helps me not worry," Artur groaned. "Bet, tell her."

But Sabine couldn't. She, too, was worried, albeit about something else entirely.

"We don't have any magic left." She wrung her hands, sinking onto a pew in the back row. Guilt flooded her like waves lapping against a dock. "What are we supposed to sell?"

"Don't be stupid, Bet." Katrynn sighed, long and low. "We're not going back to the market."

Sabine frowned. "Then what…?"

Katrynn clicked her tongue, looking exasperated. "There's only one place left to get the money we need."

Sabine's eyes went wide. Her sister couldn't be serious. "The *Black Rock*?" Surely they weren't that desperate yet. But even as she tried to convince herself otherwise, Sabine knew the truth. The Anders family bank contained all of a single copper coin. Between her father's absence, the increase in the Church's quarterly tithes, and the crown's taxes, they could hardly afford to feed themselves, let alone keep a roof over their heads. It was disheartening, the way their endless work never quite paid off. The way life always demanded just a little bit more.

Still, the idea of standing before the worst Harborside had to offer and begging for another loan was devastating. They had nothing left to barter, nothing left to give. Sabine glanced up at the portrait of the New Maiden. She'd never really been one for prayers. The Church leaders said that She was always listening, but Sabine felt silly. The New Maiden never answered. It was only Sabine's darkness that ever spoke back.

"It's our only chance, Sabine." Katrynn sat heavily down next to her sister on the pew. "If it offends you, don't come. I'll handle it. As usual," she added, under her breath.

Sabine bristled. "What does that mean?"

"You were so busy flirting with the pale girl that you gave away our only honest chance at coin," Artur added, far too brightly. His voice echoed in the empty church.

"I was *not* flirting," Sabine snapped. She glanced up again at the portrait of the New Maiden. It looked like She was judging Sabine.

Well, Sabine was judging herself, too. She had done this to them, to their family, over a stranger she would never encounter again.

All because for one beautiful, blissful moment, she had seen her emotions reflected in someone else.

But there was no time to wallow. Sabine had mistakes to mend. A family to support. Siblings to satisfy. And if that meant taking a trip to Harborside's most notorious gambling den, she was no longer in a position to refuse.

7

It was staggeringly easy to approach the queen.

For all their self-important rhetoric extolling the value of their mere presence, not a single Loyalist guard looked her way as Elodie approached a slumbering Brianne at the high table. So, too, were the clergy folk distracted, drinking with the long-bearded delegates from the Fourth and Fifth Republics. Toasting, no doubt, the Church's newly ineffable power.

Her heart beat against the vial of sleeping potion. Each step was purposeful, her scuffed silk slippers gliding silently across the polished floors. The high table was abandoned, plates splattered with thick dark sauces, half-eaten squabs with their bones exposed, cores of apples and pears leaning like fallen soldiers. Most of the cutlery hadn't been touched; forks gleamed brightly while discarded napkins were crusted with grime from soiled fingers. Elodie glanced again at the circle of holy folk with their wry smiles and too-bright eyes, the sleeves of their white robes stained with wine. Heathens, all of them.

A peacock screeched, talons scraping against the floor as a group of partygoers made a show of trying to pluck its tail feathers. In the corner of the room, one of the bears used a gigantic paw to swipe at a man who had stumbled too close to the gilded cage. His date shrieked with laughter as he stumbled away in the nick of time.

It was all just a game to these people dressed in their finest clothes, pulling meat from the bone with their molars, pouring nut wine down their throats. All of this—the transfer of power from the crown to the Church, the way the New Maiden's colors hung in the ballroom, replacing the evergreen of the Warnou family—did not affect these dignitaries in the slightest. They could still laugh loudly and provoke wild animals from the relative safety of the other side of the cage. They would remain overseers of their estates, their parliaments, their thrones.

The future of Velle did not matter to them. But it mattered greatly to Elodie.

She twirled a lock of her youngest sister's corn silk hair between her fingers. It was clean and soft and smelled like the bergamot incense burned night and day in the church. Brianne's eyes fluttered open, the soft blue of her irises like the morning sky.

"Ellie!" Brianne sprang up excitedly from the table. She had mashed potatoes on her cheek.

"I think it's time for bed," Elodie chuckled, passing Brianne a crisp white napkin.

"No," Brianne moaned, looking crestfallen. "The party is only just getting started. No one's even asked me to dance."

"You were sleeping on your supper," Elodie pointed out, as Brianne used the napkin to blot away the gravy.

"I'm awake now," her sister said sheepishly. "Oh, don't make me go, Ellie. I'm having such fun." She stared longingly out at the dance floor, her desire palpable.

"Fine," Elodie sighed, rolling back her shoulders and extending her hand.

Brianne frowned at her. "What are you doing?"

"Your Majesty," Elodie said, with an elaborate curtsy, "may I have this dance?"

Brianne's mouth fell open. "You hate dancing."

It was true. But Elodie had been raised to understand the tactical importance of sacrifice. Brianne accepted Elodie's hand, and the eldest Warnou sister swept them away from the high table and onto the dance floor. Elodie had endured dance lessons years before, Rob always her partner, the two of them constantly changing who would lead so they could assume either position.

Now, Elodie led her sister, one hand gently pressed against the queen's back, the other wrapped around Brianne's fingers. She started slowly, then began to turn them in great circles, twirling Brianne until the train of her dress fanned out in all its glory, nearly tripping a couple nearby.

"It's my turn to lead," her sister insisted, and Elodie changed her grip, letting the youngest Warnou parade her around the ballroom instead. Brianne held her head high, shoulders back, her steps thoughtful and decisive as they waltzed past the high table. "This is much more fun than being the girl." She grinned. Her laughter was so infectious—her eyes bright, her expression relaxed—that Elodie let loose a giggle of her own.

This, here, was what she was fighting to protect. This innocent child, hopeful and earnest to a fault, would not last beneath the

Chaplain's rule. That Brianne was still so bright after a childhood surrounded by the bleak-eyed clergy folk was nothing short of a miracle. But with Chaplain René in control of both Church and crown, Elodie feared that Brianne's goodness would be stripped away in favor of the power her position could offer her father. Their mother's legacy would be reduced to dust.

When the song ended, Elodie pulled her sister close, pressing a kiss to the top of Brianne's head. "Come now." She smiled, swallowing the lump rising in her throat. "I have a surprise for you."

Brianne's already bright eyes sparkled. "For me? Where?"

"Just upstairs," Elodie lied. "Will you accompany me to your rooms?"

She offered her sister an arm. Brianne hesitated.

"This isn't some trick to make me go to bed, is it?" She studied Elodie suspiciously. "I'm not tired, Ellie, I swear." She forced herself to stand up straighter. "I'm grown now. I'm the queen."

"I know, dearest." Elodie tucked a stray lock of hair behind her sister's ear. "It isn't a trick. Just a present."

Eventually, Brianne's curiosity won out, and she took her sister's arm, allowing Elodie to lead her out of the ballroom.

It was quiet in the stone hallway, the ruckus of the party muffled by the double doors. Instead of calming Elodie's nerves, the silence stoked them. She didn't know what she was going to say once she got her sister to the east tower. Really, she should just return to the party and drown her sorrows in peich-nat. It would be the easy thing to do. The right thing to do.

Then again, tomorrow she would depart for Ethliglenn, moving from one end of the map to another. Chaplain René would pivot control of her country to the Church, would do everything he could to destroy the Warnou legacy entirely. Once Elodie left Velle, she knew the Chaplain would ensure she never returned.

If she was going to intervene, it had to be tonight.

That got her moving faster. With each step she carried the weight not only of what she had to do but of the lessons she'd learned in the castle's hallowed halls. Here, she'd walked with two books atop her head to acquire the posture of royalty. There, she'd burned candles down to the wick reading about the political strategies of Velle's southeastern allies. Up the spiral staircase was the room where she'd recited the past perfect tense of verbs in six languages. But Brianne had not received the same education. More proof that she was woefully unprepared for her new role.

By the time they reached the east tower, Elodie's heart had slowed its pace. Her brain had stopped its buzzing. Brianne greeted the guards, who sheathed their swords and opened the door to the queen's chambers.

Elodie bypassed the three sitting rooms and rested on the edge of her sister's bed. Brianne flopped down beside her, sprawling out lazily like the rag dolls she loved to make. She looked so peaceful. It made Elodie pause.

Brianne was a child with no concept of the role she had inherited, whose desire to please those around her meant she was quick to agree, willing to give in for fear of disrupting the peace. No one in the Church would advocate for her. Instead, they would expect for her to parrot their word and follow their rules. No one cared about who she was beneath her title. Brianne was not just a purported reincarnated deity, but a girl of flesh and blood.

Still, even louder than Elodie's conscience was her mother's voice: *Sometimes it takes a monster to keep the beasts at bay.*

"Bri." Elodie nudged her sister before her nerves could get the better of her. She wasn't a monster. She was doing this *for* Brianne. "Do you want to see your surprise?"

Brianne's eyes fluttered open as Elodie pulled out the vial. Inside the glass, the liquid seemed to sparkle, unlike any potion Elodie had ever seen. Then again, that was what the midnight market was for: Rare objects. Oddities. Pretty apothecaries who inadvertently became accessories to treason.

"It's special," Elodie whispered around the lump rising in her throat. "The present I promised you."

Brianne's eyes caught on the bubbles. "Is that peich-nat?"

"Yes," Elodie said with relief, passing the vial to her sister for further inspection. "Your father mentioned he wouldn't let you have any, but I thought you deserved a taste in celebration."

Brianne's face lit up. "Really?"

"Of course." Elodie swallowed thickly as her sister poured the potion down her throat in one gulp. "What are sisters for?"

"It's *good*," Brianne said, her voice moony. "Fizzy." She flopped back down on the bed, tapping the place beside her. "You're good, too, Ellie."

"Am I?" Elodie leaned backward on the mattress, turning to look at her sister.

"You are," Brianne declared, her tone swaying as though she was actually drunk. "You're so smart and beautiful and I want to be just like you."

Elodie's heart clenched. "You're even better, Bri." She reached for her sister's hand.

Brianne fell asleep smiling.

Brianne

It was dark. Darker than her dreams had ever been. She could not discern her hand held up in front of her face. She could not make out the shape of the room—if it even was a room. Yet somehow her feet knew where to go. Brianne rose, her slippers slick against the stone, fingers brushing against the wall as she turned. She was in some sort of tower, the floor beneath her dipping into stairs as she descended—down, down, down.

Her stomach fluttered. The farther she walked without stumbling, the more she allowed the darkness to envelop her, the steadier she felt. Brianne had once been afraid of the dark. She had begged Pru to keep a candle burning by her bedside in case she woke without warning, an anchor reminding her of where she was. Who she was.

Sometimes, Brianne wasn't sure. Neither her father nor her mother had allowed her to consider what she wanted.

When she thought she could bear the darkness no longer, she reached a door. If this had been a nightmare, Brianne would have pounded her fists against the wood, would have clawed until her fingernails bent backward and broke. Either way, she would have been trapped.

But the door opened easily. Was this a dream, then?

The Third Daughter blinked wildly, eyes adjusting to the space beyond.

And then she stepped into the light.

Part Two

The New Maiden was powerful in a way that women from
the Lower Banks had never been before. She came from
ruins to build a brighter world. She stepped forward, Her
voice louder, Her spine straighter than those around Her.
She rolled up Her sleeves, sank to Her knees on the banks of
the river, dug Her hands into the depths of the soil. That was
how She ascended: By quelling the flames that licked at the
beams of Her town. By calling the water back to the parched
riverbank. As the current returned, the water bursting
forth from soil and from rocks, Her followers noted Her first
miracle. It would not be Her last.

—Book of the New Maiden,
verse 12

8

The *Black Rock* had not left its dock in nearly fifty years. The keel was caked with algae; barnacles and cockles clung to the warped wood hull like flies on rotting fruit. The sails were tattered and weatherworn, the once-white canvas now yellowed and crusty. The siren carved into the bow had lost her head. It was unbelievable to Sabine that the ship could still float, what with all the horror it housed.

By virtue of the ocean the *Black Rock* inhabited, its activities lay just outside the Loyalists' jurisdiction. This made the decrepit ship the most appealing gambling den in all of Harborside.

Sabine grimaced as Artur stepped onto a pigeon carcass, its bones breaking beneath his heel. A man stood scowling at the bottom of the gangway, his shoulders nearly as broad as Sabine was tall. She fell back into step with her siblings, who both looked as wary as she felt.

Sabine cleared her throat. "Hello, there?" It came out a question instead of a statement.

"No women aboard," the man guarding the gangplank grunted. A toothpick was wedged between yellowing teeth. "Don't want to offend your delicate sensibilities."

"That's absurd," Katrynn said, stepping forward. "Considering."

The man raised an eyebrow. "Considering what?"

"Considering I already know what goes on below the deck."

The man hacked a lump of phlegm into the bay behind him. It sent a ripple through the calm water. "And how would you know that?"

"Our father is Leif Anders." Artur emerged from the shadows of his sisters. He was the clincher. Both father and son had the same stocky build, same smattering of freckles, same pale blond hair.

The bruiser snorted with recognition. "Your da owes me a thousand kelbers. But seeing as he's a regular, I'm now willing to offer you access. I'll even apply the friends and family discount to your entry fee."

"And how much is that?" Artur scowled, but his attempt at bravado fell flat. Next to this man, he appeared as docile as a house cat.

"How much you got?" the man grinned, exposing a gap in his smile.

"We have to *pay* for the chance to lose money?" Katrynn growled. "Absolutely not. Let me pass."

The man snickered. "No."

Sabine didn't like the glimmer in her sister's eye. "Let's just go, Rynn."

Her father's debt was everywhere, following them around like a storm cloud. For a man who spent so much time thinking of ways to cheat men out of their coin, he was incredibly loose with his own. Leif Anders could lose money on anything. Tell him a ship would sail into the harbor at second bell, and he'd bet you it would arrive one week late. Offer him a tip that sugar would be scarce during the winter season, and he'd stock up on flour instead. It would have been comical if her father's choices didn't directly affect Sabine's life. She was a girl from Harborside, so her prospects were already bleak. But the way her family's finances were stacking up, she wouldn't be from Harborside much longer. She wouldn't belong anywhere.

Sabine's sister seemed less concerned. "How about a gamble of our own?" Katrynn was doing some of her best work, batting her long eyelashes at the man. Sabine could see his hard eyes softening some, even though his stance stayed firm. "If I leave this ship with more money than we came with, I'll give you your entry fee plus a ten percent cut."

The bruiser narrowed his eyes at her. "And what if you lose?"

Katrynn cocked an eyebrow. "I never lose." She offered him one of her rarest smiles, brighter than the lanterns at the midnight market.

The man cleared his throat, considering. "Fine," he said gruffly. "But this one stays behind." He jerked his thumb at Artur. "Collateral."

Artur spluttered with outrage. "I will not!" The man took a single step forward, glowering over Sabine's brother. The guard could crush Artur's wrist between two of his fingers without even breaking a sweat. "Okay, all right, all right," Artur acquiesced. "I guess I'm staying here." He pursed his lips, shooting Katrynn a sour look.

Katrynn ruffled Artur's hair. "Have fun, you two. Back in a jiffy." Then she grabbed Sabine's hand and led her sister around the colossus of a man and up the gangplank.

The ship's deck was deserted, save for a horde of rats swarming an empty bucket, jostling moldy mop strings, and gnawing on broken railings. Rusted knives littered the ground, bundles of shredded sails were flung haphazardly about, and suspicious stains spread across the boards beneath. The quiet made Sabine uneasy; the clutter left her itchy.

"Creepy," she said, shivering. Katrynn, who was nudging a coil of rope with her boot, nodded in agreement.

"Never gets easier, this part." Sabine's sister wrinkled her nose. "I hate it here." Katrynn's shoulders slumped, her usually brilliant smile dim in the starlight. For once, her sister looked the way that Sabine felt.

Finally, came the voice. *She acts as though she doesn't understand your feelings, that there's something wrong with* you. *But maybe the problem is her.*

"I'm sorry, Rynn," Sabine said weakly. "I didn't mean to…" She exhaled sharply. "I'm so sorry."

Katrynn shot her a weak smile. "I know you didn't mean to. Accidents happen."

That isn't the sound of forgiveness.

Anger and shame flooded Sabine in equal measure, the midnight wind freezing the sweat dripping down her neck into an uncomfortable wetness. She couldn't witness her sister's anguish any longer. So Sabine ducked into the dark of a doorway, trepidation in every step as she descended a set of creaky stairs with a loose railing. The weak starlight didn't even manage to cross the threshold down below.

Behind Sabine came the blessed sound of Katrynn's footsteps following her. "Are you okay, Bet? You're acting odd."

Sabine tightened her grip on the railing. "I'm fine." But it came out strangled through her clenched teeth.

"I'm serious." Katrynn's voice dripped with concern. "You don't seem fully...yourself."

Sabine stumbled as she reached the staircase's final step. A lantern hanging on a nail burned low, casting flickering light around the musty corridor. Her right hand fell from the railing. Katrynn gasped, gathering it between her own.

"What's on your skin?" The black in Sabine's veins had spread past the back of her hand, curling up around her wrist like a bracelet. "Bet, why is the darkness still there? You expelled it tonight, didn't you?"

Don't tell her, the darkness warned, as though there was any risk of that happening. *Not that she'd believe you anyway.*

"I'm fine."

Katrynn's brown eyes were wide with worry. "I told you it was too long," she began.

Like she has any idea what you've been through, the darkness chimed in.

"I told you," her sister continued, "that you didn't know what you were doing."

"Stop it!" Sabine snapped, wrenching her hand from her sister's grasp as the ship lurched beneath their feet.

Katrynn stumbled, letting out a small cry. "What is the matter with you, Bet?"

Sabine hurried to help steady her sister. "I'm sorry," she said, once Katrynn had found her footing. "I don't know what came over me. Can we forget it? Please?"

"Yes," came a new voice, grizzled and thick with sleep, "*please* do shut up."

Sabine jumped backward as the cabin door beside them opened to reveal an old man, his gray beard scraggly and patchy, his smell sour, his clothes caked with grime. He looked the sisters up and down dispassionately. "Give me one reason why I shouldn't remove you girls from my ship."

Katrynn, still shaken from Sabine's outburst, didn't speak. Sabine swallowed the lump in her throat. She had never snapped at anyone like that before. "We're told you may know our father."

"Your father, hmm?" The man eyed the girls. "And who might that be?"

"Leif Anders." Katrynn had found her voice.

The man blinked, surprise shading his hardened expression. "Your father has been banned from this vessel."

Sabine frowned. "What for?"

The man gave a grimace. "Your father was caught with an enchanted die during a craps game. Afraid he's not allowed back on board until we're paid damages in full. Is that why you're here?"

Sabine's heart, which had already been bobbing around her toes, found a way to sink even lower. "No, we—"

"We're not here because of him," Katrynn said quickly. "We're here for a loan."

The man tsked. "Can't double-dip from the *Rock*, girlies. Your da's in big time."

Katrynn took another step forward. "We're not here because of him," she repeated. "We're here for us. I want the loan in my name."

The man began to laugh, a wheezing, hacking sound. He laughed so long and hard that he had to clutch the doorframe to keep himself upright. "I'll be doing no such thing," he said, once he caught his breath. "But I appreciate your sense of humor, lass."

"Please." The pain in her sister's voice threatened to send Sabine's heart straight to the underworld to reside with Death himself. The man, too, stopped laughing. "Issue the loan. Keep me here as collateral. I cook. I clean. I'm a good storyteller, too, in case any of you get tired of your little games. I'll work on board until you're paid back in full. I swear on the New Maiden."

"Rynn, no," Sabine said, but she could already see the wheels turning in the man's head.

"Could use some real food in these parts. Do you know how to make blackbird pie?"

"Do I make pie?" Katrynn scoffed. "I only make the flakiest crust in all of Harborside. You're in for a treat." She giggled brightly.

"Don't I get any say in this?" Sabine felt impossibly small, like the mouse that occasionally poked its nose out between the cracks of their kitchen's baseboards.

"You don't get a say," Katrynn snapped, although she kept the bright smile plastered across her face. "Not when..." *Not when you're the reason we're here.*

"Let me stay," Sabine tried, stomach clenching as the man's eager expression slipped several notches. "I can—"

"No." Katrynn's mouth was set in a firm line. "It has to be me." She glanced pointedly at Sabine's hand. "You're the only one who can get us out of this. You're the only one with..." She bit her lip, offering her younger sister the saddest smile Sabine had ever seen, before turning her attention back to the man. "Now then," she said, clutching his arm. "We'll need gold. And a fair bit." She winked as she handed over their coin purse for him to fill.

"Katrynn—" Sabine rounded on her sister again as the man turned his back. She couldn't let this happen.

"No," her sister interrupted. "Whatever you're going to say, save it. Whatever you're feeling, use it." She glanced again at Sabine's dark veins. "Just…be careful, Bet. I mean it." The man returned, waving a significantly fuller coin purse. "And hurry back," she added, her voice brighter. Katrynn was a consummate professional, even in high-stress situations.

Sabine wished she could be more like her sister. She wasn't nearly as quick or as deadly. Katrynn was a sharpened blade to Sabine's butter knife.

"I'll be back," Sabine promised, her voice shaking. "As soon as I can. I swear it."

"I know, Sabine," Katrynn said, squeezing her sister's good hand. "I know."

"*Tassi An,*" Sabine whispered, in the secret language they'd invented when they'd been young, certain their code would be impossible to crack. But her sister had already turned away, following the man into the belly of the ship.

See, the voice whispered as Sabine slowly ascended the creaky stairs toward the moonlight, back to a desperate situation turned even worse, *she doesn't love you back.*

9

The royal chapel was outfitted with three bronze bells.

These bells served many purposes: They played a bright tune to signify the start or end of daily mass; they bellowed a low, deep toll signifying the threat of impending war; they reverberated a sad, hollow call for the death of a queen. But the incessant, endless clanging that awoke Elodie from her restless sleep only ever meant one thing: A miracle had occurred.

Elodie shot up out of Cleo's bed, the unfamiliar floral wallpaper of her sister's room jarring in the morning light. Beside her, Cleo sat up, too, eyes thick with sleep.

"What's happening?" Rob pushed himself up off the floor. Her brother's hair was a mess, his cheek pink and imprinted from where he'd fallen asleep on his mask.

After putting Brianne to bed, Elodie hadn't wanted to be alone. She'd gone back to the party, not bothering to change, the laughter even louder and the crowd even drunker than she'd left them. She'd poured herself a glass of true peich-nat, hoping the bubbles would sweep away her guilt the same way the apothecary's potion had carried her youngest sister to sleep.

When that didn't work, she'd wrapped herself around her two remaining siblings, forcing Rob to dance and Cleo to sing along with the epic ballad penned in honor of their great-grandmother, the First Warnou Woman. The three siblings had trudged back to Cleo's room in the early hours of the morning, light-headed and bone-tired.

Judging from the position of the sun, they'd been asleep only a handful of hours.

"We have to go," Cleo shouted over the clanging of the bells. "They'll be gathering in the chapel."

Elodie wasn't certain if the sour taste in her mouth was exhaustion or fear. Were Brianne truly trapped in sleep, the alarm would have sounded differently. A Loyalist would have come to whisk Elodie away, to brief her on the queen's condition and what was needed to rule in her absence.

Instead, the bells rang out through the castle grounds, alerting the entire court to the New Maiden's latest miracle. It made her nervous.

"You have makeup on your chin," Elodie told Cleo, hoping that her clipped tone would be mistaken for concern.

"Your hair is a mess," Cleo shot back, tossing her sister a hairbrush. Elodie yanked the brush quickly through her locks, smoothing the flyaways and twisting the length of it up into a bun at the top of her head.

"Let's go." Rob was hovering near the door, bouncing nervously on the soles of his feet. "I want to get a seat."

"We're the New Maiden's siblings," Elodie said, sounding more confident than she felt. "They'll save us a pew."

Still, the Warnou children hurried down the long marble hallways from Cleo's rooms in the west tower to the church in the center of the courtyard. They weren't alone. Courtiers and coronation guests flooded from their rooms draped in dressing gowns and covered in glitter. The group descended upon the church like a wave, whispers echoing against the vaulted ceiling.

Rob, Elodie, and Cleo were spotted by a bishop and guided forward to a pew in the front of the chapel. They squeezed together, the sound inside competing with the clanging of the bells. The ringing did not stop until the Chaplain, dressed in robes of aubergine threaded with gold, stood at the altar, hands clasped in prayer.

The silence that fell was electric.

"She has triumphed." The Chaplain's voice bellowed. Elodie scoured his face for insight, but his expression was the picture of serenity. Brianne was nowhere to be seen.

"Not only has the New Maiden risen," he continued, "but She has exacted a plan so perfect only She could have fathomed it. The *Book of the New Maiden* states that when our lady returns, Her reign will be everlasting." His voice was contemplative. "I read that passage daily, and yet I did not truly understand until today."

Elodie shifted on the pew's unforgiving wood. There was no hint of anguish in the Chaplain's voice. No sense of fear or urgency. Instead, he spoke as though this turn of events had always been the plan. She began to sweat. The gray dress she'd worn to the coronation clung uncomfortably, suffocatingly tight.

"This morning," Chaplain René continued, "when I entered

83

the rooms of the New Maiden, She did not stir." Beside Elodie, Rob stiffened. Cleo's face paled. Elodie took a careful breath. The potion had worked.

"At first," the Chaplin laughed lightly, "I assumed She'd had too fine a time at the coronation. But as I grew more insistent, She still would not wake."

The audience's whispers turned to murmurs, sweeping through the church like a wildfire. Cleo began to cry. Rob turned stony. Elodie wrapped a hand around her brother's clenched fist. Only days ago, their mother's life had been stolen by sleep. Now, it appeared, the same fate had befallen Brianne. The courtiers seemed to have come to the same conclusion. Several had fallen from their seats onto their knees, calling out to the New Maiden.

The Chaplain held up a hand and the room immediately quieted. His eyes glimmered. Elodie frowned. He didn't look nearly as humbled as she'd expected.

"We called the doctor, of course, who examined her thoroughly. No sign of poison. No sign of illness. No," he said, each word piercing as a blade, "your queen is not dead. In fact," he said, lowering his voice just enough that the entire room leaned forward, "She has found a way to live forever."

The throng began to buzz as insistently as insects.

"It's a miracle," a man called from the crowd. As Elodie watched the Chaplain's face fold into a smile, she thought she might be sick.

"Yes," the Chaplain said, teeth gleaming in the morning sun, "it is indeed. Our lady, as She exists above us and now, among us, has perfectly preserved Herself in sleep. She is not living, She is not dead. She has ensured her reign will never end."

Gasps echoed up from the pews. Beside Elodie, her siblings were studying the Chaplain intently. Cleo chewed on her bottom lip, while Rob's foot jiggled incessantly. Elodie's fingers were numb. The Chaplain had turned her haphazard plan into something divinely promised. He spoke of the situation so simply, as though this outcome had always been the New Maiden's intent.

Elodie ought to have expected it. Chaplain René spoke for the New Maiden even when Brianne was standing beside him. *I knew you before you were born,* Elodie recalled him telling his daughter. *I know you better than you know yourself. Let me do your work.* Even with Brianne indisposed, he seemed prepared to maintain his control.

"She came to me in a dream," the Chaplain continued, his tone softening, "and told me, 'Father, there is no one I trust to speak for me but you.'" He paused, head bowed. When he looked up, his eyes were glistening. "She begged me to speak for Her, still. And so, citizens of Velle, I humbly ask that you accept the New Maiden's request. That you let me be Her voice and ensure Her will is done."

This time, the shouting of the crowd was joyful. Applause and heartfelt cheers filled the church as the sun peeked through the stained glass windows, casting glittering rainbows across the floor. Under any other circumstances, it would have been beautiful.

But Elodie was frozen, trapped in bindings of her own making. Instead of freeing Velle from the clergy, she had further tightened its grip. She had not considered all possible outcomes. Had underestimated the Chaplain's ability to manipulate political situations for the benefit of his Church.

"The New Maiden," the Chaplain shouted from the pulpit, clutching his heart, "says, 'You must trust in the voices of those I value. I am with you,' She said, 'always and forever in the hearts of righteous men.'"

The gathered crowd murmured their assent. A few even repeated the Chaplain's words back to him. But as Elodie sat, stewing over the impossible mess she had made, something grated on her even more than the Chaplain's triumphant tone: She had read the *Book of the New Maiden* cover to cover nearly ten times, and nowhere in the text was there a line akin to the one the Chaplain had just spoken.

10

Harborside was waking up. The sun began to peek above the horizon as Sabine led her brother home. Clouds clustered above the dock, but a faint golden light pushed through, shining in such a way that the sea seemed to be made of stars.

Sabine kept her head down, chewing on her lip so hard she tasted blood. Artur was at her heels, his exhaustion palpable. He looked as though he'd been awake for a week straight.

"I don't understand," he said, for the tenth time since Sabine had emerged from the ship alone. Katrynn's absence swelled between them like the sea during a storm.

"I told you," Sabine said, ensuring her hand was buried deep in the pocket of her skirt. "She didn't give me a choice." The bag of coins jingled with every step, lighter only for the bruiser's cut, which Katrynn had already factored into their loan.

"But we're getting her back?" Artur pressed.

"Obviously." It wasn't even a question.

"How long will that take?"

Sabine sighed as they continued their way down the harbor, wind at their backs. The gulls cried out like hungry babes and the waves sloshed against ships with a rhythmic lulling. It nearly sent Sabine into a stupor. Their situation was so dire it was almost incomprehensible. How was she supposed to move forward with such a crushing anticipation hanging over her?

"You didn't answer my question," Artur harped, as they turned down an empty alleyway. His voice had taken on the particular whine of a slighted child, his feet shuffling across the stone streets. *He's never had to sacrifice. Never had to give up anything in his life.*

"That's because I don't know, Artur," Sabine snapped, braiding her hair into a messy plait to keep it out of her eyes. She hated admitting defeat, but unless they were going to rob a nobleperson's manor or hold the crew of a cargo ship for ransom, it didn't seem like there were any viable solutions but to save up her sadness. Sabine would happily sell her soul to Death, but she didn't think even he had that sort of money lying around. "Perhaps you'd care to contribute for once in your life?"

Her brother recoiled, like he'd been stung by a wasp. "What is that supposed to mean?"

Sabine threw her hands up exasperatedly. "Just as I said. You spend all your time gallivanting about, drinking with your friends, and committing petty theft. You're hardly ever home, you barely help at the market, you just pop by every time you need a hot meal, then you disappear again to participate in some alleyway brawl. You're as bad as our father, and if you're not careful, maybe one day you'll be worse."

Artur stopped walking. "Don't you dare speak to me that way, Bet." He flexed his fingers into fists, more out of habit than any sort of threat. "You don't know what you're talking about. Spending all day in that rat-infested house hiding under a blanket pretending that'll keep you safe. Maybe you're so sad because you can't accept the truth: You're a Harborside girl. This is all there will ever be for you, so you just give in." He rubbed his neck. "At the very least, perhaps you'll be happier." He gave her a long look before turning away, stalking back toward the docks.

Sabine kicked the alley wall, her anger so loud she didn't register the pain at first. Then her toe began to throb. She let out a strangled yell, her self-loathing a hot, slippery thing. *Stupid, stupid, stupid.*

She hobbled the rest of the way home, feeling sorry for herself on several counts. The worst part, though, was that Artur was right. She was afraid. Terrified this was all she'd amount to—selling tears, letting darkness swirl within her, only ever just scraping by.

Maybe for some, for Artur even, it was enough. But Sabine wanted more. She wanted a cozy cottage somewhere far away. Four walls that fully belonged to her, no neighbors yelling on the other side of the floor. No darting down alleyways avoiding the hawkish eyes of a Loyalist. She'd often dreamed of living on the coast of a quaint seaside town with no docks, only sandy beaches. Places she'd heard about in stories. Sabine needed the salt water, but she could do without the rest of Velle. She'd hoped that one day she could be rid of this queendom once and for all.

Why don't you run, then? The thought blipped across her mind like the flash of green across the ocean during a sunset. Brief, fleeting. Impossible to ignore. *You've got a full coin purse. No one to witness you leave. They'd never be able to find you.*

Sabine shook her head sharply, desperate to scrub the thought away, like the effort of removing an oil stain from wool. Katrynn was being held captive on the *Black Rock*. She couldn't walk away from her family. From Harborside. From her life.

Isn't that what you wanted? The voice sounded disappointed. *Artur's right. You are a coward.*

"Shut up," Sabine muttered. Her dark veins bulged beneath her hand as she turned the doorknob and entered the family's apartment.

"What's that now?" Her mother looked up from poking at the embers in the hearth.

"Mama, it's early." Sabine frowned. "Why are you awake?"

Her mother offered her a small smile. "Couldn't sleep. I love celebrating the spoils of market day. How did you make out?" When Sabine didn't answer, her mother's smile faltered. "Where are your siblings?"

"Ah." Sabine tugged a loose thread on her sleeve. "There were some..."—*absolute disasters*—"unexpected issues. We had to..."—*sacrifice your favorite daughter to Harborside's vilest in order for the family's biggest disappointment to have a chance to repair her damages*—"go to the *Black Rock*."

Sabine's mother shook her head uncomprehendingly. "I don't understand. You siphoned out more than enough of your magic. It should have earned you plenty of coin."

Yes, hissed the voice. *It should have.*

Sabine took a shaky breath. "I lost the vial before we could sell it all."

Her mother's face paled. "You *what*?" It was hardly more than a whisper.

"I accidentally swapped it with a potion." Sabine wished she could melt and disappear beneath the floorboards.

"A patron has it?" Her mother clutched the back of the chair. "Bet, there's no telling how that sort of concentrated magic might affect them." She pushed herself away from the table and buried her face in her curio cabinet.

Sabine's throat tightened. Her undiluted magic treated every person differently. Katrynn had been the first to try, a finger brushed casually through her sister's tears, the salt placed on her tongue. She had giggled for an hour straight, babbling about the stars and the patterns in the dust on the wall. Artur had been bolder, taking an entire mouthful, and ended up with a fever that kept him bedridden for six days. There was no way to know what might happen to the pale girl with the sharp gray eyes should she choose to imbibe.

"Maybe it isn't anything." Sabine's voice broke as her mother began moving bottles about, the glass clinking and clattering. "Maybe she'll be fine."

Or maybe not. Maybe you murdered someone with your carelessness. You shouldn't be allowed to leave the house.

"What sort of potion did she purchase? Perhaps she hasn't used it yet. Maybe there's still time to track her down and get it back. Oh"— her mother grimaced, cheeks paling as she turned away from the cupboard—"please tell me it wasn't a preventive tonic. Or an anti-nausea brew."

"Nope," Sabine said through clenched teeth. "Wasn't that."

"Well, what did she purchase?" Her mother waved a drooping bundle of chamomile flowers about like a flag.

"It was, ah, henbane?" Sabine bit down on her tongue so hard she tasted blood. "She wanted a sleeping draught."

"Oh, Bet." Her mother's eyes were glassy with tears. "How could you let this happen?"

See, said the voice. *She isn't even surprised. She knew she couldn't trust you. Knew you'd do something irreversible if only you were given the chance.*

"I'm sorry, Mama." But the words felt too small. Sorry was for spilling tea on a sweater, or running late to dinner, or cursing your brother when he pulled your hair. It wasn't for ruining lives, for forcing your sister to hold herself hostage so the family could keep a roof over their heads. It wasn't for preventable mistakes with devastating consequences.

"Where is your sister? And Artur?" That her mother did not even acknowledge the apology set the corners of Sabine's eyes prickling. She blinked back the tears, choked down the emotion rising in her throat. She had to hold it close. She had to save it, had to swim in it, envelop it, if she was ever going to get the family out of this mess.

You'll only muck this up further, came the unwelcome voice. *You'll never be the victor. The savior. You're nothing. No one.*

"Katrynn is being held on the *Black Rock* as collateral. Artur is pouting down by the docks." Sabine dumped the coin purse on the table with an indelicate clang. "Here's rent. Now I need to find a way to pay it back plus ten percent to get her free." Her mother's jaw dropped.

She hates you. She wishes you were the one held captive and Katrynn was here. Hot shame crept up Sabine's spine. If her mother was already so disappointed, why not disappoint her more?

"And you should probably know Da owes them money, too." Sabine's heart twisted at the pain that flashed across her mother's face. "More than I do. I'm sorry."

That word again. *Sorry.* So useless in the face of trial. A person couldn't eat *sorry.* Couldn't pay debt with apologies.

"I'll fix this, Mama. I swear it." Sabine's voice shook, but she swallowed the sadness again. It needed time to fester. Ferment. "I'm already working on a new batch." She laughed, too brightly. "And in the meantime, I'm going back."

"Back where?" Orla slammed the curio cabinet shut with a thud of finality, her expression impossible to read.

"To the market," Sabine said, even as she swayed with exhaustion. "I'm going to find that girl if it's the last thing I do."

At this rate, it very well might be, came the darkness's scathing reply.

11

Brianne's chambers were thick with incense, the bergamot fragrant and sweet. All the curtains were drawn; a single candle flickered wildly, casting weak light on the faces of Elodie's siblings. Rob and Cleo were huddled together on one side of Brianne's bed, Elodie on the other, all staring down at the queen's sleeping figure.

"She looks like a doll," Cleo whispered, almost reverently.

Brianne's chest rose and fell steadily, but the rest of her was still. Her eyelids did not flutter. Her fingers did not twitch. She remained in the exact same position she had been in when Elodie left her the night before.

"She looks dead," Rob said flatly, staring down at his youngest sister. Elodie knelt beside the bed, taking Brianne's limp hand in her own. *Wake up*, she urged.

She had imagined this day so differently. A summons to the grand hall. A swift coronation. Four years of protecting and preserving the Warnou legacy. Then, on Brianne's seventeenth birthday, sneaking off to wake her up and returning the crown. She would explain it all gently, would give her sister room to understand not only what Elodie had done but why.

Instead, she had turned Brianne into the perfect figurehead for a corrupt Church clamoring for the crown. The Chaplain could pass the title from clergyperson to clergyperson until Warnou rule was nothing but a distant memory. Until the New Maiden's prophecy had been manipulated to accommodate the Church's every desire. Unless, of course, Elodie could wake her up now.

Elodie dropped her sister's hand and leapt to her feet, ignoring her siblings' cries of confusion. She hurried toward the vanity in the second sitting room and sorted through bottles of perfume and face paint, containers clanking as she searched for the smelling salts her mother had always kept on hand. She found them finally, shoved in the back of a drawer.

She returned to the bedside, the bottle clutched carefully in her palm.

"Elodie, what—?"

Her siblings watched, eyes wide, as she frantically uncapped the bottle of amber-colored crystals and shoved them beneath Brianne's nose. Their sister's chest rose and fell as she breathed in and out. In and out. In and out.

She did not stir.

Elodie frowned, positioning the bottle so close to her sister's nose that it nudged her head. She was absolutely certain the apothecary had said smelling salts would reverse the potion's effects.

"Ellie," Cleo said, frowning, "what are you doing?"

"She needs to wake up," Elodie said, her voice catching. She tapped the bottle of smelling salts against her palm, loosening three small crystals, which she then held up to her sister's face. Perhaps the glass was muffling the scent.

But even as Brianne continued to breathe, she did not wake.

"Wake up," Elodie said, abandoning the smelling salts altogether and reaching for her youngest sister's shoulder. "Brianne, baby, you need to wake up *now*."

Panic rose in her chest as Brianne remained unconscious. This was wrong. The apothecary had told her, had promised her, this would work, but Brianne was still asleep and the Church now controlled the Warnou crown.

"Elodie, stop," Rob pleaded, but her siblings' cries rolled off her like rain.

She shook Brianne again, harder this time, both hands on her sister's shoulders, until Rob rushed around the bed and hauled Elodie off, wrapping his arms around her in a half restraint, half embrace.

Rob's chest shook with sobs as she fought half-heartedly against his tight grip. Eventually she let herself be held, and the two of them stood together, weeping, while Cleo bit her nails until they bled. Everything was wrong and it was all Elodie's fault.

"Mama died in her sleep," Cleo whispered, her brown eyes bloodshot. "Now it's come for Bri. I'm never sleeping again." She shook her head vehemently.

"'Sleep comes for us all in the end,'" Rob quoted the words spoken immediately after the New Maiden's death by one of Her Favoreds, Sebastien. Cleo's face fell.

"Rob!" Elodie chided her brother, but there was no animosity in her tone. Only defeat. Their mother had been dead less than a week. Now Elodie was the reason her siblings had to mourn Brianne, too.

Rob looked dejected. "I'm just trying to think what She would tell us."

"*Brianne* would tell us that she'll only wake for hot tea and fresh cakes," Cleo laughed softly. "Has anyone tried that?"

"I assure you, Cleodette, we were very thorough."

The siblings jumped at the sound of Chaplain René's voice. He had changed out of his purple robes into an all-black uniform. His eyes were bright, his beard freshly trimmed. He was accompanied by two red-clad Loyalists.

"Elodie." He turned his attention to the eldest Warnou daughter. "What are you doing here?"

Her stomach dropped to her toes as the Loyalists took a step toward her. There was no way the Chaplain could know what she had done. Elodie had shattered the glass vial that had contained the sleeping potion. Each shard had been carefully disposed of in different receptacles: one piece in the ballroom's fireplace, another in the rosebush outside Cleo's bedroom window, a third wrapped in a cloth napkin she'd discarded on a tea tray. *Never give anyone the entire truth*, Tal had told her once, as they hurried to remove all evidence of a clandestine trip to the midnight market. *Offer only enough evidence so they may begin to question themselves.*

"We just wanted to see Brianne," Cleo chimed in, chin jutted out defiantly. She was always quick to rebut, quick to throw herself into the middle of any fight.

"After all, Chaplain," Elodie said, swallowing her fear and letting it digest into anger, "seeing is believing."

The Chaplain bristled at her irreverence. "I am not here to reprimand," he said tersely. "Only to remind you that your carriage departs at the next bell."

Elodie frowned. "My carriage?"

"To Ethliglenn." The Chaplain's smile sent a chill up her spine. "Surely you have not forgotten." Elodie had.

"Percy and Mott will escort you to the Ethliglenn cohort." He nodded to the Loyalists. "To ensure you don't get...lost."

Elodie glowered at him. She had been born in this castle, had run down every hallway, had opened every door to ensure she knew where it led. The Chaplain hailed from the Highlands. He'd been promoted to the palace only after gaining favor as the New Maiden's voice. This was her home, not his.

No, he wanted to ensure she was supervised. That he would truly be rid of her, once and for all.

"I don't know that I should depart Velle, Chaplain," Elodie said, trying her best not to let her voice waver. "Considering." She cast a pointed glance at Brianne.

"Considering what, Elodie?" The Chaplain had the audacity to look confused. "The New Maiden has made Her wishes abundantly clear. Perhaps if you had bothered to cultivate your faith, to be a true member of Her following, you would not question Her methods. Perhaps you would hear Her voice, too."

Elodie curled her shaking hands into fists. "I don't accept this."

"You doubt Her judgment, Elodie Warnou?" The Chaplain's voice was sharp.

"No." Elodie swallowed the lump rising in her throat. "I doubt yours."

"We are one," the Chaplain sneered. "I am the Sebastien to Brianne's New Maiden."

Elodie opened her mouth to tell the Chaplain exactly what she thought of Sebastien and all the other men who spoke for the New Maiden, but Rob put a hand on her arm to stop her from further blaspheming.

"El," her brother said dejectedly. "Just let it go."

"Yes, Elodie," the Chaplain trilled. "You'd be wise to listen to your brother."

Elodie clenched her teeth until her jaw ached. It would do her no good to get into a sparring match with the Chaplain, not now that he held so much power. He had been shrewd to publicly proclaim his divine right. Still, it unnerved her how fast he had prepared his sermon. How unconcerned he seemed by the sleep-induced state of his only daughter.

But then, the Chaplain had always been quick on his feet. It was the reason he was so revered, why worshippers traveled for miles to hear his proselytizing. He was able to pivot seamlessly, to make his preaching feel personal. He knew just how to make people believe they mattered. At least until he had taken all that he needed from them.

"Time to go, Miss."

"Princess," Elodie corrected the guard, a person called Mott.

The Chaplain raised an eyebrow but did not respond to it. "Goodbye, Elodie. We look forward to your reports from the Sixth Republic. Perhaps, if you're lucky, the New Maiden will find your future countryfolk worthy of Her favor."

He dismissed her with a wave. The Loyalists took the lead, armor creaking as they moved. Rob and Cleo rushed to either side of her, and the three remaining Warnou siblings exited the queen's chambers.

Elodie had assumed that leaving the castle would be strange and unsettling, but as they moved through the corridors it felt like any other day. The only indication of Velle's new reality was in the form of the ballroom, wrecked by the aftermath of the coronation. Sleeping dignitaries and nobles snored in corners using the tapestries that had once lined the walls as blankets, the stench of bile and peich-nat lingering like a hazy perfume. The swan made from ice was all but melted: Three lone tail feathers remained on the pedestal above a puddle on the floor.

"Wild night," Elodie muttered, wrinkling her nose.

"El…" Cleo's voice was hesitant. "What if the Chaplain is wrong? What if this isn't part of the prophecy? What if"—she cast a glance around at the wreckage—"someone gave something to Brianne at the ball?"

Elodie stopped walking. "What do you mean?" She hoped her sister could not hear the way her heart had stuttered in her chest.

"Yesterday she was fine. Today she's somewhere between the living and the dead? It doesn't make sense. That doesn't just happen."

"Are you questioning the New Maiden's methods?" Elodie hoped the sarcasm covered any waver in her voice. "The Chaplain seems certain that this was predestined."

Cleo's expression soured. "That's a pot of dung, El, and you know it. Brianne is thirteen. Even if she is the reincarnation of a goddess, that reincarnation is just a girl. No." She shook her head determinedly. "Someone did this."

"You took her to bed." Rob's eyes widened. "Did you see anyone in the corridor?"

Elodie's stomach churned. Her siblings would be devastated if they learned what she had done. "No, I..." She worried her bottom lip between her teeth. "Only the guards. I think it was Reirson and Posey." The silence felt incomplete. She needed to cover her tracks. "But you're right. All night she was exhausted. Almost went face-first in the potatoes." She paused, counting to three in her head so that it appeared as though she was struck with an idea out of the blue. "What if there was something in her goblet?"

Rob inhaled sharply. "You think Brianne was poisoned?"

"'The Third Daughter is always in danger,'" Elodie quoted Queen Tera. "Perhaps Mother was right."

"Who would have the motive to do this?" Rob's face was pale.

"My money's on the person standing at that pulpit this morning," Cleo said darkly.

Ten feet ahead of them, the Loyalists cleared their throats. "Get a move on, Princess."

If Elodie hadn't been the one to hand her sister the sleeping potion, she would have agreed. "Lady above and among us, I can't believe I have to go."

"First Mother, then Brianne, now you." Cleo shook her head.

"We're dropping like flies," Rob sighed.

"You two will be fine," Elodie said, more confidently than she felt. "Just keep your heads up. Try to put this all behind you. The Chaplain may be slimy, but he isn't stupid. So be careful."

Elodie dropped her siblings' hands, gave them each a long, tight embrace, then strode out into the early morning light. The day was crisp, like the first bite of a pink apple, and she pulled her cloak tighter as she stood in the shadows of the courtyard, surveying the scene. Footmen scurried about, tying her trunks to the top of the six green carriages that lay in wait. Maids fanned the Ethliglenn cohort, who did not seem to share Elodie's chill. She caught a glimpse of fiery red hair and quickly ducked behind a column.

Her stomach churned. She'd told her siblings to put it all behind them, but Elodie could not do the same. She was in too deep, twined to Brianne's condition and the Chaplain's interpretation like one fiber of a braided rope. She couldn't leave it alone. And she certainly couldn't extract the throne from the Church's clutches all the way from Ethliglenn.

She couldn't leave. Not now, when her country was in danger because of *her* actions. She had put Brianne to sleep, which meant she had to be the one to wake her. The only question now was how?

The brown-haired apothecary from the market would know the answer. The girl with her blushing pink cheeks, her tiny vials, and her faulty antidotes. Likely a local, judging by the shape of her vowels and the way her hair was caked with salt. Elodie would track her down and find out how to wake her sister and expose the Church's greed.

Then, at least, Elodie would be able to repair what was broken. Clear her conscience. Assuage her guilt. But in order to set things right, Elodie would need to commit one final wrong. Which was why, when Edgar's carriage finally departed for Ethliglenn, Elodie was not on board.

12

The city's center was different by day. Without the masquerade's patrons and their head-to-toe finery, the market was underwhelmingly ordinary. Harried housekeepers bartered with pinched-faced vendors while children ran circles around their legs, shoes slapping the cobblestones, shrieks echoing in the air. The scent of spice and roasting meat floated up and down the crowded aisles, turning Sabine's stomach. Without the breeze off the water, the autumn morning was stale.

Sabine hardly ever made it to the market during the day. She spent most mornings buried under blankets, listening to Katrynn mopping, clinking bottles, wringing water from the washing—everything necessary to keep the household running, keep her mother from mourning, her brother from brawling, and Sabine from spiraling.

It's no wonder Katrynn resents you. You're no better than your brother. Perhaps even more useless. You deserve their anger.

Sabine squeezed her eyes shut. The sunlight was orange through her closed lids. As someone who lived in tight quarters, who shared one threadbare quilt with her sister, who woke up to elbows in her side every morning, Sabine had very little experience being alone. It surprised her how quickly loneliness could bowl a person over.

Sabine opened her eyes, but the unease did not leave her. The hair on her arms was raised, goose bumps dotted her skin, and she shivered, despite the sunlight pooling on the cobblestones. As she stood, stock-still, someone ran into her, knocking her sideways. Sabine caught a flash of blond hair, the same shade as Artur's. Sabine was tempted to follow the blur, to find her brother and apologize. To make it so that there was at least one person in her family who did not resent her.

Focus, Sabine. There was no time. She needed to find the girl from the midnight market, although there was no guarantee her patron even lived in Velle. It was far more likely she had attended the masquerade and already departed back to her real life, none the wiser about the vial that held Sabine's precious tears.

Then again, the girl hadn't been wearing a mask, making it more likely she was just one of Velle's many citizens, the type of person who might come to the morning market for a fresh cut of meat or a skein of berry-stained yarn. She might be here even now. Perhaps this wasn't a complete waste of time. Perhaps she could even return home triumphant, vial in hand.

Sabine wandered up and down the rows of stalls, pretending to examine a bracelet here, a spyglass there, as she took in the customers around her shouting and shopping and stealing. Snippets of the vendors' conversations floated by on the wind.

"Did you hear them? Clanging on and on for an hour at least," said a florist to the baker at the stall to their left.

"The bells?" The baker reached for a long loaf of pumpernickel, her fingers dusted with a light coat of flour. "I heard them, too!"

"What does the clanging mean?" A chandler who stank of beef tallow leaned forward over their stall to shout across the aisle. "I never can remember."

The baker gasped, her mouth forming a perfectly round O. "Clanging is for miracles. Was there a miracle?" She clutched a basket of biscuits close to her chest. "What do you think happened?"

"I hope the New Maiden struck down all the attendees from the Fifth Republic," said the florist. "Awful folk. They plucked petals from my flowers and tore my fairy lights to pieces."

"But what do they have to do with the miracle?" The baker's biscuits had crumbled all down her front.

"Well, I'm sure I don't know." The chandler shrugged. "But Merv might."

A man sauntered forward, his skin beautifully tanned, his nails caked with dirt and grime. "The queen is indisposed," he announced to the crowd. The vendors stared at him, startled into collective surprise.

"That doesn't sound like a miracle to me," the florist finally said, raising an eyebrow. The baker fanned herself with her hat.

"Indisposed? What does that even mean?" A produce seller to Sabine's right stopped her stacking mid-apple. "You work in the castle, for Maiden's sake, Merv. We demand better intel than that."

Sabine thought she ought to walk away. *Stay*, the darkness urged.

She took a step closer, the better to hear, pretending to study a large vase with intricate floral stenciling.

"The Chaplain *says* it's a miracle." The man called Merv shrugged. "Gave a whole sermon this morning. Apparently the queen won't wake up, which means the New Maiden's reign will last forever."

"So she's dead?" the florist chimed in, clutching a fistful of baby's breath. The baker let out a loud sob.

Merv shook his head. "Not dead, but not alive, either. Not fully. Suspended in sleep, they said, somewhere in between. Like I said: *indisposed.*"

The crowd scattered after that, satisfied their gossip had been successfully spread thick like preserves. After all, there were customers still left to serve.

Sabine, alone, stayed where she stood. She couldn't shake the discomfort that draped around her like a scarf. *A vial of magic goes missing, and now your country's queen will not wake? Perhaps, Sabine, you're more powerful than you think.*

That wasn't the sort of power Sabine wanted. No, it was only a coincidence, she told herself. A coincidence that a vial of pure magic had been handed off to a stranger searching for a sleeping potion. That the queen now lingered somewhere between life and death.

You don't have even the faintest idea what you can do. You've never bothered to learn. You simply sit and stagnate, wasting what I've offered you.

Sabine swallowed. She'd never had the energy to explore the depths of her power. Not while the slippery, shadowy voice prowled about, circling her like prey. Smothering her hope, her curiosity, her joy.

I'm only giving voice to what you already feel.

That wasn't true. Usually, once Sabine had siphoned out her magic, she returned to herself, pushing the darkness far from thought until it next came time to brew. Sabine feared what might happen if she looked too closely at the root of her power. She'd done her best to never think of her sadness as anything more than a moneymaker, working hard not to wonder about those patrons who used her emotion to supplement their own needs and desires.

Selling off her magic was the best way to make sure she didn't lose herself to the darkness entirely. The voice tried to tempt her, seduce her toward its own wants. It took over her mind. Directed her to anger, envy, and fear.

Sabine carried on, more purposeful this time as she stalked the aisles. Whispers rippled through the market, stronger than before, like wind rustling the brown autumn leaves.

"Is that the—?"

"Couldn't be."

"Why would she—?"

"The eldest daughter."

"*Princess*, you mean."

Sabine frowned. She didn't know much about the royal family, besides the face of the departed Queen Tera, which decorated their coins. She could hardly recall the names of Tera's children other than the Third Daughter, Brianne. If she passed a princess here, in the middle of the market, Sabine might never know it.

Not that she would care much, anyway. All the monarchy seemed to be good for was unleashing the Loyalists on Harborside and increasing taxes in tandem with the Church's high tithes. They were so cold. Regimented. Indeed, Queen Tera had been dead for only a week, yet another already sat on the throne. And *that* queen was now indisposed.

Royal politics were too convoluted for Sabine's liking. In

Harborside, if someone wanted you dead, you knew who they were and how they'd come for you. It was civil. Respectable. The way conflict ought to be handled.

"Thought she'd be the Queen's Regent," continued the whispering.

"But the Chaplain—"

"I heard she's to be married."

"But then why is she *here*?"

So, there *was* a princess at the market. Sabine looked around with interest, expecting to find a dozen red-clad Loyalists flanking a regal young woman in a sparkling tiara. Instead, she saw the same colorless face she had been searching for. The crowd parted like curtains for the girl; some of them even kneeled. But she didn't seem to notice. Her eyes never left Sabine.

Sabine moved toward her, even as she pieced together the impossible reality of her situation. The girl who had taken the vial of her tears was a princess. A princess who had been armed with Sabine's magic the night before the new queen ended up indisposed.

A coincidence seemed less and less likely with every passing second.

13

The marketplace was overflowing with momentum—vendors shouting, children yelling, dogs peeing, vegetables rotting. It should have been impossible to locate a familiar face amidst the madness. Yet there she was, gaping like a fish served whole, scales shining on its silver platter: the girl who would summon Brianne back to the realm of the living.

Elodie's relief was palpable as she hurried forward, trying not to trip over the hem of her silver dress, which had already sent her tumbling onto the market's cobblestones once before.

In just a handful of minutes, this would all be over. She'd have instructions on how to wake the maiden-queen, and then she could storm the castle, revive her sister, and put her back on the throne. She could pretend as though none of this had even happened. Everything would be as it was.

Velle would still be compromised, but her sister would have a voice. Elodie could use her influence to illuminate the Church's corruption for Brianne to see. This time it would be different. But first she needed the antidote.

She returned her attention to the apothecary's sad eyes. Her beauty was in that sadness, the way that it turned her lips down ever so slightly, the way it sent her fidgeting, a finger twisting a long strand of brown hair away from her face, exposing her pale neck. Elodie could almost see the cloud of gray that lingered above the apothecary's head.

But there was no time for her to envy the way this girl's emotion spilled across her face like red wine on a white tablecloth. Elodie needed answers.

"You." Face-to-face with the girl, Elodie found her sadness even more intriguing. Her brown eyes were wide and deep, like the sea at night or fresh earth after the rain. Even now, confronted with royalty, her expression did not shift. Her emotion blanketed her, and Elodie found herself wishing she could wrap herself up in it, too.

"I've been looking for you." The girl's voice was huskier than Elodie remembered. Her breath sweeter, too. Elodie took a tentative step back, bothered by the curiosity that flared up in her chest. She tried not to feel flattered.

She failed. "You have?"

The girl had yet to blink. "You didn't tell me you were a princess."

That caught Elodie by surprise. "I didn't think it was relevant."

The girl considered this, then, after a moment, seemed to agree. "I suppose not."

"Is that why you were looking for me?" She didn't want it to be. While she was proud of her name, Elodie had never sought to be known simply for her title.

"No." The apothecary bit her lip, as though worried she had offered the wrong answer.

"Good." Elodie exhaled sharply.

The girl smiled hesitantly. "Is it?"

"Yes." It was exhausting trying to navigate her status among citizens. Elodie had never had the fortune of being allowed to merely exist. "Why *were* you looking for me?"

"Oh." The girl tugged on her fingers nervously. "I…wanted to make sure you were okay."

Elodie had almost forgotten her tumble amidst the chaos of the coronation. "My hands are fine." She held them out as proof, the once-bright-red scrapes now a muted brown as they began to scab over.

"No." The girl swallowed thickly, avoiding Elodie's eye. "The sleeping draught."

Her skin prickled. It concerned her that the apothecary had brought up the potion entirely unprompted. It was like when the royal chef apologized before serving a stew that then sent a wave of illness through the court. "Was there something wrong with it?"

The girl seemed to brighten. "You haven't used it, then?"

"Oh no," Elodie chuckled darkly. "I've used it."

The girl's face fell. "All of it?"

"Yes," Elodie said. "All of it." The girl looked somehow even sadder. "Which is why I need your help," Elodie continued, willing the girl to meet her eye. "I gave it to someone."

The apothecary's face shuffled through myriad emotions. "It wasn't for you?" She seemed to settle on disappointment. "Are they all right?"

"Well, they're asleep," Elodie said. The girl looked at her with trepidation. "But they won't wake up."

The girl's face paled. "The smelling salts didn't work?"

Elodie shook her head gravely. "Alas, they did not."

"This isn't…I mean, you didn't…" The girl bit down on her lip. "Did you dose the Queen of Velle with henbane?"

Elodie looked over her shoulder. The longer she spent in the market, the more whispers she would inspire, and the more likely it was that her tenuous plan would dissolve and someone would inform the Chaplain that the first daughter was not where she belonged.

"I…" She grabbed the girl's wrist, dragging her into an alleyway that stank of fish and rotting cabbage. "Yes. The maiden-queen gulped down your sleeping draught, and now she will not wake."

"Why?" The apothecary began to pace, lifting her skirt just enough so it wouldn't drag in the sewer sludge.

"Because the smelling salts did not work," Elodie said, exasperatedly. "I already told you."

"No." The girl looked up, eyes narrowed. "I mean, why did you put the queen to sleep?" She studied Elodie intently.

"I'm not here for your judgment," Elodie muttered, uncomfortable beneath the girl's stare. "I'm here for your help."

The girl stopped pacing. "But isn't this what you intended?" She cleared her throat. "When you purchased the potion?"

Elodie paused. "It was," she answered carefully.

The girl frowned. "What changed?"

It was a loaded question. One she had not earned the answer to.

"Everything," Elodie finally offered. "So you see why I need your help…" She squinted. "What's your name?"

The girl looked nervous. "Sabine."

"Sabine." Her name tasted like salt, like the ocean's waves during a storm. "I need your help to wake the queen."

"I—"

"You cannot possibly refuse," Elodie interjected, trying to get ahead of the other girl's line of questioning. She could not admit to this stranger the political machinations that were at play. "The queen of our country is indisposed because of your mangled brew." She turned her haughtiest glare on the girl. "What was in that vial?"

Sabine simply stared at her, lips pressed into a firm, pale line.

"It wasn't the henbane I purchased," Elodie continued. "Of that much I am certain."

Although she didn't speak, Sabine's expression flickered, threatening a frown.

"The Queen of Velle lies between life and death, in a state of preservation," Elodie whispered, almost reverently. "And you're the only one who knows why."

The apothecary's eyes widened, then shuttered. "I'm not in a position to assist at the moment," she finally said. "Your predicament is not my problem."

Elodie frowned. "I'm afraid you've mistaken my command for a request. I am not asking for your help. I demand it."

Sabine eyed her steadily, expression flat. "I'm not the one who poured a sleeping draught down my sister's throat. That doesn't particularly inspire confidence in your partnership." She fidgeted with her sleeve. "Why should I trust you?"

Elodie pursed her lips, thinking of Brianne. "She drank the potion willingly, if you must know."

The apothecary cocked an eyebrow. "That doesn't answer my question."

Elodie wanted to scream. "If you won't help me out of duty, perhaps I can sweeten the deal. What do you require, Sabine, to make this worth your while?"

Sabine blinked rapidly, then spoke. "Ten thousand kelbers."

Elodie blanched. "Surely you're not serious."

Sabine laughed, a half-baked, feral thing. "As serious as my debt, Princess."

Elodie glanced over her shoulder. "Call me Elodie, please."

The girl squinted at her. "My sister is on a gambling ship, Elodie." Her tone was pointed. "She's being detained as collateral, and that is the sum which will free her."

Elodie shook her head. "There are no gambling ships in Velle."

That coaxed a true laugh from Sabine. "Oh, Princess." She smiled wryly. "Everything exists in Harborside."

"Ten thousand kelbers," Elodie repeated.

It wasn't really so much money, all things considered. She'd worn gowns that had cost more. The issue was access to funds. With her hand offered in marriage, the royal coin was less accessible. She was now supposed to go to her husband for spending money. But Sabine didn't need to know that.

"And what if I say no?" Elodie wasn't planning on it, but she didn't need to concede so easily.

Sabine bit her lip nervously. "You won't."

"Oh, really?" Elodie appreciated the combat. It seemed outside the apothecary's nature and therefore important.

"A sister for a sister." Sabine nodded, as though that was the end of it.

"Seems fair," Elodie acquiesced, as though she had another choice. "But you *can* wake her?"

Sabine did not miss a beat. "Of course." She held out a hand. "I can and I will."

"Okay." Elodie wrapped her fingers around the other girl's, chest tight with anticipation. "We have a deal."

114

14

Sabine's father had always been a gambler. He spent his nights haunting the lower deck of the *Black Rock*, throwing money away like it was dice on the craps table. Sabine's earliest memory of Leif Anders was the angle at which his head hung dejectedly while he told his wife how many coins he had lost.

Sabine had hated him then. Hated the way he stank of smoke and rotting apples, hated the way the ink from his gambling ledger smeared along the side of his hand and onto his shirtsleeve. Sometimes, when Sabine scrubbed away the stains from his shirts, the water turning murky in the same cauldron her mother used for brewing, she would silently swear at him. Curse the way her father continued to soil their lives with his selfishness and poor decisions.

Sabine swore she would never be like him, would never make a bet that put her family at risk. But five minutes in front of a princess with sharp eyes and starlight hair, and she had broken that promise. Worse, if this was what it felt like for her father at the craps table, she was starting to understand his predilection for gambling. She'd never felt so powerful. One moment, she held nothing but uncertainty and fear. The next, she was risking her life for the chance to free Katrynn.

All you have to do is wake the Third Daughter. The darkness was even more condescending than usual. It was as sobering as the buckets of water Orla sloshed over her drunken husband's head when he stumbled through their front door at dawn.

Sabine had agreed to help a girl who had put her own sister to sleep. If Elodie was willing to do something so sinister to her own kin, what might she do once she learned that Sabine had absolutely no idea how to bring the Third Daughter back? This was the part of the gamble that felt like a punch to the gut. Like wind knocked out of lungs, or torn sails flapping uselessly in a breeze. The fear.

"So, where do we begin?" Elodie—the *princess*, that foul darkness reminded her—was looking at her expectantly. "Your house?"

Sabine blanched. She couldn't take the Princess of Velle to her family's cramped, crooked apartment. She had already overpromised on her magic—she refused to lose the final dregs of dignity to which she perilously clutched.

"Shouldn't we go to the castle?" She tried to keep her voice from wavering, as though it was perfectly normal to invite herself to Castle Warnou. "That's where your sister is, isn't it?"

For the first time since she'd stalked toward her with fiery eyes, Elodie seemed to dull—the flame from a taper momentarily stolen by a breeze. "I'm afraid that isn't possible," she said, eyes trained on the cobblestones at their feet. "As far as everyone in the castle is concerned, I am currently in a carriage on the way to Ethliglenn."

Sabine wrinkled her nose. "Where's that?" She instantly regretted airing her ignorance.

She thinks you're a fool, warned the voice. *If you don't even know simple geography, how can she trust you to hold up your end of the bargain?*

But instead of laughing or rolling her eyes, Elodie pressed her lips into a grim line. "Exactly what I said."

The tightness in Sabine's chest loosened some. *She's using you. Don't get too comfortable.*

"All right, then. Neither of us can go home." Elodie glanced dispassionately around the alley. "And we certainly can't stay here. So, Sabine"—Elodie turned the full force of her gaze toward her—"where would no one care what we do or why we do it?"

Sabine laughed softly. That, at least, she knew. There was no better place to disappear than Harborside.

Shadows ushered the young women away from the city center. The salt assailed them, and the breeze tousled their hair the closer they stepped to the sea. The princess shivered the moment her silk-slippered foot hit the broken cobblestones. Her face scrunched up into a grimace.

"What's wrong?" Sabine cast a glance over her shoulder. "Are we being followed?"

"No." Elodie shook her head. "No, it's just that..." She looked desperately about. "Why is it so filthy?" She gestured to the piles of rubbish, the bones picked clean, the onion skins shriveled and shrunken, the insects hovering like storm clouds.

Sabine frowned. It was not as though anyone enjoyed living in squalor. Between working for paltry wages, feeding hungry children, and falling victim to vices, the people of Harborside hardly had time to sweep the streets with soap. "You tell me. We pay our taxes, but none of that money comes back to serve us." Sabine stared at Elodie, eyebrows raised. "The Church claims that we have fallen out of favor with the New Maiden, but that doesn't explain why the crown has abandoned our infrastructure."

The princess's expression darkened. "The Church claims many things," she said, the bitterness in her voice soothing Sabine's frustration some. "But tithes and taxes are different. Your taxes are still used for safety initiatives. Beautification. Celebrations."

"If by safety you mean putting more Loyalists on patrol, please stop." Sabine pressed on. "You can keep your parades, too. The route never crosses this far east anyway."

Sometimes, long after the parades had passed, once the carriages were parked and the horses fed and tacked, Sabine would walk the route, kicking at the crepe paper confetti littering the cobblestones, collecting crumpled flowers for her mother so she could crush the petals into her potions. But she'd never seen a parade in all its fanfare. She always arrived too late, was too short to see past the gathered heads of the crowd, too tall to peek through the gaps in elbows. It was a taunt without a taste, like every other experience she'd ever had with a crown-sanctioned event.

Judging by Elodie's expression, she was equally disillusioned with Sabine's world. The princess grimaced as a muffled roar shook the peeling green door of the Weeping Weevil. The tavern's windows were fogged with condensation, but Sabine could make out a thick throng of bodies. Too many witnesses. That simply wouldn't do.

They walked on, past several hovels and gambling dens, Elodie studying each with a morbid fascination. Sabine, too, surveyed their surroundings with a keen eye. Artur and his friends were known to haunt several of this street's establishments.

She was ill at ease with the way things had been left with her brother. His words stuck to her heart: She was afraid; she did not contribute. Well, if she could pull off this swindle, he'd have to eat those words. She would show him.

"Here." Sabine paused before the bright red door of the Pained Pig, a dodgy inn with steaming rye bread and itchy bedding. "This will do."

Elodie examined the sign, which featured a knife stuck in the side of a squealing hog. "Lady above and among us," she swore.

Bold of her to invoke the Third Daughter, considering.

"That's the first time you've mentioned Her," Sabine said darkly. She still mistrusted the other girl's intentions. Actions were better proof than promises, and Elodie's actions were deeply indefensible.

"Who?"

"Your sister." Sabine frowned. "The Third Daughter. The New Maiden. I'm not sure what to call Her."

Elodie didn't answer. Instead, she glanced up again at the tavern sign swinging in the wind. She looked completely out of her depths. "Is this... I mean, are we safe here?"

Sabine shrugged. "Harborside isn't where you feel safe. It's where you disappear. Speaking of..." Sabine slid off her dingy cloak and wrapped it around Elodie's shoulders. The harsh weave of the fabric lessened the vibrant effect of her dress.

"What are you—?" Elodie spluttered as Sabine ruffled her hair until it was frizzy and out of place.

"You looked too refined." Sabine led the girl inside. "Someone was bound to try and swindle you."

The innkeeper barely looked up from his place behind the bar, where he dabbed at a puddle of something brown with a rag that stank of vinegar and soot. "What?"

Elodie looked affronted. "Excuse me, I—"

Sabine slammed an elbow into her rib cage. That wasn't the way to speak to these types of men. They would lunge at any sign of weakness. Instead, she placed both palms on the bar top and leaned forward, pitching her voice low, like Katrynn had taught her. "Need a room for one week. Third floor. With a window."

The innkeeper scowled at her. "Don't have one."

He's lying, her darkness whispered. *I know his type. It's in the eyes. In the rubble. The ashes.*

Sabine glanced over her shoulder at the empty dining room. Bar stools lay overturned, tables with tankards sat abandoned. "Liar. All the vultures from the coronation have returned home. You're sitting on at least ten empty rooms."

"Not all of 'em," he grunted as two towering men descended the staircase, hoods drawn close to hide their faces.

"Fine," Sabine sniffed. "Then we'll take our coin elsewhere. Come on." She tugged Elodie's sleeve, careful to expose the fine fabric of her dress.

She hadn't taken but a single step when she heard the innkeeper's strangled call.

"Wait." Back turned, Sabine smiled. "I've just remembered," the man continued. "I have one room. Second floor. Window sticks. Five coppers a day."

Sabine turned back to face him, offering a hand. "Three, and you've got a deal." She glanced at the princess. "We'll stay for a week. She's paying."

Elodie grumbled something under her breath as she reached into her pocket for the coins. But Sabine didn't care how she felt about the decision. This was the perfect place to hide. No one would know to look for them here. They would be safe. Or as safe as one could be in Harborside.

Their bill paid and key in hand, Sabine led the way up the stairs. The floorboards moaned beneath their feet as they walked down the long hall. The lock stuck. When it finally clicked open, Elodie gasped in horror.

But Sabine didn't see what was so objectionable. There was a window, caked with grime, but the bed was made, the floor hastily swept, and the candles were only burned halfway down. She'd seen worse. She'd slept in worse.

"Three coppers don't get you very far around here, do they?" Elodie remarked.

"Three coppers don't get you very far anywhere."

Elodie removed Sabine's cloak and spread it over the bed's quilt before perching herself daintily on the edge of the mattress. She grimaced. "Is this thing stuffed with rocks?"

Sabine sat beside her. The mattress sank like the straw pallet she slept on at home. "Probably not like what you're used to in Castle Warnou. Welcome to Harborside. This is what we have."

Sabine had always judged the royal family from afar, criticizing their fine clothes and boundless feasts, so it was almost validating how disconnected Elodie appeared to be from reality. But it was hurtful, too. Everything in the small room—the grime, the lumpy mattress, the threadbare fabrics—was Sabine's reality. For the princess to turn up her nose at the only lifestyle Sabine had ever known made it feel like Elodie was turning her nose up at her, too.

The wooden bed frame squeaked as Elodie readjusted her seat on the mattress. She licked her plump lips. Cast her eyes at the floor. Then turned the full force of her gaze directly toward Sabine. "All right. Tell me what you need."

It had been so long since anyone had asked about her own wants or desires. Had asked about anything other than her magic.

Don't be naive, came that unwelcome whisper. *She is asking about your magic. She wants to know what you need to wake the Third Daughter. Which you might want to consider, yourself.*

Flying fish. She hadn't a single hunch how to undo what she had done. But she'd made the gamble. Now she had to see it through. So, in a desperate attempt to save face, Sabine took another page out of her father's book, and she lied.

Brianne

Once her eyes adjusted to the light, Brianne noted three things. The first: an arched window in the small room, displaying a night sky as black as ink and stars that shone like silver.

The second: a table set for two, the plate closest to her loaded with bread and cheese and honey and fruit—dried apricots, just the way she liked, with their shriveled skin and plump, gummy flesh.

She was starving. She hadn't eaten much at her coronation feast, so busy was she meeting dignitaries, shaking the hands of strange, leering men and trying to please her father. No matter where the Chaplain was, Brianne could always feel his eyes trained on her. His faith manifested in attention so intense that Brianne was nervous all the time, afraid she would slip up and embarrass him, would tarnish the name of the New Maiden. This paranoia made her appear foolish when she was simply too attuned to her surroundings. Brianne especially hated the way she always seemed to stumble when Elodie was watching.

Her eldest sister had such disdain for the clergy. As the daughter of the Chaplain, raised by the Church, sometimes Brianne feared her sister's contempt extended to her, too.

Hoping to distract herself, Brianne took an interest in the cheese, the soft creamy center like silk on her tongue.

She was so sick of wearing silks. She envied the sharp, careful cuts of Rob's clothing, the buttons down the front instead of up the back. She longed for the freedom of pants, the ease of shoes with no heels. Those were clothes she could dance in. Those were clothes she could live in.

Instead, she was given garments to wear: dresses of purple and white, soft, flowing things that made her feel more ornament than human. She struggled to find room for herself amidst her role as the New Maiden. Amidst the expectations placed upon her by family and Church. Sometimes, she wondered who she might be without the prophecy. Without the precedent of a deity. Without the attention.

But Brianne was not sure she would ever find out.

The third thing took the longest to notice. Distracted by the delicacies, it did not become clear until she caught the barest hint of movement reflected in the window glass.

"Hello, Brianne." A girl sat across the table from her, licking honey from her fingertip. She was a few years older than Brianne, perhaps around Elodie's age. She looked like a charcoal drawing— her outline sharp, her center hazy—more concept than person. "We've been waiting for you."

The bite of bread stuck in Brianne's throat. A shiver ran down her spine.

The third thing Brianne noted was inarguably the most important: Wherever she was, she was not alone.

PART THREE

*The New Maiden's Favoreds spanned many walks of life.
Not all had taken an honest path to join Her, but the New
Maiden was not concerned with who people had been so
much as who they could be.*

*Petra and her sister Hera had been friends with the New
Maiden since birth. There was never any question of their
loyalty to Her, even in Her earliest hours when nonbelievers
were loud and plentiful.*

*Beck had stumbled upon Her camp in the middle of the
night, bloody and bruised. She had since blossomed into the
New Maiden's gentlest follower, though she never spoke of
where she had been before.*

*Ruti had abandoned Her, at first. She had followed the
doubters away from the ruins of their home. But when she
finally witnessed proof of the New Maiden's work, she returned
to the Lower Banks and was welcomed back with open arms.*

*Theo and Mol had come to the Lower Banks after She had
revived the land. Her word had begun to spread, and they
had laid down their tools at Her feet, promising to use them
only in service of Her work.*

*Although Sebastien was among the first to join Her fold, he
was the last to pledge his loyalty. He pressed and balked and
fought Her word, but the New Maiden delighted in every
battle. His scrutiny ultimately bolstered Her strength and
enduring work. Once he fell into Her favor, none could say
he had not earned his place by Her side.*

—Book of the New Maiden,
verse 75

15

They were halfway to the Garden District before Elodie could accurately recite the list of Sabine's required ingredients.

The apothecary had protested when Elodie said they were leaving their cramped quarters and venturing back out into the city. They were supposed to be keeping a low profile, she argued. They could hide between the nut trees, Elodie insisted. There were only a few hours left of daylight, and they simply did not have time to waste. Every minute Brianne remained encased in sleep, Chaplain René's claim to the crown grew stronger. Elodie had now witnessed the deprivation in Harborside. She could not bear to watch the Chaplain continue to pilfer taxes and tithes from the people of Velle only to reward his contacts in the outer republics. The first daughter had to protect her country. And that meant waking her sister.

"How much farther?" Sabine asked for the fifth time.

"Just a little way past the western bridge." Elodie gestured vaguely. "You've really never been to the Garden District? It's so close."

Sabine shrugged. "We've always just grown herbs in the sill of our kitchen window. Picked the dried petals from the alley behind the funeral parlor or off the street after a parade. Never had the means to purchase greenery new."

Dried petals from behind the funeral parlor. It was so unbearably sad. Any time she wished, Elodie could go pluck a rose, no matter the season. Fresh flowers littered every room in the castle, their perfume wafting through the halls, sweet to the point of being sickly. Sometimes even the most elaborate arrangements fell into the background of her consciousness, like curtains or throw pillows. Just another decoration. One more thing to take for granted.

If the Chaplain and the Church remained in possession of the crown, who was to say how many more of Velle's citizens would be denied such pleasures?

Elodie put a hand in her pocket, feeling for the remaining coins she had. They clanked merrily enough, but for the first time in her life she was focused on how much she didn't have, rather than what was there.

She didn't like the tiny thread of panic this new perspective inspired—the way it fluttered uncomfortably in her chest like a songbird on its perch. Impossible to ignore.

She focused on something she could control: information. "What are the items again?"

"A dried mushroom from the Nettle region. A lily pad plucked from the swamps of Redfell. A starflower bloomed beneath the light of a full moon. A pinch of earth from the Forest of Ipswall." Sabine listed them easily, despite the tongue-twisting nature of the ask. "That's the tenth time you've asked me."

"It's just so...specific." Elodie repeated the ingredients again. She hadn't the faintest idea how these elements would wake

Brianne, but then, she supposed it didn't matter. She merely had to procure the pieces to this puzzle. Sabine would do the rest.

They carried on through Harborside, where the dockhands bellowed curses just as foul as the smell of horse stables. It was all so loud, harsh like the scrubbing brush that sloughed off her skin in the bath each season. Salt settled on her tongue, the wind whipping her disheveled hair into the back of her throat.

The gusts settled as they crossed the canal by way of a short stone bridge and entered the Iron District. Here the noise was more consistent, clanging and clamoring, but all in time, like one of Rob's compositions. The smell was searing and metallic as swords were forged all around them. Elodie was practically bowled over by sense memory. Tal had always smelled of steel, had carried that sharp, cruel scent in the fibers of his clothes and hair no matter how many ways he tried to disguise it. It had been at odds with his playful smile and easy nature. The way he'd thrown back his head to laugh at Elodie's every joke, even when they weren't funny. She missed him terribly. Her predicament could greatly benefit from his tactical mind. Instead, she had only the apothecary.

Elodie watched the way Sabine walked, eyes trained on the cobblestones. Even with her head down, she moved as fluidly as a fish through water. Still, her dress did not hang quite right, the waistline a bit tight, the hem too short. She looked like Brianne when she'd dress up in their mother's clothing. Putting on an act. Struggling desperately to look the part.

This close, she could see signs of weariness in the bags beneath Sabine's eyes, in the way her hair hung limply, sea sprayed and slick. In the silence they shared, Elodie realized for the first time exactly how much faith she was putting in another person.

Elodie had always taken after her mother. Her devotion was to country, not Church. To places, not people. But now, assigning so much trust to Sabine, a girl she only knew from a mistake...it frightened her. She needed to ensure that this time, everything went smoothly.

"What went wrong?" Elodie asked the apothecary, as they left the Iron District behind.

Sabine looked at her warily. "That's quite the loaded question."

Elodie smiled, very nearly charmed. "With the sleeping potion, I mean. Why didn't the smelling salts wake my sister?"

The apothecary bit her lip. She seemed to be silently warring with herself, eyes darting back and forth as she considered. "I'm not sure you want to know."

Elodie raised her eyebrows. "Now you have to tell me. I've got quite a bit of coin on the line, after all."

"Are you getting cold feet, Princess?" Sabine's attempt at teasing was hesitant, and Elodie felt a flush of tenderness toward the girl. It was refreshing to be with someone who did not seem to have an ulterior motive. Someone who was exactly who they said they were.

"Information is power. I'm sure you can understand."

"I sometimes wish I could know fewer things," Sabine said softly, that signature sadness pooling in her eyes.

Elodie considered the girl beside her. Sabine was haunted by something. She contained a level of emotion Elodie could not fathom, having been raised by a cold, calculated mother. Yet she was attracted to the apothecary's feelings. She wanted to know all about them.

"You don't have to tell me." Elodie shifted focus, now invested in shooing away Sabine's sadness. "But if you wanted to, you could."

Another war took place behind the apothecary's eyes. This time, she waited several minutes to respond. "I gave you the wrong vial."

Elodie frowned. "But it still put my sister to sleep."

Sabine nodded, sucking her lips into her mouth as though to keep herself silent.

"So what did you give me?" Trepidation creeped up Elodie's spine. "What did she drink?"

Elodie, who thought she was decently well-read and worldly, was still not prepared for Sabine's answer: "My tears."

"Your...?" Elodie had never heard of such a thing. "I don't understand."

Sabine, who had seemed to brace herself for a harsher reaction, exhaled. "I don't, either, really. But when I bottle up my emotions, let them stew and simmer, my tears have...power."

Elodie squinted at her. "Like...magic?"

She'd never had much use for magic. She had never needed it to reveal her deepest desires or influence her heart. She had always known what she wanted, had always been surrounded by everything she needed. But for someone in Sabine's circumstances, she could see how it might make all the difference.

Sabine nodded, looking relieved. "Exactly. They accelerate the efficacy of potions. I"—she cleared her throat—"added a few drops to your henbane. Usually we charge extra, but..." She shrugged, cheeks turning pink.

"You did?" Elodie was oddly touched. She was used to scrutinizing all favors, to working out what the other person wanted from her. But Sabine had helped her for no reason at all.

"When you said you wished you could sleep until the world was different," Sabine said softly, "until *you* were different. I..." She looked pointedly at the cobblestones beneath their feet. "Let's just say, I understood."

"Oh, Sabine—" Elodie began, but the apothecary cut her off.

"Then I picked up the wrong vial in our handoff and sent you away with all the tears instead. Once my family realized what I'd done, we had nothing of value left to sell, and, well..." She sniffed. "My sister sacrificed herself for my mistake. All of this is my fault."

Elodie's stomach squirmed uncomfortably. She felt exposed by Sabine's confession.

"You're not the only one at fault," Elodie said softly. "I was trying to protect my sister—protect Velle—from the Chaplain, but I only served to make him stronger. If I had simply accepted defeat, none of this would be happening."

"You don't seem like the kind of person to accept defeat." The corners of Sabine's mouth twitched as her eyes met Elodie's. "You're too fierce for that."

Heat flooded Elodie's cheeks. She was the first to look away.

As they crossed the western bridge into the Garden District, Elodie found herself grateful for the shade, for the long-limbed branches that tenderly brushed the cobblestones. It allowed the blush to fade from her cheeks. Gave her a moment to tuck away the flutter in her stomach.

The air was laced with perfume and the rich, luxurious spread of soil. In shop windows, ferns and other flora bent toward the autumn sun. Stalls lined with freshly cut flowers radiated with delicate petals and sweet fragrances. The district was lush, green, and earthy, a feather pillow upon which to rest one's head. Elodie desperately needed a nap.

Beside her, Sabine had softened in their new surroundings. Elodie led them around a corner, down a clean stone street where tiny potted plants lined the road. A stretch of storefronts with wide windows boasted dried herbs and bundles of pressed flowers.

Sabine turned instinctively to a bright green door of a shop stenciled with the name THE HERBALIST.

A bell tinkled above the shop door as they made their way inside, the air bright with the bite of herbs. A woman looked up from behind the counter, glasses perched precariously on the end of her nose. Curiosity and skepticism flashed across her face at the sight of them. It set Elodie on edge. She'd never been greeted with suspicion. Beside her, Sabine shrank slightly, her height disguised by the way she slouched, hunching her shoulders forward as she drew into herself.

There was a glassy look in Sabine's eye. Almost as though she was losing an argument with herself. Elodie hated to see her made small and wanted to fix it, to draw her back out and beg her to take up the space she deserved.

"Pardon me," she used her most uninterested voice, "we are looking for a particular mushroom. From the Nettle region. Dried, preferably, as—"

"What do you want them for?" the woman interrupted, eyes squinting. "Those mushrooms aren't for chewing like cud and laughing while the stars dance before your eyes. It's expensive to import from Nettle." Her eyes darted quickly at a glass jar on the highest shelf. "They're valuable."

Elodie gaped at her. Never in her life had she been so callously dismissed. "Hence why I seek them," she said, through gritted teeth. "Do you think that I would part with the coin I can tell you overcharge just to chew on stale mushrooms that have spent three seasons drying in the sharp Nettle sun? I am no fool. Shame on you for painting me as such."

Elodie removed the dingy cloak from her shoulders to reveal the fine gown underneath. She watched with satisfaction as the woman behind the counter pulled her glasses higher up her nose.

"Ah, I…I only meant to warn…I didn't mean to offend…" She finally deigned to step out from behind the counter, wringing her pale hands.

"I only mean to spend my coin elsewhere, then." Elodie batted her eyelashes, offering the woman a winning smile. "Goodbye."

Before the shopkeeper could do more than splutter, Elodie had taken Sabine by the hand and pulled her out the door. She laughed brightly, the autumn breeze sweeping her hair and tickling her neck. But when she turned back to Sabine, the girl was frowning and asking, "What was that?"

Elodie licked her lips. "A consequence."

"You shouldn't have said anything." Her expression was dark.

"Why in the Maiden's name not?"

Sabine exhaled sharply. "Because it was embarrassing. People with money love to act as though I'm no better than a bug beneath a boot. But if you acknowledge it, they win. You let the shopkeeper win."

Elodie threw her hands up in the air. She'd only been trying to help. "We'll go back in, then."

Sabine looked horrified. "The only thing worse than what you just did would be going back there."

"Fine," Elodie said, trying not to let the sting of Sabine's disappointment settle. "Let's just pick another vendor and be done with it." She chose a storefront at random, landing on one with a red-bricked exterior and tangled ivy across the window that obscured the stenciled gold lettering over the door.

"Fine," Sabine huffed, storming toward the shop. Elodie, starting to fear she was in over her head, wearily followed.

16

It was darker in the second shop. Here, there was no merry entrance bell, just the watchful eyes of a lizard perched upon the counter that was made from the wood of the peich-nat trees, the brown of the bark lined with ash-gray rings. From the back doorway slithered forth a shadow—no, a lithe, spindly man whose posture mirrored that of his scaly pet to an alarming degree.

He took in the faces of the two girls standing before him. Unlike the woman up the street, he did not shudder or shrug. Instead, he narrowed his eyes, as the pink tongue of his lizard flitted out lazily.

"Hello." The man peered curiously at them. "How might I help you?" He cocked his head, examining Elodie. "Dandelion roots for a detoxifying tea? Purge your demons and your pores?" He shifted his gaze to Sabine. "Or perhaps yarrow blossom for anxiety? Quiet all the . . . noise?" His eyes felt a bit too knowing.

The shopkeeper seemed to recognize her suspicion. "I have a knack, they tell me." He smiled apologetically. "Of looking too closely. Seeing too much. Hence my empty store. My accuracy frightens folks."

"Or maybe it's the lizard," Elodie muttered under her breath.

"Actually, I…" Sabine took a deep breath. She reviewed the list of ingredients one more time. She braced herself for the expression of incredulity that would paint the man's face when she told him what she sought. In fact, she was counting on it.

When Elodie had asked what Sabine needed, her mind had gone blank. At first she'd considered an endless list of ingredients, but then she pictured herself surrounded by wilted herbs with no idea what to do with them. So instead, she'd gone for specificity. Items so unique and rare that their cost could hardly be justified. Items she could never dream of procuring. Surely that would buy her time enough to figure out what, exactly, she was going to do.

"I'm looking for some very specific ingredients." Sabine listed them out, waiting for the blessed moment when the man's too-bright smile would turn into a frown. But it never came.

Instead of scowling, the shopkeeper jumped to attention. "I don't know what you're planning, but I'm certainly interested. No one tends to disturb those shelves." He glanced up at the glass jars that lined the back wall. "But I think I have nearly everything you need. Might have to check the latitude of the soil, though I'm certain it's from the outskirts of the Forest of Ipswall, at the very least. May cost you a pretty penny, though."

Elodie's face brightened. "Cost is no concern." Her gray eyes settled on Sabine, who tried to combat the nerves swirling in her stomach.

She wondered what it might feel like to be so thoughtless about money. To close her eyes and no longer see the thick black lines of her father's ledger, the years he had to spend at sea to pay back what he owed. She wanted to go to the market and buy an apple, to bite into the crisp pink skin and let the juice run down her chin without thinking about where that coin was supposed to go, and if her family could survive without it.

The shopkeeper dug through his potted plants, soil falling on the countertop like snow as he worked to extract the starflower's roots fully intact, while Elodie looked on gleefully. Sabine didn't like how serene the princess appeared. As though all their problems had been solved in one fell swoop.

As far as she's concerned, it's true, the darkness confirmed. *Liar.*

That she was. Sabine had been a liar as she paced the well-worn floorboards of the Pained Pig, and she was a liar now, as she reached for the supplies carefully curated by the shopkeeper. She was a liar as she watched Elodie count out the coins they owed, more money on the counter than Sabine had ever held, but rather than scream, she smiled.

The shopkeeper handed over their wares. Sabine watched her own fingers close around the handle of the supply bag, heard her voice thank the shopkeeper, felt her feet shuffle out the door behind the Princess of Velle, a girl who had placed all her faith in Sabine. The apothecary refused to consider how much it was going to hurt when she inevitably let Elodie down.

The air in the Garden District was sumptuous to the point of suffocation, as though she was breathing the thick clouds of fresh perfumed air through cloth. Sabine missed the bite of sea and salt. It was hard to believe that such a quiet, rich area could exist in Velle, only two bridges away from the bustle of Harborside.

It might as well have been a different world. *But you don't belong here, do you, Sabine? The first shopkeeper made that abundantly clear.*

"Sabine?" Elodie was looking at her with concern.

Sabine felt her cheeks heat up with the full force of her attention. "Yes?"

"What's the matter?" A red-gold leaf blew up from the street and lodged itself in Elodie's messy hair. Her voice was heavy with concern.

Sabine tugged at her sleeves, and her heart sank. The black swirling through her veins had crept higher, up her forearm and toward her elbow, as though she was wearing a glove.

"I'm…fine," she said, trying to sound nonchalant. Instead, an odd warmth circled in her chest at the princess's attention.

She had opened herself up, shared the truth of her confusing, endless well of emotions, but Elodie had not laughed, had not made her feel small or lesser, the way Artur and Katrynn did. Instead, she had admitted failings of her own.

That this strong, powerful girl could sometimes feel just as helpless as Sabine did made her think perhaps she wasn't as weak as she'd always believed.

"Are you sure? Your eyes looked…" Elodie frowned. "Never mind." But she didn't seem convinced. "This way."

Sabine clutched the supply bag closer as she followed, the aroma of the ingredients settling her some. The floral notes of the starflower made her think of her mother, the way she used to pack satchels of herbs to be tucked beneath her children's pillows. *Sweet scents for sweet dreams*, Sabine remembered her saying, even though it was obvious her mother was simply trying to mask the city's smell.

They'd never had much, but they'd always had love. *But now you've gone and bungled that, too. Your mother doesn't respect you. You cursed out your brother; you sacrificed your sister. Your mistake has put your entire family at risk.*

The once-fresh fragrance now set her stomach roiling. Katrynn was stuck in the seedy underbelly of the *Black Rock* while Sabine gallivanted around the Garden District with a princess. She needed to focus on the real task at hand: getting her sister free.

Sabine quickened her step to catch up with Elodie. The trees that lined the street were beginning to thin, opening up to reveal regal stone buildings towering above the quaint street. Pink streaked the sky as the sun began to sink, dark blue spreading like dye on linen. She turned to Elodie. "This isn't the way we came."

Elodie snickered. "Well spotted."

"Where are you taking me?"

"Don't ask how I know this, but the taverns in the Commerce District have some of the best pies in Velle."

Sabine blinked at her, nonplussed. "Pies?"

"For supper," Elodie said. "I'm not eating at that inn. They probably grill rats and stuff them between bread."

"The bread there is actually quite good," Sabine said softly, but Elodie had already forged onward toward a building with lightly frosted windows and a roaring fire flickering through the panes. Even before Elodie opened the door, Sabine's stomach growled. The mouthwatering scent of roasted meat and browning butter filled her nose.

They were the sort of smells she'd stolen while wandering the market with Katrynn and Artur, looking for their next mark, swallowing the drool that puddled in her mouth as she imagined the richness of true butter instead of the curd her family spread on toast. It had only ever been an olfactory dream and nothing more. But as she stepped into the tavern, she was nearly bowled over by her appetite.

The Wiltern was a cozy, dimly lit place with long tapers and wooden tabletops ringed with condensation stains. There was a smattering of people sprawled across long benches. Not enough to be claustrophobic, but enough to speak to the quality of the place.

"Come, come." Elodie waved Sabine over to an empty table. She swung her leg over the bench, combing out her tangled bun with her fingers, pale skin fading into the white silk of her hair. It fell perfectly around her face. In the warm firelight of the sunken afternoon, she looked almost soft.

Gone was the cut-blade sharpness of hammer striking anvil, the angle of Elodie's cheekbones and harsh line of her jaw shifting into something feather-soft and inviting. Sabine had never looked upon the faces of boys with such interest, had never needed to reckon with herself about what her heart wanted. She had always known, however hypothetical the knowing might be, that she longed for the touch of another girl. Now that she sat across the table from one so beautiful, sharing dinner in a charming tavern, she very nearly forgot herself and reached for Elodie. She wanted to know if the princess's skin was as smooth as it looked, if the pink of her cheeks when she ran out of breath were as sweet as the berries they resembled. Instead, Sabine smoothed her skirt, busying her hands and catching an unwelcome glimpse of the black veins creeping up her arm. She pushed her sleeve over it, twisting the cuff in her palm.

You can hide, Sabine, but you cannot run.

"Sabine?" She looked up to find Elodie watching her. There was something behind her eyes that made Sabine pause. Made her feel warm, too. "Do you want wine with your pie?"

"I..." Sabine glanced up at the tavern girl, who had twisted a curl around her finger as she spoke to Elodie.

She's very pretty, isn't she? The warmth faded, like a fire extinguished. Of course Elodie would find someone to flirt with. Someone gregarious with a wide smile, someone whose every thought, every action, every instinct wasn't dictated by a blooming darkness.

140

Jealous? No. Sabine was not jealous. She was merely pragmatic. Unfortunately, the two instincts often led to the same result.

"I've…never had wine," she finally managed. She'd only been able to afford peich-nat and flat mead. Wine was a luxury. The serving girl let out a surprised laugh. Elodie didn't.

"Wine for us both, then." It was an order and a dismissal, so curt and contained that even the serving girl looked stunned. She extracted the finger from her curl, dropped the warmth from her smile, and stalked away, tray tucked beneath her arm.

"You certainly know how to command a room." It was an off-handed comment, but Sabine thrilled as she saw something like pride flash across Elodie's face.

"I've been in training my entire life." Elodie's expression fell slightly. "Not that it got me anywhere when it truly counted…" Her voice was bitter.

"Aren't you worried someone here will recognize you?" Sabine glanced around the tavern, although none of the other patrons seemed to offer them a whit of attention.

"Not at all." Elodie laughed. "I loom in the shadows of the Third Daughter." Her expression flickered. "The lithograph they made of my face to put on coins is long destroyed." She ran the back of her hand down the length of her cheek. Sabine wanted to follow that line with her own finger, forehead to clavicle, one sweeping motion.

And then pluck her eyelashes and put them in a bottle. She did have strange impulses around Elodie. Sabine sat on her hands, just to be safe.

The serving girl returned, balancing glasses and steaming plates on a wide tray. She placed the dishes down on the tabletop with a *thunk.* She did not look at Elodie, but she glowered at Sabine.

She can see you don't belong together. Everyone knows it.

Elodie, however, did not appear bothered. She had shoved a steaming bite of pie into her mouth, stuffing dripping down her chin. "Umfff," Elodie moaned through a mouthful of stewed meat. "As good as I remembered."

Sabine set to work eating a bit more daintily. That is, until she swallowed her first bite. Only then did she realize how ravenous she was, after a day and night and another day of brewing, selling, scheming, and buying, with nary a thought of food or sleep in between. As she made her way through the pie and the wine—the liquid like velvet on her tongue—she felt the knots between her shoulders loosen slightly, felt the buzzing in her brain quiet.

"You haven't said much."

Sabine glanced up, fork halfway to her mouth, shocked to find her plate nearly empty, her goblet drained. "Sorry," she mumbled through a bite of flaky pastry crust. "Distracted, I guess."

"It's good, isn't it?" It was a question, not a command. It left room for Sabine. But she didn't know how to fill it.

So she nodded, mouth full and tongue slightly burnt in her eagerness, numbing any potential response. That silence was a gift, rather than a hindrance. For at the table opposite them a group of patrons, red-faced and brooding, were speaking. The smallest man among the bunch, the one with the longest, wildest beard, held his compatriots enrapt. Other necks craned toward them, and it was clear that the evening's entertainment would not be a poet or musician but a storyteller.

"Concerning this," the storyteller went on, stroking his beard in a way that seemed orchestrated, "that the Third Daughter is indisposed. Doesn't ring true of the New Maiden, who found Her way to power with much more gravitas."

"He's going to tell it again, isn't he?" grumbled one of the man's companions.

"Griffin can't help himself," said another, downing the remaining contents of his tankard.

"That means he's buying," chimed in a third. When Griffin opened his mouth to protest, his friend stared him down. "We agreed. You made a pact last time."

"Fine," Griffin sounded dejected.

"Barkeep!" The table hollered for another round, their laughter so infectious Sabine found herself smiling.

Griffin, meanwhile, got to his feet, scanning the room for listeners. Although Elodie was more interested in her pie, Sabine couldn't contain her curiosity. She'd only heard the priests' droning text at the Holy Day masses her mother once dragged them to. She'd never been privy to the whispered stories passed along by people in taverns.

As if he could sense her attention, the storyteller met Sabine's eyes. He smiled. Then he began to speak:

The New Maiden was not, until She was. Like flint struck against stone to make a spark—darkness dissipated to make room for the light. And indeed, it was flame that brought the New Maiden forth. Once a girl, whose town was ravaged by a warring province. Whose bedroom was burned by orange-yellow-red-hot fire. Who emerged—odd and awed like a baby bird—from the ashes. A woman born. And She wiped the soot from Her eyes and said, "We shall start again."

It was slow going, to rebuild the world. Even before the pillage, the Lower Banks had been mere remnants of their namesake; the water that had once lapped against their shores was long gone. Silt and sand filled the beds where the river had been. The earth had shriveled and cracked, and neither hoe nor trowel could coax it back to life. Still, the New Maiden would not give up.

"This is our darkness," the New Maiden said, "and it is up to us to bring forth the light." She was a scrawny girl of seventeen, yet Her sheer belief was enough to inspire. It was also enough to turn nonbelievers away. The people of the Lower Banks divided quickly into two factions.

The first chose to leave in search of arable land, a better home amidst the vast, wide world. For so long they had existed in their enclave, sending out hunters and scavengers who always returned with bounty. But beyond those borders, they knew not what they'd find. Most were willing to take that risk, were willing to put their lives on the line, rather than stay and rebuild.

The second faction was firmly devoted to the New Maiden's vision. Energized by Her words, Her encouragement. They chose to stay and help Her manifest the better world they had always dreamed of.

Before the fire, mind you, the New Maiden was just a girl. She cooked and cleaned and tended to the hearth in the center of the village, which kept them all fed and warm. She was not a beautiful girl, but Her hard work made Her valuable all the same.

And so, the village divided—there were those off to seek their future elsewhere, and those committed to the New Maiden's word. The latter group was much smaller—only three remained in the Lower Banks with Her. Two who stayed—a set of sisters—were no surprise. They had been close to the New Maiden since birth. But the third defector stunned the group. The youngest son of the Lower Banks' leader chose to break away from his father and remain. Even the New Maiden Herself seemed astonished he would stay.

Ten days into their journey onward, the group from the Lower Banks stumbled into the camp of those who'd pillaged and burned their home. A massacre ensued. Only one girl escaped unharmed. She said that all through the violence, the Lower Banks glowed, like a beacon, calling her home.

When she returned to her village, she found it changed. Though they'd been gone only a short while, the river flowed again, the earth bore fruit, and in the center, where once there had been a hearth, sat an altar.

None who had remained would tell the girl what the New Maiden had done. But it was clear: Divine power had been awakened. With such inarguable proof she stayed, devoting herself to the New Maiden and vowing to record every word of Her good work. That girl was Ruti, and that record became the Book of the New Maiden. *Ruti joined Petra, Hera, and Sebastien by the New Maiden's side. And the New Maiden was glad. For this was only the beginning of Her work, and the more who followed, the more would believe.*

The room was silent when Griffin finished his tale, save for the crackling fire. Elodie had even put down her fork to listen, cradling her cheeks in her hands.

Sabine sat, stunned. She had spent years in church thinking the New Maiden was nothing more than another powerful being who would never be relevant to those on the margins. But after Griffin's story, Sabine found herself yearning for someone she'd never known. Yearning for the sort of magic that healed others, instead of magic that hurt her.

Now, now, Sabine, the darkness interrupted, *don't go pretending that I'm a hindrance to you, when I'm the only thing that makes you special.*

Sabine let out a tiny sigh. It was right, in a way. Besides, her magic was nothing like the New Maiden's. Sabine would never inspire belief in others. She could only ever serve the darkness.

Sabine bit her tongue as she accompanied the princess back to the Pained Pig. She wanted to talk to Elodie about the story of the New

Maiden. Wanted to ask if she'd felt that same yearning, that same hope swelling in her chest. But she didn't want to give the princess the chance to dismiss the connection she'd felt, to roll her eyes the way Katrynn would, to tell her she shouldn't be so bold as to relate to a deity, the way Artur would. The ridicule would hurt that much more from Elodie.

And so Sabine stayed silent, endeavoring to match the unbothered air of the princess, who took the stairs up to their room two at a time and flung the door open haphazardly, collapsing onto the bed with a sigh.

But her attempt at calm lasted only seconds. There was a pressing problem: The room contained only one bed. She froze beneath the doorframe, scrambling for a solution. Just like her hesitation about the New Maiden, Sabine could not bear for Elodie to misunderstand her intentions if she were to suggest sharing the lumpy mattress. And so, rather than setting herself up for disappointment, Sabine took control of the situation and disappointed herself.

"I'll just"—she gestured vaguely toward the floor—"sleep here, then." It wasn't such an unfamiliar position. She and Katrynn shared a thin bedroll they laid out in front of the hearth.

"Oh." Elodie sat up quickly, sounding taken aback. "Are you sure?"

"I just assumed…" Sabine frowned at her. "Do you not want the bed?"

"That's not what I said," the other girl clarified right away. She exhaled, shifting slightly. "You could…" She waved idly at the space beside her on the rumpled sheets. But Sabine shook her head. The bed wasn't much bigger than the bedroll she shared with her sister, and she'd woken up too many times with Katrynn's elbow in her back to accept.

Yes, that's the reason you don't want to share a bed. The darkness cut right through her excuses. It made Sabine shiver, knowing this thing in her head could see the tentative blooming of interest in her heart. She had no privacy. No safety.

"I'll be all right." Sabine's stomach squirmed guiltily as Elodie's open expression shuttered. Her tone had been harsher than she'd intended. She swiped a pillow from the bed and curled up on her side toward the wall, draping her cloak over herself as a blanket. The room's candle flickered like a lone ember in her family's fireplace. It was almost familiar, the floor rigid beneath her shoulder, the aching loneliness in her heart. She heard the soft hitch of Elodie's breath, and then the room plunged into darkness. The princess shifted on the bed, the sheets rustling like a whisper, a secret Sabine was not privy to.

You bemoan your own fear, Sabine. Your own weakness. Her darkness sounded almost exasperated.

Sabine bristled. She wasn't weak. In fact, it was the opposite. That she had claimed the floor rather than slipping into bed beside a beautiful girl was really a showcase of her fortitude.

The silence was interrupted by Elodie. "This is ridiculous." The princess sounded annoyed, as though the situation was Sabine's fault. "I can't sleep with you lying on the ground. Those floorboards are likely infested with mites and mold." Sabine could practically hear her shudder. "Just...come up here." She sighed, the sheets rustling again as she shifted. "There's space. Sort of."

"Elodie—"

"I'm exhausted, and you're keeping me awake," the princess said, stifling a yawn. "This is not a conversation, it's a command."

It's not about you at all, the darkness said snarkily. But that offered Sabine some relief. If it wasn't an imposition, she did not need to wring her hands at the idea of accepting comfort. Sabine lay down, straight as a broom's handle and as stiff as its bristles. She made sure not to offer Elodie even a hint of a touch. She kept herself isolated, tense, alone—positioned carefully on top of the bed's thin sheets. The outline of Elodie's body beneath it was suggestive enough.

"You can move over." The room was dark, Elodie's voice hesitant. Still, the offer felt too close to her own wanting, which made Sabine fear it was a joke at her expense.

"I'm fine."

"You're hanging halfway off the bed," Elodie said tersely. Sabine sat up quickly. The princess could only know that if she was paying as close attention to Sabine's body as Sabine was to hers. "Are you all right?" Elodie asked, sitting up, too. "I didn't mean to startle you."

"You didn't." There was no way Sabine could tell the princess that the real surprise was the full force of her attention. "I'm all right."

Elodie moved over, the mattress sinking beneath them both. As Sabine tried to settle, she thought again of the story of the New Maiden's origin. The devotion She'd earned from Her Favoreds, the awe She'd inspired in Ruti, the loyalty She'd earned from Sebastien. The idea of that sort of enduring companionship was unfamiliar to Sabine.

Or it had been, before she'd met Elodie. The princess shifted again, her body beneath the sheets while Sabine stayed resolutely above. This way, there was no fear of touching.

"Aren't you cold?"

"I'm fine," Sabine answered immediately. If Elodie was as tired as she claimed, why was she still talking?

"You're lying."

Sabine's breath caught in her throat. She lied to everyone: her mother, her siblings, her darkness. Herself. It was easier that way, even though it hurt. But Elodie was the first person to notice. The first person to challenge her. The first person curious enough to know the truth.

"Fine." Sabine shimmied awkwardly beneath the blanket. The warmth radiating from Elodie settled her some. Still, she kept her limbs close, arms pinned tightly to her sides, her heart tucked away.

Elodie shifted again, brushing Sabine's hand with her pinky finger. Sabine did her best to maintain the careful boundaries constructed around her emotions, but she fought a losing battle. Her skin sparked beneath the princess's touch. Her stomach fluttered. Her heart ached for more.

Sabine kept her hand where it was. Even as her effortful composure threatened to come undone, she did not move, for fear it would reveal to Elodie that she wanted this. Or, even worse, that it would appear as though she did not.

To Sabine's immense relief, Elodie did not move, either. Instead, they remained side by side, fingers barely touching, their breathing hesitant and slow. Sabine struggled to stay awake, to revel in the spark between them, until finally she could fight it no longer and slipped softly into sleep.

17

The apothecary was quiet all throughout breakfast.

"Cat got your tongue?" Elodie raised an eyebrow at Sabine as she stabbed her sausage. Grease oozed out in a little puddle. Served her right for ordering meat at an inn called the Pained Pig. She pushed her plate away, turning her attention to the tea that tasted of dishwater.

She wished Sabine would have let them find sustenance elsewhere. But the girl was nearly as suspicious as Cleo, all deep frowns and sidelong glances each time they strayed from the confines of their small quarters. Even now, they were the only two patrons in the main room and she was still scowling at the front door. The inn, which had been a boisterous den of chaos when they'd returned the night before, was silent at sunrise.

"Just thinking," the other girl said, turning her fork over in her fingers. She had barely touched her biscuit.

"Do elaborate." Elodie did her best to tamp down her nerves. She'd taken a risk the night before, had indulged in the tentative exploration of touch, and while the apothecary had not moved her hand away, perhaps she saw things differently in the morning light.

"What do you believe happened"—Sabine rested her chin on her left hand—"in the Lower Banks?"

Elodie's nerves melted. She found herself disappointed and relieved in equal measure that Sabine's dreamy, faraway look had nothing to do with her. She did not have time for a distraction, however pretty she might be. "You're talking about the New Maiden?" The tale recounted in the tavern had left her with some questions, too.

The storyteller's New Maiden seemed a fierce, powerful woman. Not much like the "delicate girl from the Lower Banks" the clergy worshipped. Elodie pondered the contrast. There was no doubt the Church needed the New Maiden to appear welcoming and accessible, but to alter Her characterization so much that She became unrecognizable was suspicious to a much larger degree.

Sabine nodded. "The Church hardly mentions Her early life." She shifted on the bench. "I can't help but wonder who She was before. What made Her special enough to ascend?"

"Power, I suppose." Elodie shrugged. "Or persuasion." She had seen the Chaplain utilize the latter to gain the former. But the New Maiden had also seemed to possess something more ethereal. "Maybe magic."

The Church never used that word to describe the New Maiden's miracles, but Elodie found it fitting. It didn't seem so different from what the apothecary could do.

But Sabine stiffened. "You're mocking me."

Elodie frowned. "I'm not."

"No?" The apothecary chuckled dismissively. "You wouldn't be the first." The hurt in her voice was palpable.

"Your family ridicules you?"

"I suppose it's not so much the magic as what it takes to make it." She stared down at her plate. "They're ashamed of me."

A lump formed in Elodie's throat. While her mother had been standoffish, she had still taken Elodie under her wing. The first daughter had been blessed with a father who adored her, siblings who were her constant companions, and a best friend who not only appreciated her ambition but encouraged it. Sabine's life sounded terribly lonely. "Surely that's not how they feel. What you do seems brave."

Sabine smiled self-deprecatingly. "You're only saying that because you need something from me."

Everyone in Elodie's life was so calculated. No one gave in to their emotions for fear of being painted as weak. Lady above, her mother had died only days ago and Elodie had yet to truly grieve. She could learn a thing or two from Sabine and her sorrowful eyes.

"I'm saying it because it's true. I wish I knew how to feel."

"Trust me, Princess," Sabine said, "it's not nearly as nice as it sounds." As she reached for her teacup, the sleeve of her cloak slipped and revealed her pale skin. Threads of black snaked their way up her right arm from fingers to elbow. Where the faintest glimmer of blue blood shone up from Elodie's wrist, Sabine's veins were dark as ink.

"What is that?" Elodie gestured at Sabine's hand.

Sabine's eyes widened, even rounder than they always were. "Nothing." She tugged her sleeve down to cover her fingers, but it was too late.

"Liar."

Sabine's face darkened. That same strange battle seemed to take place behind her eyes. Elodie watched in silence.

"As I said," the apothecary finally answered before taking a sip of tea. "Feeling isn't nearly as nice as it sounds."

Elodie considered this. She supposed her own avoidance was essentially armor, the ability to repress what ought to hurt—her mother's passing, her sister's dismissal. She wanted to offer Sabine the same reprieve, and so she changed the subject.

"When will you begin to brew?"

But the new topic did not seem to settle Sabine. Instead, she appeared to retreat inside herself again, eyes flashing amber in the morning light. Elodie didn't want the girl to fight another internal battle. Each time she emerged looking sadder still.

"Come back," she said quickly.

Sabine blinked, and the amber in her eyes disappeared. "What?"

Elodie was suddenly embarrassed. She'd been watching the other girl too closely, had observed too keenly, and now, Sabine would think her strange and overeager. "Nothing, I…"

"No." The girl's gaze was unwavering, impossible to ignore. "What did you say?"

"Your eyes looked different." Elodie scratched at a nonexistent itch on her nose. She needed a reason to look away.

"Different?"

"They were amber. Now they're brown again." Lady above, she was acting so odd. Sabine would think her a fool.

"No." Sabine shook her head. "You said, 'Come back.' What did you mean?"

"I don't know why you asked if you heard me the first time," Elodie grumbled, even as heat flooded her cheeks. This girl was making her sweat.

"Elodie?" Sabine asked gently.

"Sometimes…" Elodie ran a hand through her hair, uncertain how to explain it. "It's like you disappear. You're present, of course, but not really. Your attention is inside. Almost like you're fighting off an attacker or arguing with an enemy. There's nothing wrong with that, of course," she said quickly, as Sabine's expression changed, "it's just, whenever you return to yourself, you always seem worse off."

Elodie shifted her attention to the tabletop, tracing the initials carved into the scuffed wood. Just like the many gamblers who had sat here before her, she had revealed her hand too soon.

"You're not wrong." Sabine sounded as hesitant as Elodie felt. Elodie met the apothecary's eyes. They were that deep, mournful brown she had come to know. "But I'm not ready to tell you exactly why you're right."

Elodie smiled, despite herself, and Sabine returned it. The tension settled into a comfortable compatibility. But the silence lasted only a minute.

The inn's front door flung open, the morning's pale light shuddering where it met the shadows. A small boy, no older than eight, paused on the threshold. "Hear ye, hear ye," he called to the room. When he found only the two girls inside, his face fell.

Sabine pushed back her stool and got to her feet. "Any news?"

The boy cocked an eyebrow. "Any coins?"

Elodie snorted, charmed by his cheekiness. It reminded her of Tal. The boy turned his attention to her, sizing her up. "You look like you've got money. Your hair's shiny."

Elodie rooted about in her pocket, coming up with a copper coin. "Tell me what you know."

"Procession through the North Quarter. The Chaplain calls

upon Velle's citizens to look upon the Third Daughter and hear Her plea."

Elodie frowned. "That can't be right."

The boy scowled. "I don't spread lies." He took a step forward. "Now pay up."

She held the coin just out of his reach. "Where did you get your information?"

"Town crier, in the Commerce District." The boy plucked the coin from between Elodie's fingers. "They don't come here if they can help it."

Sabine made a soft noise of assent, and the boy was gone just as quickly as he came.

"What do you think it means, 'look upon the Third Daughter'? You said she was asleep."

Elodie sighed. Knowing the Chaplain, this display would be elaborately plotted and theatrical. Yet another way to extol his claim to the crown, to disseminate the lies spoken that fateful morning in the royal chapel.

Elodie couldn't bear to watch him repeat his fabricated story, but she knew they had to attend. She needed to know exactly what his propaganda entailed, so she could rebut and rebuff it as soon as she was able to wake Brianne.

She had to do as her mother had taught her and stay two steps ahead of her opponent.

"Let's go," she said, getting to her feet.

"What?" Sabine blinked at her. "Where?"

"Didn't you hear, Sabine?" Elodie exhaled sharply, turning her attention to the front door where the boy had stood only moments ago. "We've been called to look upon our queen."

18

Elodie Warnou was terrible at lying low. It had been all of one day and already she was dragging Sabine out the front door of the Pained Pig, the hood of Sabine's borrowed cloak pulled over her head in a weak attempt at disguise.

Sabine didn't think that anything could truly conceal Elodie's distinctive look, especially not the cloak's threadbare flax, which was fraying at the seams.

She wasn't pretty, exactly. Pretty implied an easiness on the eyes. It was for clouds or flower petals. Pretty was soft. Serene. So no, Elodie wasn't pretty. Elodie was striking. Sharp-featured and stark in her coloring. Handsome, almost, in that her appearance was not delicate, but intentional.

You're so enamored by this girl, and for what? There's nothing special about her beyond the luck of being born to the right mother at the right time. Sabine's darkness sounded annoyed.

She didn't know why it cared. The more time she spent with Elodie, the more obvious it was that she had absolutely no idea how to wake the Third Daughter, that she would bungle her part of their bargain and would end up delivered to the Loyalists on one of Castle Warnou's silver platters. Surely, Elodie had noticed the way Sabine shrank away from her line of questioning.

But then, they were also growing closer. She had known the princess barely a day, but already Elodie saw beyond Sabine's hesitant exterior, could tell when she was lying, noticed when she took a moment to respond to the darkness's incessant babbling—something that even her siblings and her mother had never paid attention to.

Because they're too embarrassed to look, too disgusted by your emotion, the darkness chimed in.

But that meant Elodie wasn't. This strong, thoughtful whirlwind of a girl saw Sabine's sadness and instead of turning away, she kept watch. She witnessed Sabine war with herself, and she was waiting on the other side.

The air off the harbor was brisk and bright, drying the sweat on the back of her neck. Leaves tumbled from the trees, crunching underfoot. The streets were empty—either she and the princess had missed the rush of the clamoring crowd on their way to the procession or, more likely, no one in Harborside cared to attend.

They passed the bridge that would take them to the Iron District and instead forged forward, along the circular path down toward the castle on the hill. The trees that lined the High Road were lush, older, and more sprawling in their coverage than the sickly trunks of Harborside. These trees leaned lazily, painting the ground gold with turning leaves.

As the road snaked to the left, a chorus of cheers erupted and Sabine caught sight of the crowd, thousands deep, spilling through the city square. All the market stalls had been broken down, folded up, and stored in alleyways, disrupting the rats. It was astounding how many people could cram into the marketplace. It made the space feel smaller, somehow.

"Citizens of Velle," a voice boomed from the top of the bell tower in the same church where Sabine and her siblings had sought shelter only two days prior. "The New Maiden has called, and you have answered." A man stood, clutching the balcony with knuckles so white Sabine could see them from where she stood at the very back of the crowd. The same place where she'd witnessed every other parade before.

"The New Maiden promised that She would return," the man continued. Atop his head was a monstrous crown the size of a baby, crushed purple velvet enveloped by gold leaf, glittering in the morning sun. "But none could predict the way She would do so. Your Maiden, your queen, has made the ultimate sacrifice. She has given Her life for us. For you. For Velle."

Gasps echoed up from the crowd. Sabine turned frantically to Elodie. "She's dead?"

But the princess shook her head, looking furious. "Just wait. He's baiting the crowd."

"Oh, no, good people of Velle," the man said, holding up a hand. "She is not gone. She has merely fallen into eternal slumber, ensuring that She will always be here. Will always speak for you. To you."

"How can she speak if she's asleep?" Sabine whispered. Beside her, Elodie was glowering up at the man, her nose scrunched and her jaw set.

The two of them might have been unlikely allies, but Sabine

was grateful to have someone beside her who felt the same disillusionment.

"She has chosen me to be Her voice!" The man's words echoed with resounding bravado, his excitement so vivid it almost sounded like fear. "I have proven my devotion, my dedication to Her word. After all, the New Maiden is discerning." He paused, ceremoniously, to allow for the murmurs that ricocheted through the crowd.

Sabine noticed Elodie roll her eyes. Even the darkness was skeptical. *He's awfully sure of himself, speaking on behalf of a woman with no voice.*

Sabine didn't know if she should be worried that she was now consistently agreeing with her sadness.

"And now, Velle"—the man clasped his hands together joyfully— "I shall present your eternal queen!"

Trumpets blared. The shock of brass blasting in Sabine's ears compromised her balance. When she regained her senses, she was clutching Elodie's arm tight enough to bruise. But the princess didn't shrug her off or push her away. Instead, one of Elodie's pale hands wrapped around Sabine's own.

Her veins were a clear blue. *Not like yours.* Sabine pulled away, and then the festivities began.

Even from her limited vantage point, she could see the way the clergy folk burst forward, flowing from the doors of the church, draped in white robes, sharp slashes of purple across their chests like gambling debts in a ledger, gold pendants glittering about their necks. They looked like a procession of ghosts. The smaller ones carried leather-bound books, flipping through pages to murmur passages beneath their breath. Behind them came the stronger ones with shoulders broad enough to carry a giant glass box, nearly blinding in the sunlight. Black spots danced in the forefront of Sabine's vision, impossible to dissolve, even as she furiously batted her eyes open and closed.

When her vision finally cleared, Sabine realized with horror what was being carried: the body of a girl, dressed all in white, her blonde hair fanned out across a bed of roses. Someone had painted her cheeks and lips with red. She looked garish lying there, too bright even in her in-between state.

The Third Daughter. The New Maiden laid out in all her glory.

It was disturbing, the way that the crowd shouted and clamored as Brianne's body passed, the glass coffin sparkling in the sun, gleaming with the confidence of a sharp smile. Although the girl's expression was serene, Sabine couldn't help but note the way her jaw was clenched ever so slightly. She was just a child.

Still, Sabine couldn't stop staring at the motionless body of the New Maiden. Her magic had done this. *She* had done this. She didn't know if she should be terrified or proud.

Terrified, her heart said. But the velvet voice of her darkness told her: *proud*. Sabine had always wanted to be something. Some*one*. And now she was, however invisibly. Not a single person in this crowd knew Sabine, but they were humbled by what she had done. *Isn't that almost the same thing?*

"This is impossibly vulgar," Elodie whispered, as the glass coffin came closer to where they stood. The white-robed clergy folk did not seem to struggle beneath the box's weight.

"It's awful." Sabine tore her eyes from the glittering glass box. "Why are they doing this?"

"Seeing is believing, Sabine," the princess muttered darkly. "Ironic, considering."

"Faith is sightless?"

"Faith is not based in reason or proof. It's ridiculous."

"Hmm." Sabine made a half-hearted noise.

"What?" Elodie snapped. "I heard the judgment in your... sound."

Sabine scratched her neck, which was warm beneath her hand. "Isn't that what the monarchy expects, too?"

Elodie looked incredulously at her. "Of course not."

Sabine raised her eyebrows. "Church and crown are not so different. They promise greater good, then take all our money to buy outlandish headpieces." She nodded up at the Chaplain, who stood above, surveying the crowd. His crown had slipped forward, over his brow. His beard was disheveled, eyes bright.

"That I can't dispute. Ridiculous, pathetic man," Elodie said, shaking her head, fist tightened around the velvet of her dress.

"What is this all for?"

"For that." Elodie was still staring up at the Chaplain. "For him to feel tall. For him to speak to his people on behalf of the voiceless New Maiden. To claim Velle's throne so he can indulge his own interests, not Hers." She sighed darkly. "This is what I was trying to avoid. Instead I made it worse."

"What's his story, anyway?" The man was dressed in holy robes, his gold pendant flashing sharply in the sunlight, yet his eyes seemed cloudier than those of the clergy folk. Perhaps they were simply reflecting the deep purple of his cloth, but Sabine thought there may be more to that granite gaze.

Nothing good comes from men made of stone.

Elodie's face twisted into a grim smile. "Don't you know? The Chaplain is the Third Daughter's father."

Sabine raised an eyebrow. "Does that mean he's your—?"

"Lady above, no," Elodie sounded incensed. "My father is a delight. He runs a cluster of farms in the Highlands. Keeps horses and bees. He'd never orchestrate a coup." She shook her head. "In fact, all of my siblings have different fathers. This one just happens to be the worst."

Sabine looked up at the Chaplain with renewed scrutiny. She was no stranger to slimy men. To the kind who slicked their greasy hair back with long fingers and pointed glances. The kind who tossed a coin, flipping head over tail over head again, in the direction of any pretty girl they passed. But the Chaplain's slime was subtler. Harder to detect and therefore more repugnant once it was known.

A glimmer of gold caught Sabine's eye as a red-clad Loyalist stepped out of the shadows behind the Chaplain. Sunlight flashed across the medal pinned to his chest as he peered down at the gathered crowd. For a single second, the Loyalist's gaze met hers.

Her darkness began to scream.

19

Sabine went slack, the full weight of her crashing into Elodie before stumbling sideways into the man beside her. His face was buried behind a gigantic brown beard, but his eyes were kind, shifting quickly from surprise to concern as he spotted the apothecary clutching her head, her face twisted in pain.

"That's all right, there you are," the stranger said, hoisting Sabine's arm over his shoulder to keep her upright. The girl's skin was pale, and wisps of her brown hair stuck to her sweaty forehead. She was, rather decidedly, not all right. "What's the matter with her?" Elodie hadn't the faintest idea.

"Too much peich-nat," she lied. The air was filled with the sickly sweet scent of nut wine, and glass bottles clinked under cloaks as the people of Velle celebrated the New Maiden's everlasting reign. It was a plausible explanation if ever there was one.

"I'm sorry," the apothecary croaked, turning toward Elodie. Her eyes were darker than Elodie had ever seen them. Instead of their usual bright brown, they were murky, almost muddy. "I think I'm going to be sick."

The bearded man cleared his throat, glancing over his shoulder at the group he was with. They were cheering and hollering, shouting for the New Maiden. "Can you carry her?"

Elodie searched the faces of the crowd desperately, as though a solution might emerge. But she had only herself to rely on.

"Please," Sabine croaked. She sounded so pained it very nearly broke Elodie's heart.

"Give her here."

The man moved Sabine from his shoulder onto Elodie's. She was several inches shorter than the other girl yet had no choice but to make do. Sabine's arm was flung around her neck, and Elodie could smell Sabine's bright bite of herbs, the floral grassiness of the dirt beneath her fingernails, the salinity of the sweat that pooled above her lip.

She shifted her shoulder, adjusting Sabine, whose head had lolled against her neck. The apothecary's skin was still a ghostly white, and her expression had not improved. Her face was scrunched up in agony, and her teeth chattered as though she had been left out in the snow for hours and her bones had been infected with a deep-rooted chill.

All around them, bodies pushed closer as the glass casket came their way. Elodie searched for an exit, but every break in the crowd revealed a flash of bright red. Loyalists. They were posted everywhere—at the doors of the chapel, standing watch at the corners of the High Road, lingering six steps behind Chaplain René, whose arms were still spread wide above the crowd, a hawk using its full wingspan to intimidate its prey. Once, Elodie would have run toward the guards. Now, she shrank away.

She'd never been so aware of a color before. Red was for flowers, for vegetable soups, for velvet gowns. But here it set her heart racing with fear as it flashed in her peripheral vision. While she did not know every Loyalist's face, they certainly knew hers. And Elodie Warnou's face was supposed to be in Ethliglenn, along with the rest of her.

She buried herself deeper into Sabine's cloak as she tried to keep the apothecary upright. The thin garment wasn't much of a shield, but having something to hide behind offered her a sliver of comfort as she snaked the two of them through the masses.

"Sabine," she hissed, sweat dripping down her spine even as a sharp breeze whipped at her neck. "Are you all right? Can you speak?"

The other girl squeezed her eyes shut. "No." She gritted her teeth, shaking her head sharply. "Pain."

Elodie tried to remember the moment before Sabine had slumped, tried to fathom what might have happened to send her into such a state. Sabine had been speaking, standing, studying the Chaplain, and then suddenly, something was wrong. It was almost as though his poison extended far beyond his silver tongue.

Sabine groaned, huddling even closer, her breath warm on Elodie's exposed clavicle. Elodie's arms were beginning to shake from supporting the other girl's full weight, but she refused to let go. When she nearly rammed into the broad back of an ironsmith, Elodie realized with a panic that she'd led them into the depths of the crowd, rather than away from it. All around her, the whispers grew like frenzied birdcalls, clamoring for the New Maiden, thanking the New Maiden, praising the New Maiden.

It was strange, hearing the calls for the New Maiden, when all

Elodie could see in the glass coffin was her youngest sibling. She'd never thought of Brianne as anything but her silly little sister, despite the fact that she fulfilled the prophecy. She was the New Maiden first, monarch second. And it showed in her education, her demeanor, her personality.

Brianne had been raised by the Church, tutored by the Chaplain, fawned over by the clergy folk. Tera Warnou had argued with the Chaplain countless times about the need for Brianne's education to cover a more robust portfolio of subjects and strategies. But it was a fight she'd never won.

If Elodie hadn't known better, it might have even seemed like the queen had found relief in the distance between herself and her third daughter. In Brianne's absence, Elodie had been trained to do the job the youngest Warnou would one day inherit. The problem was that on the other side of the castle, Chaplain René had been scheming even harder.

He had campaigned too intently and gloated too loudly over his appointment as the Queen's Regent for it to have been incidental. Had Elodie been less focused on her bruised ego and more perceptive of his agenda, this entire mess could have been avoided.

She had to get them out of there, out of the main square, the public eye. She'd put herself at risk far too much already. If the Chaplain caught wind of her disobedience, Elodie would be shipped off to Ethliglenn accompanied by a guard. She would never find a way to wake Brianne.

She managed to duck down a side street teeming with rubbish. A fowl carcass was splayed out beside a stone wall, its bones nearly picked clean. A dash of soup, possibly regurgitated, was splattered across the concrete, beans and vegetables pale and lifeless. Elodie shuddered as she passed, Sabine still sagging beside her.

"Sabine," Elodie pleaded, as she accidentally kicked what looked like a pig vertebra, "do you think that you can stand on your own?"

Sabine leaned over and vomited on the cobblestones, right beside the soup.

"I'll take that as a no." Elodie sighed, stepping delicately around the mess. "That's fine. No trouble." She hoisted Sabine even higher on her shoulder. "Please, wake up."

"I'm awake," Sabine snapped. "But I . . . oh no." She paused. Put a hand to her mouth. Then she pulled away from Elodie and retched again.

The alley ended abruptly, the space between buildings boarded up with thick slabs of maple and pine. Sabine had sunk to the ground, slumped like one of Brianne's dolls. Elodie's skin crawled imagining the sort of filth soaking into the other girl's skirt.

She used her foot to delicately nudge Sabine's knee. "What happened to you?" One minute, the other girl had been a competent ally. The next, she was deadweight.

"Those eyes . . ." the apothecary was babbling, her words unintelligible. Elodie hadn't the slightest idea whose eyes. "I—"

"It's fine," Elodie interjected quickly. If Sabine had been lovestruck by some fool, she didn't care to know. "Save your energy. We're safe here."

"I suppose that depends on your definition of safe," came a voice behind her, "but I'd say this isn't the sort of place you'd want to frequent at night." The speaker possessed a brash self-assurance that Elodie might have appreciated, were it not challenging her directly.

Instead, she bristled. She'd managed to navigate them away from the crowd, from the Loyalists at every corner, only to be cornered in an alleyway by some guard wanting to play intimidation tactics with her. Well, it wasn't going to work.

She turned away from Sabine, ready to bite back, but the words died on her tongue as she took in the face before her, so familiar, even with the added years. Even though it was deeper now, she should have known, without looking, the voice of the boy who had once been her best friend.

Tal was a man now, standing there in a deep red uniform that fit snugly across his chest, the color striking against his skin. His mop of curly hair still fell across his eye playfully, but the rest of him was different. Harder. Sharper.

"Elodie."

She shivered as her eyes met his. She could see him remembering, too—dueling together in the courtyard, his arm always wavering at the last minute, letting her win. She could smell the pastry his mother baked, spread thick with cardamom and cinnamon filling that they would share when they sat up in the tree that overlooked the queen's chambers. She could hear the words he spoke when he told her he was joining the First Army under Rob's father, marching off to war. She remembered the betrayal she'd felt when he disappeared without saying goodbye.

"Tal." She felt something release within her—a fear, hard and round like one of Cleo's thimbles, dislodging from her chest. She wanted to run to him. She wanted to hit him.

"I have to sound the alarm."

It caught her unawares, like a slap or a splash of cold water. She'd been expecting a reunion. But that boy who had been her best friend, the only person who had ever seen her, had been replaced by a red-clad Loyalist. This wasn't Tal. This was a supporter of the state. Not a person, but a profession.

"What if you walked away instead?"

"I left you, once." Tal's eyes were grim. "I won't make the same mistake twice."

In any other circumstance, the words would have soothed her. She had cried for days after Tal had left, uncertain what she had done to offend. Not knowing if she would ever see him again. But this was not the reunion she had hoped for.

Elodie glanced back at Sabine, who was, mercifully, not paying attention in the least. The other girl's head was still in her hands.

She took a step toward Tal, desperation in her voice. "If you care about me at all, please, don't tell."

Tal was nothing if not loyal. But judging by the look on his face, his loyalty no longer belonged to her. He looked down at his uniform, red like a sunrise. Like a warning sign. "I have to, Lo."

"Don't call me Lo, then," Elodie bristled at the nickname that had only ever been just for him.

"But, Princess—"

"Better yet, don't call me anything at all." She knelt down to shake Sabine. "We have to go." She wrapped one of the girl's arms around her shoulders and groaned as she hauled her to her feet. By the time she managed to right them both, Tal was gone.

The knot in her stomach untangled itself, leaving a hollow ache in its stead. But it was replaced one moment later by the white fire of betrayal as his whistle sliced through the air, loud and bright and deadly.

20

The darkness would not stop shrieking. The sound was sharp, stark, like the clang of steel against steel, and uninterrupted. It set Sabine's teeth on edge, made her want to peel off her skin, the high screech like a bird of prey. There was nothing in Sabine's stomach—all she had left to retch was bile. Still, that offered no reprieve from the screaming; it only left a bitter taste on her tongue.

Sabine could feel Elodie's insistent tug on her arm, but she couldn't react, couldn't get her limbs to follow. Her voice and her mind were rendered useless by the endless noise in her head. She still didn't know what exactly had set it off. One moment, she'd been looking up at the Chaplain and his Loyalist guards; the next, the darkness unleashed a scream so loud and furious and feral that Sabine thought her skull might explode.

"Come *on*." It was like Elodie was speaking to her from underwater. Sabine reached desperately for the words, for the response of her body, for the ability to put one foot in front of the other.

They needed to move, that much was obvious based on the

flash of red in her peripheral vision. But the sun was too bright. The screaming too loud. The grip on her wrist too tight. Then the shrieking was outside her mind, too. The shouting rose to a fever pitch, the voices mingling, high and deep and loud, and then, slicing through it all like a knife through butter: a whistle.

Sabine knew that whistle. It was the severe shriek that echoed through Harborside late at night, early in the morning—the sort of alarm that sounded just before the worst, before the Loyalist guards came to take someone away. Suddenly, the grip on her wrist made sense, the urgency in Elodie's words cut through the noise, and the hair on her arms stood at attention. It was fight-or-flight. Sabine shook her head, trying to clear it. She squeezed her hands into fists. Blinked to clear the spots from her vision.

And then she chose flight. They ran, the world a blur of red uniforms and white-gloved hands reaching, reaching. Fingers grabbed a fistful of her dress and she let it rip, let them pull her apart, whatever they could take without slowing her down. Elodie gasped as she was strangled by the cloak tied tight around her neck. Her fingers loosened around Sabine's as she was pulled backward, toward those many grabbing hands. Sabine tugged the tie free, letting the cloak fall from the princess's shoulders, into the hands of the enemy.

Elodie readjusted her hold on Sabine. Her palm was slick with sweat, so Sabine twined her fingers through the princess's for a better grip. She couldn't tell if the thrill that moved through her was illness or excitement.

"Welcome back," Elodie wheezed, tugging Sabine sharply to the left. "Now, do you trust me?"

Sabine glanced around the corner behind her at the furious Loyalists in pursuit. "Not sure I have a choice," she said.

"Good." Elodie stopped abruptly to duck behind a stack of crates. Sabine held her breath as the thundering steps of predators continued past their hiding place. Once the footsteps had faded, Elodie started to push at the crates. "Help me."

The shrieking in her head had faded to a low, consistent buzz, like a gnat or a bee was stuck in her ear. "Help you do what?"

"Move these." Elodie grunted as she pushed the boxes away to reveal a trapdoor. She knelt down to pull at the handle.

"What in our lady's name are you doing?"

Elodie swung the door open to reveal a stone staircase. "Getting us out of here. Now come on, let's go." She disappeared down into the shadows.

Even Sabine's darkness was silent with surprise. Sabine scurried down after her, swinging the trapdoor closed with a dull *thunk*.

"Elodie?" Sabine couldn't see her hand in front of her face. She didn't know where the princess was—if she was even still here or had left her behind.

"Right here," the princess called, her voice echoing eerily. "I wouldn't leave you to roam the sewer system alone." That explained the smell.

"Why *are* we in the sewer system?" Sabine said, pinching her nose closed as she descended the steps carefully.

"These sewers were built as an escape route. A way to flee the castle undetected."

"Must they be in use, though?"

Elodie snickered. "We have to keep the disguise convincing."

"Could have warned me there was a turn," she said dryly, as she walked into a wall.

"Here." Elodie held out her hand. "I'll guide you. I've gotten good at it." Sabine fumbled for the princess's hand, which was cold and clammy. "What happened to you back there, anyway?"

Sabine hesitated. *You can't tell her.* The darkness had regained its voice. *She'll think you're mad.*

Sabine was fairly convinced she was. Between the hissing darkness and the inky black spreading in her veins, she was starting to experience lapses in judgment, starting to feud with herself each time someone asked something of her.

Strangest of all was that Elodie seemed to *notice*. The moments where Sabine was struck by the echoing darkness, where it chided her or insulted her or made her paranoid, Elodie seemed to sense the transgression. As though she knew there was more unfolding beneath the surface.

Sabine had always been treated like a puddle, impure and contained. Yet when Elodie looked at her, Sabine felt like the ocean: vast, complex, and unending.

You cannot truly believe that girl sees anything in you. The laughter was high-pitched and cold.

"Sabine?"

She shrank away, even though there was no way Elodie could see her face in the darkness.

"Can the Loyalists find us here? They're the Queen's Guard, after all."

"Some things stay secret." But Elodie's voice was not as confident as her words, and Sabine noted that she picked up her pace.

"Where are we going?"

"Somewhere no one would ever think to search for me," she said softly.

Sabine, grateful that Elodie had dropped her own line of inquiry, decided not to press. After a period of silence Elodie stopped, fumbling about until there was the sharp scrape of metal. Sunlight came flooding through the sewers, sending spots across her vision. Sabine ascended the ladder and stepped out into the light, taking grateful gulps of oxygen. Early afternoon air had never tasted so sweet.

They emerged among rolling hills littered with leaves every color of a blazing fire—soft golds, harsh reds, gentle oranges, their points sharp and crisp even as they began the slow shrivel toward brown. Soon the slopes would be covered in snow and sleet, but today, as the breeze ruffled the trees and shook loose more leaves, Sabine couldn't help but sigh with contentment. Even if she hadn't just been freed from a stinking sewer, the scene would have been beautiful. These particular circumstances had simply made it more so.

When she turned back to look at where they'd come from, Sabine saw only Elodie and the smooth side of another hill. No indication that they'd emerged from anywhere at all.

"Eerie, isn't it?" Elodie seemed to delight in her confusion. "You'd never guess the door was there unless you knew exactly where to look."

Sabine squinted at the hill but couldn't see anything other than browning grass. "I'll have to stick close to you, I suppose."

"Rule number one, always make yourself essential to the cause."

Sabine's heart clenched. Her family's rules had once been her guiding light, but she felt worlds apart from them in this glittering, glistening field. If Katrynn were here she would frolic through piles of leaves. Artur would jump in them. They'd all laugh, like the children they still were. But they'd never had time to explore the country they lived in. They were always hustling, always running after the next coin. Which left them empty. Wanting.

"This place is so serene." Sabine closed her eyes, the soft breeze cooling her sweaty brow. "But where are we, exactly?"

"The one place in the world no one would ever think to look for me." Elodie gestured down a leaf-riddled path to a small white building built of stone. "Church." She gave a self-deprecating chuckle. "I'm surprised you've never been here. Visiting Velle's First Church of the New Maiden is usually a worshipper's rite of passage."

"I hardly ever leave Harborside," Sabine admitted, falling into step with Elodie. "I've seen more of this country in the last couple of days than I ever have in my life."

"But we've hardly left the city." Elodie frowned. "Is that…quite typical for people like you?"

Sabine snorted. "What does that mean?"

"People who are, you know…" Elodie struggled for a moment, searching for the right word. "Ordinary."

She sees you for exactly what you are, Sabine. Nothing special. Sabine made a soft noise in the back of her throat.

"Oh, come now." Elodie sighed heavily. "I didn't mean it like that."

"No?" Sabine cocked an eyebrow at her. "Then tell me what you meant."

"I meant someone who isn't royalty. Someone who lives in the real world."

Sabine frowned. "You live in the world."

"I'm not so certain of that." Elodie shivered. She wrapped her arms around her own shoulders like a hug, leaves crunching underfoot.

Sabine had begun to notice a hesitancy, a reticence in Elodie that had not animated their initial interactions. The princess seemed sad. The way her gaze softened when she thought Sabine wasn't looking. The way her sighs sounded like fire bellows deflating. If there was one thing Sabine knew, it was sadness. Perhaps she had more in common with the princess than she'd thought.

Elodie turned toward Sabine. "Want to go inside?" They had paused at the front steps of the church, which up close looked just as small as it had when they'd emerged from the sewers. It was built of fine stone, but the roof was warped, the doorframes were worn, and the windows boasted a cloak of dust. It didn't seem as though anyone had disturbed the place for some time.

Elodie tried the door, which gave a deep groan, hinges weary from disuse. The church was just as small from the inside, only a few rows of hard wooden pews and an aisle that led up to the altar. There rested a sculpture, a statue of the New Maiden with Her long hair and open arms proclaiming Her church a place for all.

It was a gesture at odds with Her clergy's actions. At odds with the padlock that secured the doors of Harborside's small chapel. The Chaplain claimed the New Maiden had sacrificed Herself for Velle, but it was clear by the lush greenery of the Garden District and the fine food in the Commerce District that Her favor came at a price. One Sabine's neighbors could not afford.

Tapers glimmered along the wall of the small church, the white wax of the three lit candles glistening as beads of sweat dripped down the length of them. Most of the tapers, however, were unlit, their bare wicks standing at attention like soldiers waiting for orders.

Whoever had lit the candles, though, was long gone. The church was empty and the air was very still, a perfectly preserved tableau disturbed by their presence. Each step Elodie took forward sounded to Sabine like a scream, a declaration of their trespassing.

"There's no one here." Sabine's words echoed as though she were giving the sermon.

"Exactly my point." Rather than collapsing into one of the pews, the way Sabine wanted to, Elodie floated down the aisle, like a queen on her coronation day.

"Where are you going?" Sabine was fairly certain only the clergy were supposed to set foot on the altar. But that didn't concern Elodie in the slightest. She strode forward, footsteps muffled by the velvet that covered the stairs to the pulpit. Suddenly the princess was above Sabine, glowering out at the empty pews. She was beautifully commanding, her gray eyes no longer like ice, but iron.

Sabine had the sudden urge to kneel before her, to recite her prayers not to the New Maiden but to Elodie. She scrubbed her eyes wildly. She was losing control of her senses, her impulses running wild from the stress and screaming and sweat. Even if she did feel something for Elodie, it would never be reciprocated. Her darkness was right: She was nothing compared to the other girl's fire.

"And lo, the New Maiden bequeathed Her legacy to men like worms, and the world wept." The bite in Elodie's voice could tear meat from the bone. Sabine thought again of the Chaplain, standing on the dais of the bell tower, his steely eyes catching hers. She shivered. Not wanting to give her darkness an opportunity to start screaming again, she hurried to join Elodie on the stage.

Resting on the pulpit was a copy of the *Book of the New Maiden*. Sabine leafed slowly through the pages, thin as skin, notes penciled into the margins. The words were cramped together, spidering across the page as though they'd been copied in a hurry.

"What are you doing on my altar, Princess?" A new voice, spindly and cracked with age, echoed through the small church. It was an old woman, back hunched as she hobbled forward, her cane tapping regally against the stone floor with every step. She'd emerged as though from thin air, and she was squinting at them with guarded curiosity.

Elodie frowned as she watched the woman approach. "How do you know who I am?"

The woman let out a cackle. Or it might have been a cough. "I know everything." The cane tapped three times as she continued forward. "That's my job."

"And who, exactly, are you?" Sabine clutched the *Book of the New Maiden* to her chest.

"They call me the Archivist, girl from Harborside." When the woman turned her way, Sabine shivered. Her irises were black. It felt as though the Archivist was seeing all the way down to her soul.

Even Elodie looked shaken. "How did you know that?"

"I know this country like the back of my hand," the woman said. "Wrinkles and all." She chuckled. "Besides, it's in the way she lilts up at the end of her sentences," she continued. "All Harborsiders speak just like the sea." Sabine felt self-conscious beneath the old woman's knowing gaze. "But you didn't come here to talk to me now, did you?" The Archivist hardly bothered to phrase this as a question.

"We carry Her word in our heart," Elodie answered, before Sabine could tell her about the procession. Sabine frowned. Elodie had admitted that she found the Church untrustworthy, yet in this moment she sounded like a devotee.

"Ah." The Archivist's face went carefully blank. "And what truth do you seek?"

"We seek the truth only She can provide." Elodie dipped her head reverently.

Sabine had almost certainly missed something. She'd thought they had simply stumbled into this church, but she ought to have known better. Elodie always seemed to be a few steps ahead.

A corner of the Archivist's mouth quirked upward. "You look too much like your mother not to have inherited her curiosity as well." She nodded toward Sabine. "Can she be trusted?"

Even though she had no idea what was going on, it still sent a jolt through Sabine when Elodie nodded her assent.

"What—?" Sabine looked to Elodie, but it was the Archivist who answered her.

"The princess spoke the royal code," the old woman said, leaning on her cane. "And so"—she began to make her way down the long aisle, cane clunking against the stone—"you may follow me below."

21

Warnou women always had a plan.

The moment Elodie had stepped foot in the sewers, she knew where they needed to go. What she had told Sabine was true—no one, not Loyalist guards, not Chaplain René himself, would ever think to look for her in a church—but that was merely a benefit, not the motivator. A memory burned in the back of her mind was the reason they were here.

Elodie had been thirteen and standing in front of her mother's sitting room door, the tea tray she'd swiped from the chambermaid shaking in her hands. On the other side was Chaplain René, snarling the royal code at Tera Warnou as he cornered her on a couch. Brianne knew her origins, he'd spat. Her mother, *the New Maiden's vessel*, ought to familiarize herself with the sacred history, too.

Tera snapped back at him just as viciously, refusing the history lesson. Elodie filed away both the code and the insult, certain they would each come in handy one day.

Knowledge was power, after all, her most insufferable tutor

liked to say. Jervis had taught her ancient languages, most of them unusable in any sort of conversation. The only thing of value Elodie had ever learned from Jervis was the location of the *Book of the New Maiden*, the first edition transcribed by Ruti, the girl who had returned to the Lower Banks to witness and record the New Maiden's prowess. It lived in the Archives of Velle's First Church of the New Maiden, the small chapel with a dusty, sprawling underground library that housed every record kept by the Church. The Archives for which Elodie had the code.

Still, she couldn't believe that it had worked, that the Archivist was now leading them down a winding spiral staircase. It might as well have been winter down below, the air thin and sharp with cold. Deeper and deeper they went, so many steps that Elodie soon lost count. At one point she grew so dizzy she paused abruptly, entangling Sabine into a near collision. Sabine steadied herself, but not before brushing a hand against Elodie's own, which sent a shiver up the princess's spine.

She'd taken lovers before, of course. Being royal made seduction easy enough. So yes, Elodie had unsnapped corsets in closets, had been pressed up against the endless spines of books on the library shelves, had darted her tongue in soft, seashell-shaped ears as she whispered pretty nothings they would both soon forget. But then, as they always did, the girls departed, either to their home countries, to marry princes, or to the war or the ranks of the Loyalists. Elodie had never been able to keep anything but her solitude for longer than a month at a time.

She flexed her fingers, trying to shake off the quiver. It was distressing, to feel for even a moment like her pain or pleasure were at the mercy of someone else. It seemed absurd to assign any additional meaning to the innocent brush of skin against skin, no matter how much she might want to. She kept descending, the darkness all around them turning inward, the cold settling into her bones.

The Archivist's cane echoed dully as they neared the ground. Elodie was fascinated by the woman, the way she had been so quick to identify Sabine simply by her accent. Sabine *did* sound like the sea, steady and soothing. Elodie wondered if that meant she herself sounded as hollow and cold as the castle's long marble corridors.

She didn't see the final step coming, so dim was it when they made it to the ground. She stumbled and skidded, sprawling helplessly at the Archivist's feet. Her palms, which were still raw from the spill she'd taken in front of Sabine's market stall, screamed.

"Here." Sabine, who was somehow still standing, offered Elodie a hand. There it was again, that shiver all the way from the base of her neck to the bottom of her spine. A chill that felt like sparks instead of snow.

"You all right?" Sabine asked, her eyes barely discernible in the darkness.

"Fine," Elodie said tersely. "Just cold."

"It's freezing," Sabine agreed, rubbing her hands together. "Why's the temperature so stark down here?"

"Preservation," the Archivist said, and with the strike of a match she began to carefully light the lanterns along the walls. In the center of the circular room was a large table, stacked with books and pages of blank paper. There were rows of shelves piled with volumes and loose pages covered in black ink. "This room holds the oldest known texts pertaining to the New Maiden. This is my life's work, and I'd do anything to protect it. Including freeze."

"Better safe than sorry," Sabine confirmed with a gentle smile.

"I keep the original over here." The Archivist led Sabine to the table, to a thin black leather-bound book that sat alone. "It stays in my sight. Always available to reference."

"Original what?" Sabine looked curiously at the woman.

"*Book of the New Maiden*, dear," the Archivist said.

Sabine's eyes widened as the woman offered her the document. She received it tentatively, eyes moving slowing across the words scrawled on the page. Elodie, not wanting to get too close lest that intoxicating shiver return, began to study the shelves. She scoured the spines before pulling a tome at random, flipping through pages upon pages of what looked like names, the letters scrambling in the weak light.

"What are these?" She looked up, putting a finger between the pages to hold her place. "I don't recognize these names from Her book."

The Archivist was suddenly behind her, silent as sin. "Those aren't for your eyes," she snapped, tugging at the tome.

She was surprisingly strong for such an old woman. Although she emerged from the scuffle triumphant, book tucked beneath her arm, several loose pages of parchment floated to the floor.

A thick slash of ink caught Elodie's eye. She stooped down to collect the paper in question, which revealed a giant black X drawn atop a name on a line of ancestry. As she gathered the rest of the spilled pages, she saw X after X in the same space on each family tree.

"What is all this?" She stared up at the Archivist.

The woman didn't look worried, exactly, but she did look wary. "Those are the country's records. I've kept track of every birth and death in Velle since I was old enough to hold a pen. My mother before me and her mother before her have all been tasked with this meticulous duty."

"Every single birth and death in Velle? Since its inception?"

"The Church was understandably anxious to find the New Maiden's chosen reincarnation. We record the lineage of all Velle citizens with three daughters or more. This responsibility began with our family's matriarch, the New Maiden's Favored, Ruti."

Ruti, the record keeper. It was no surprise then, that her descendant would be tasked with guarding all the Church's secrets.

"*This* is how they tracked potential Third Daughters?" Sabine had tucked the *Book of the New Maiden* under her arm and come to join them in the center of the room. "Can I see one?" Elodie handed over a stack of pages. "What does the X mean?" Sabine frowned down at the thick black lines. "Is this just the identifier for each third?"

"No, dear," the Archivist said softly. "That means they died."

Sabine looked horrified as she leafed through the stack she held. "But there are so many. So many girls gone."

The woman was now uncomfortable. "Death comes for us all."

"But this is concentrated, even you must admit. The likelihood of a third daughter's third daughter is already rare. For them to be born only to pass on feels...wrong."

The Archivist shrugged. "The New Maiden works in mysterious ways."

Sabine opened her mouth, then closed it. But Elodie could see something written across her face, something more than frustration. Something like suspicion. Eagerness fluttered in Elodie's chest. It was the same skepticism and distrust that brewed within herself.

"You said the Church was monitoring all of these births? To

seek out the third daughters?" Elodie glanced at the pages in her hands as well. "The clergy folk would have known about all of these girls." She peered down at the name on her page cut through with that deadly black X: *Aribelle Hoghlin of Lakeshore Common*. A tiny northern province. Nothing there but farmland and wolves.

Elodie flipped to another page. *Nachtia Luken, of Eastern Hill on Dale*. A trading post halfway between the Queen's City proper and the outer provinces. Good for purchasing cheap furs and very little else. These third daughters had been born to parents of no great regard, in locations of even less. And none of them had survived.

None remained, save for Brianne. The daughter of the queen. The daughter of the Royal Chaplain. Someone who could be used for the Church's cause. Someone who was easily controlled.

"Of course they knew, dear." The Archivist might as well have been underwater for all Elodie heard her. Now that she saw it all laid out on paper, the truth was so obvious as to be offensive. The Chaplain's romancing of her mother. His warmth turned cold as soon as the queen, a third daughter, bore a third daughter herself. The path cleared, ready and waiting for Her arrival. Which meant the prophecy had not chosen Brianne as the New Maiden. The clergy had.

Brianne

The girl wouldn't tell Brianne her name. It had been hours, or perhaps days—time was confusing here, as after the first meal she didn't long to eat or drink or sleep or relieve herself—and although they had spent every moment together, Brianne knew very little about her companion.

This wasn't a nightmare; that much was obvious. But it wasn't a dream, either. When Brianne dreamed, there was a sparkling, warm quality, like summer mornings in the royal garden where she'd sip dew off pink rose petals.

She was suspended somewhere in between panic and safety, an uncertainty that kept her shoulders straight and her heart pounding. But no matter how hard she tried—whether by digging her fingernails into her palms until she winced with pain, by jumping from the table to the floor, or by shouting at the top of her lungs—Brianne could not seem to wake herself up.

She pushed her chair away from the table, eyeing the strange, shimmering girl with skepticism. "If you won't tell me who you are, perhaps you'll tell me where I am?"

The girl smiled sadly. "We don't call it anything. It's an…in between, I suppose. Not quite a beginning. Certainly not the end."

"Why am I here?"

The girl laughed brightly, eyes smudged, as though the artist who had sketched her had smeared the charcoal with the side of their hand. "That's the right question, Brianne."

Suddenly the door flung open and the glass window shattered. Shadows began pouring into the room, each taking the form of a girl as they settled in. They leaned against the wall, curled up in corners, stood in small huddles, staring at Brianne, their pale mouths open, their wide eyes desperate, longing. Each of them reached out a hand, as though to caress her. As though to hold on to her tightly and never let go.

"What is this?" Brianne whispered, scrambling backward until she herself was pressed against the wall.

The first girl pushed back her chair and took her place among the shadows. She looked Brianne in the eye and smiled sadly. "The truth."

Part Four

*The New Maiden was not always beloved. She was
questioned along the way by those afraid of Her, those who
would battle Her, those who were embittered by Her, and
even those who would follow Her. It was strange, to witness
a young girl commanding an audience, Her Favoreds
never more than ten steps behind. Her power was intrinsic.
Unforeseen, yes, but impossible to deny. "I may not be
what the world expects," She told Her Favoreds, after they
were turned away from yet another town whose citizens
worshipped the Old Gods, "but what a person wants and
what a person needs are often two very different things.
One day, they will see that I am the constant, despite the
darkness. I am the guiding light."*

—Book of the New Maiden,
verse 104

22

The *Book of the New Maiden* was warm in Sabine's hands. The pages were yellowed and faded, thin as a fine layer of frost, the ink splattered where Ruti had scrawled hastily to record everything the New Maiden had done. But Sabine wasn't focused on the *Book*'s word. She was too busy looking at the records Elodie had uncovered. At the giant black Xs over third daughters, as menacing as the thick black tally lines on her father's debt ledger. There was something so cold about those marks. Something incredibly final.

The Archivist's expression was pained, but Elodie was aflame, eyes blazing like a polished sword. Ready to strike. Ready to kill.

"Why did no one stop them?" Elodie asked, tone careful. The question hung heavy in the air between them.

The woman swallowed. "I do not deign to understand the clergy. I trust only what is written. Her word. My records. This is the truth I know." Silence settled like dust around them. Sabine watched Elodie filter through several expressions, but no words came.

Sabine glanced down at the book in her hands, flipping back one page to find a quote she'd noted. "And the New Maiden rose, and said, 'I am for beginnings, not ends.'" Sabine cleared her throat uncomfortably. "Why would the clergy stray so far from Her word?"

The Archivist's face darkened. "That I cannot explain. Now put away the self-righteous sparkle in your eyes, both of you." She shook her head sadly. "Your knowledge of their actions changes nothing. No one trusts girls from Harborside."

Sabine's chest tightened. The Archivist hadn't said anything she didn't already know. Still, it didn't hurt any less to hear it spoken out loud.

"I hold a considerably higher station. Perhaps I might intervene?" Elodie was shuffling through the pages, stacking them into a careful pile. "As soon as the world sees this, the Chaplain will be forced to step down."

"I cannot allow you to take my records." The woman shook her head sharply. "They do not leave this room."

Elodie's face fell. "But Velle needs to know the truth. Our people need to know what he's done."

"Are you so naive?" the Archivist said, her voice mightier than Sabine thought possible. It was the heave of fire bellows, the tightening of a knot, the tug of a rope. It set Sabine on edge. "It does not matter what you do. This is bigger than one person—larger, even, than the New Maiden. It was set in motion long ago. No. It is too late." She looked unbearably sad. "You are too late."

Elodie's face went frighteningly blank. "Fine." She dropped the careful stack of parchment, pages flying every which way. "Be on the wrong side of history, then." She glanced at Sabine before turning on her heel. "Coming?"

Sabine, who had bent down to gather the pages, jumped quickly to attention. "Thank you," she said half-heartedly to the woman, handing her the mess of paper and the *Book of the New Maiden*.

The climb back up the staircase was much more difficult than their descent.

"This is bad," Elodie muttered, between huffs. "This is very bad."

"It isn't good," Sabine was forced to admit. "But you heard her. Who would believe us?"

Elodie stopped walking. "Where is your loyalty to Velle? To the New Maiden?"

"Where was yours?" Sabine had done her best to repress her judgment toward Elodie's decision to send her sister to sleep. But she would not allow the princess to call *her* disloyal without raising a mirror up to her actions, too.

"What did you say?" Elodie's voice was dangerous.

"I just meant..." Sabine hated the way she shrank into herself, shoulders hunching up toward her ears, stomach twisting into knots, even as they continued to climb. "You used a sleeping potion to incapacitate the Third Daughter."

"Yes," Elodie said darkly. "I did."

Sabine sighed with frustration. "How is that any different from—"

"It's *entirely* different." Elodie rounded on her. "The fact that you can't see that means you're even more naive than I thought."

"Well, you're crueler than *I* thought," Sabine snapped back. "I tried to give you the benefit of the doubt, to partner with you despite the fact that you would compromise your own sister, but—"

"I did not do this for myself," Elodie sniffed. "I did it for Velle."

"Ah, yes, the age-old adage," Sabine's voice dripped with sarcasm, "'country before family.'"

They'd made it to the top of the steps, back in the hallway that led into the tiny church. It was just as empty as when they'd arrived, the Archivist still down at the bottom of the cellar pit surrounded by her pages and her secrets. Before Sabine could stop her, Elodie blew out the three lit tapers, the flames extinguished with a single breath.

"Elodie." Sabine herself wasn't religious, but she'd seen her mother drop a precious copper into the offering box before striking a match to send her wishes straight to the New Maiden's ear. These votives were meaningful, especially to those whose day-to-day lives offered little hope. Sometimes a prayer was all a person could afford. A flicker of flame amidst the darkness. And Elodie had swatted them away as though they were nothing more than gnats upon her shoe. It was the same disregard she'd displayed by using Sabine's tears on the Third Daughter.

"What." It wasn't a question so much as a threat. Elodie turned on her heel and pushed her way back into the autumn air. With shaking hands, Sabine relit the candles before she followed her out.

Elodie didn't speak to Sabine the rest of the evening.

Sabine's darkness was delighted by this turn of events. *Now you've done it*, it laughed. *You didn't even need my help.*

Sabine tried her best to ignore the dark, velvety voice, bitter like the mead her father used to drink from the flask he wore at his hip, offering a taste to his younger daughter when she was no more than four, barefoot, curly haired and curious about why he always smelled like smoke and spice when he finally found his way home.

The inky-black veins had moved even farther up her arm, past her bicep and toward her shoulder, her entire right arm annexed by the sadness stewing within her. All she needed to do was take a seat, let the darkness step forth and run the show, to speak the words that lived in the foulest parts of her heart. She was tempted. Even though she had seen more of Velle than she ever had before, even though she'd spent the day with a princess whose eyes sparkled like iron, Sabine was still sad.

She had never been apart from Katrynn and Artur for longer than a day. She'd never suffered the berating voice of her darkness anywhere other than on her straw-stuffed pallet, in the cramped front room, listening to familiar footsteps from beneath her blanket. Now, although a ragged quilt was pulled up over her eyes on the shared bed at the Pained Pig, all Sabine could hear was Elodie. Her sharp huffs. Her furious sighs. There was no burning tension between them this time. Only anger. It made Sabine feel even more alone, trapped in a tiny room with no ally. With someone who could never truly understand her heart.

You're never alone, dear. Sabine didn't know if she would ever escape this darkness. She didn't know if she'd ever fully possess her own mind again.

She turned on her side, tracing the walk back through the sewer system from the church, the silence hanging about them like an ill-fitting cloak. Sabine knew they were both reflecting on the horrors of what the Church had done.

You'll never be ruthless enough to make a difference in this world, offered the darkness unhelpfully. Sabine realized that's why Elodie was so fascinating to her—she seized opportunities, even those she didn't fully understand. She was daring, was willing to go out not with a whimper but a scream. Ruthless enough to be powerful.

Of course, Elodie also had the privilege of never truly facing a consequence. Never really reaching an end. If Sabine was identified as the apothecary whose potion had enchanted the Third Daughter, her life would be stripped from her the way Artur skinned the mice he caught by their tails, their matted gray pelts dripping with blood. She shivered.

"What is the matter with you," Elodie interrupted her thoughts. It was becoming clear to Sabine that the princess did not ask questions so much as demand answers.

Good question, added the darkness.

"Shut up."

"Excuse me?" The blanket was yanked away from over Sabine's head, letting in the warm candlelight and Elodie's glowering expression. "Don't speak to me like that."

"Don't pretend you don't like it." Sabine rolled her eyes, hoping her flippancy would cover up the embarrassment of responding to her darkness out loud.

Elodie opened her mouth, then closed it. She gave Sabine a look that was indescribable, so Sabine focused instead on the glimmer in her gray eyes. She let it simmer and stew, like a pot over a flame. The longer it cooked, the better it would taste.

She held Elodie's eyes. After several breathless seconds, the princess blushed and looked away. Sabine felt as though she'd just played the winning hand at the card table. Like she'd won a pile of gold. She wanted to reach for Elodie's hand. To hold tightly to her victory. Instead, she pulled the blanket back over her head.

When Sabine next woke, the room was deserted, the sheets flung to the side, tousled with sweat. She cracked her neck, rolling her shoulders in hopes of loosening the knots that had formed. They weren't new but they were painful, the tension radiating all the way up through her jaw. With difficulty, Sabine unclenched her teeth. She couldn't believe Elodie had left her here alone.

Exactly what you deserve, isn't it? You abandoned your family and now the princess has abandoned you.

Sabine sank into the smooth, silky feeling of her sadness, letting it drape around her like a scarf, like ribbons painstakingly braided into her hair. She could almost feel her veins darkening further, the inky black sweeping toward her left arm, blooming in her chest like a poisonous flower. The darkness was spreading more quickly than it ever had before, faster even than it did after months of careful, tender stewing. Its voice was more calculating, too. Crueler.

It frightened her to think that she might never fully have control of her mind again. That she might always be at the mercy of something darker brewing beneath. It made her wonder about the sanctity of her soul. With all this focus on the New Maiden and Her word, Sabine began to consider how little she knew about anything beyond the mortal world. How little she cared. How disconnected she was to anything beyond survival.

Sabine pulled herself from the bed and took to the window. Below, Harborside was bustling, the red of the Loyalists' coats striking amidst the drab grays and browns of the dockhands and laborers. The pink of morning light was settling into the crisp blue of the sky. That was what she worshipped: the next day. Every new dawn was a blessing. Every sunrise a psalm. All Sabine wanted, all she believed in, really, was hope. But that hope felt more and more distant by the day.

The door rattled, and then Elodie entered the room, carrying two steaming cups of tea. She brought with her the fresh, herbal warmth of peppermint, the brightness out of place in the dingy room. It wasn't until one of the warm mugs was forced into Sabine's hand that she realized it was for her.

"Thank you." It was more habit than anything else, her manners. She still begrudged Elodie her actions and attitude the night before. Even so, she wanted to cover Elodie's hand with her own.

Elodie grunted, taking a sip, then swearing as she burned her tongue. When finally she recovered, her expression stayed grim. "Have I buttered you up enough with the tea?"

Sabine raised an eyebrow, answering sarcasm with sarcasm. "I can't afford butter. Only berry-skin jam for dipping our dry crusts of bread."

Elodie reached into her pocket, offering Sabine a crumpled piece of paper. Sabine unfolded it curiously, breath catching as she found Elodie's face staring up at her, words scrawled beneath.

"You're bunking with a convict," Elodie laughed humorlessly. "I'm wanted."

Sabine frowned down at the parchment. "For what?"

"For treason." Elodie traced the words beneath her face. "For abandoning my post as a spy in the Sixth Republic." She was acting rather glib, all things told. Sabine knew what it felt like to be wanted for her sheer existence. Those third daughters, murdered as babes, knew more about being wanted, being *hunted*. For all of Elodie's posturing, at least the artist had taken care to get her eyes right on the flyer.

"These are plastered everywhere," Elodie continued. "I won't be able to move about without someone turning me in."

How much? A soft slither. Sabine wanted to know, too.

"How much?"

"A hundred thousand kelbers." Elodie wrinkled her nose in distaste as she flung herself onto the bed. "Surely I'm worth more than that?"

Sabine didn't believe there was anything in the world worth more than that.

Do it, then. Do what you were too afraid to do before. No. Sabine would not play fast and loose. Not even when her gut was screaming at her to be ruthless, once and for all. *Looks like your father's gambling genes are finally paying off.*

But Sabine had been punished by life-changing bets before. She knew exactly her father's sorrow when he shuffled in at sunrise, pockets empty. "Double or nothing," he'd murmur softly before stumbling up the four stairs that led to the next floor, falling, unwashed, into bed.

Double of nothing is still nothing, though, the darkness warned her. *Don't do something you'll regret.*

As Sabine peered over at the bed, Elodie's white hair spilling over the side of the mattress like a frozen river, she realized with deep discomfort that she wasn't scared of a squandered bet. No, it was Elodie she was far more afraid to lose.

23

Elodie couldn't stop staring at the etching of her face. Her own cold eyes looked up at her. Studying her. Judging her. Holding people to impossibly high standards was Elodie's specialty, after all.

She sat up, accidentally crumpling the page in the process. Sabine was sitting on the floor, eyes closed, right hand pressed against her head, expression grim. The darkness beneath her skin was impossible to ignore, so starkly in contrast with the blue and purple veins of her left hand. There was something under Sabine's surface, like a cauldron about to bubble over.

"What's wrong? Planning to give me up?" Elodie had meant it as a joke, but the smile died on her lips when Sabine opened her eyes.

"I don't want to," she whispered, and her expression made it seem so. "But what if I don't have a choice?"

Elodie cocked an eyebrow. "You always have a choice. It's weak to pretend otherwise."

"Easy for you to say," Sabine said. "You've never needed to make a difficult choice out of desperation."

Elodie's intended laugh came out like a splutter. "We're here because I incapacitated the Third Daughter. If that's not a regrettable decision made out of desperation, I don't know what is."

Sabine blinked up at her, eyes round with sorrow but dry from tears. "You're clearly not the only person who wanted to eliminate third daughters."

Elodie leaned back on the bed, fingers grazing her wanted poster. "Ironic, then, that *I'm* the only one wanted for treason."

"Why do you think the Church did it?"

"Power." Elodie shrugged. "Control. All the same reasons I don't trust them with the crown."

"But what do they stand to accomplish?" Sabine shifted on the floor. "The Third Daughter is supposedly the New Maiden reincarnate. Why would they want to prevent Her return?"

Elodie shook her head, frustrated. Sabine could be so naive.

"Don't you see?" Elodie asked, squeezing the sheets in her fist. This was so much bigger than she'd realized. Chaplain René had not been operating solely on his own behalf. This was a plot to put the Church in power. A Third Daughter born of a clergyman was the perfect way to ensure they fulfilled the prophecy on their own terms. Elodie's dosing of Brianne hadn't put a snag in the Chaplain's plan for Velle. She'd merely expedited it.

"If I hadn't eliminated Brianne, the Church would have— perhaps more permanently."

Sabine's expression twisted into something grotesque and grim. "All this violence and betrayal, to what end? What is the reward?"

"To win." Elodie's shoulders quirked up and down again. When

Sabine opened her mouth to protest, she held up a hand. "I'm not saying it's right, but I'm telling you what it is."

"Everybody thinks they're destined to win," Sabine muttered softly, "which makes the losing hurt all the more."

"So you see, dear Sabine," Elodie said, "you *do* have a choice. You can turn me in. You can take the money and free your sister and pay your rent, and you can believe you've won. Until, that is, the Chaplain shrugs off all pretense and you're subjected to a murderous sect, a corrupt Church pilfering money from its own people, and a disempowered queen." She eyed Sabine, unwavering. The other girl didn't flinch. "Or you can help me burn those bastards to the ground."

Sabine's lips parted just the slightest, just enough that Elodie wanted to separate them with her tongue, pry them open, and let the other girl swallow her whole. "So, I help *you* win."

"No." Elodie smiled, a thrill running through her that had only vaguely to do with the idea of winning and more to do with the girl who would be by her side. "*We* win."

"And what do I win?" Elodie didn't think it was her imagination, the way Sabine was staring up at her from beneath her eyelashes. Like she was daring her to take the next step closer.

"Me," Elodie said, testing the strength of the tenuous string between them. For a moment, neither of them moved. Neither of them breathed. "When I am the Queen's Regent, you can have anything your heart desires." She took her chapped bottom lip between her teeth.

Sabine shifted again. Elodie could practically feel the heat radiating from where she sat on the ground.

"You don't need to stay down there, you know," Elodie said, scooting over to make room on the lumpy mattress.

"Are you trying to seduce me, Princess?" Sabine asked, voice low.

"That depends," Elodie said, trying to ignore the fluttering in her stomach.

"On what?" Sabine shifted forward slightly, elbows anchored into the mattress, her chin resting in her hands.

Elodie flipped over onto her stomach so her face was directly in front of Sabine's. "If it's working."

For a moment, neither of them moved. The air was charged. Then Sabine pulled away. When her eyes met Elodie's, she looked conflicted. Ashamed. Her brown eyes had an amber ring around them.

"What's happening?" Elodie made to reach for Sabine, then thought better of it.

"I…" Sabine twisted her hair through her fingers. "I'm sorry, I can't."

Elodie's heart sank. She was used to rejection, but for her status, not herself. Yet only moments ago, Sabine's irises were brown. She had been leaning forward, eyes wide.

"You can't, or *it* can't?"

Sabine's face paled, making the creeping black vein in her neck even more prominent. "What are you talking about?"

"You know what I'm talking about. The darkness in your veins. The war with yourself. The amber in your eye."

"I didn't know about that last one." Sabine's voice was light as a feather. Fearful as a ghost.

"Sabine." Elodie passed the other girl's name through her lips like a prayer. "Tell me."

"I don't know what's happening to me." She squeezed her eyes shut. Grimaced. Opened her eyes to blink once, twice, four times, and then the amber ring was gone. "It's my magic. My sadness. Usually it leaves when I brew, but on the night of the midnight market, it stayed. And over the last few days, it's only gotten worse." She held out her right hand for Elodie to examine.

Tentatively, Elodie reached for her. She was surprised how soft Sabine's skin was. She slowly traced the dark lines running down Sabine's fingers, up her wrists and forearms. Sabine shivered beneath her touch.

"It's spreading." Elodie hesitantly reached her other hand to hover over Sabine's neck.

Sabine's eyes opened even wider. Her sadness was vast and vicious. Elodie wanted to kiss her. But Sabine had pulled away just now, and Elodie was determined to respect her. She would not overstep. She would wait. Waiting had never been her strong suit, but Elodie knew that her patience mattered more in this moment than it ever had before.

Elodie could hear her own heartbeat, a rush of blood as she stared down at the crooked needlework on the quilt beneath her, counting stitches one by one, until she thought she could bear it no longer and finally felt Sabine's cold fingers on her jaw, pulling her forward until their lips met.

There was no soft, careful consideration. No tender exploration. No tentative touch. Instead, they crashed together, kindling catching fire. Elodie pulled Sabine up from where she rested on her knees, onto the thin mattress, a tangle of limbs and long hair and layers as they dove into the deep.

But even as Elodie raked her fingers through Sabine's hair, as Sabine nipped at her neck, Elodie saw flashes of darkness on Sabine's skin. The sadness was spreading. Sadness Elodie desperately needed if they were going to wake Brianne. Would a moment of intimacy extinguish the swirling sadness Sabine had been harvesting?

Or would being with Elodie somehow exacerbate her emotions, making her magic more powerful? Was this a tryst? Or did it mean more?

She didn't know why she was trying to evaluate the entirety of their relationship while Sabine's hand was on her thigh. Elodie had never been one to overthink. If anything, she was an overdoer. She shouldn't be fretting over logistics. She should be reveling.

Elodie had lost herself in lovers before. It was a way to take her mind off the dread of her day-to-day life. But the thrill of those distractions faded as soon as the last lingering heat of their touch had finally dissipated. And then Elodie was always right back where she started—complacent and unfulfilled.

But with Sabine, she wanted more. She wanted this to last longer than just a moment. She wanted it to be more than just soft lips and body heat.

She yelped as Sabine nipped her ear. Elodie had never been so distracted before, and it was hardly fair considering Sabine was doing excellent work. She turned herself back to the matter at hand. To the girl whose fingers were creeping higher. As she kissed Sabine deeper, her mouth warm, a touch of mint and honey still on the other girl's tongue, Elodie gave herself permission to linger in this moment before she worried about the next.

24

Elodie Warnou seemed to have a death wish. Any rational person with a mark on their head would have stayed in bed, letting the morning light of a new day filter through the grimy window as Sabine tugged lazily on a strand of her pale hair. Instead, the princess had slipped quietly from the room, leaving Sabine alone.

You sentimental fool, the darkness had chastised. *She will keep you wanting now that she knows she can.* But Sabine hardly had a chance to reflect on their tryst and everything after—their bodies pressed together as they slipped in and out of sleep, scavenging for food before returning their attention to each other—when the princess returned, looking chagrined. She had, of course, been spotted.

"Lost him in an alleyway," the princess had panted as she flung herself back onto the thin mattress.

But Sabine knew better. One hundred thousand kelbers wasn't a sum anyone in Harborside would let slip away. She'd started gathering their things. "We have to go."

"You worry too much," Elodie had said, fingers grazing Sabine's sleeve as she tried to draw her back to the bed.

"You don't worry enough," Sabine muttered, shaking her off.

"Where are we going, then?" The princess begrudgingly got to her feet.

Sabine sighed. There was only one place in Velle where she truly felt safe. But she had never brought home a girl before. Sure, there had been the occasional friend, another girl with patches sewn into her skirt, with greasy hair and gaps in her teeth, who knew what it was like to go to sleep on an empty stomach and to wake to a beetle scuttling across a forearm.

Still, it wasn't the same as she felt now, walking swiftly down the streets of Harborside, Elodie at her heels. She was trying to mentally prepare for her mother's reaction after days away. Even worse was the idea of Elodie's judgmental eyes laid upon her family home, the place where Sabine had been born and grown, where she had spent days upon weeks upon months tossing and turning on a thin pallet as the darkness crept in.

"Remind me again why venturing out seemed like a good idea?" Sabine asked bitterly.

"I wanted to know if anyone was talking about the Chaplain." Elodie shrugged. "After that stunt he pulled, parading Brianne about."

"And?" That didn't seem a good enough reason.

Elodie's face soured. "Not a word. It's as though no one even cares."

"Most of us don't have the luxury of keeping tabs on royal antics." Sabine turned down an alleyway, dodging a bucket of murky water that fell onto the cobblestones. "We only know that there is someone we answer to. That's trouble enough."

At her family's front door, Sabine paused.

"What are we waiting for?" Elodie unwrapped the scarf she had wound around her face as a disguise.

"I'm afraid." Sabine's honesty scared her. Even her darkness was silent.

"Of what?" Elodie's voice was soft. Almost sincere. It was unsettling.

Sabine cleared her throat. She didn't need to give the princess more cause to pity her, especially given what she was about to see. "Nothing. Let's go." Sabine turned the knob and pushed open the door. It didn't open all the way. Instead, it caught after opening only a slight gap. A thick chain held it closed.

"What in the twelve hells?"

The sharp sound of a knife unsheathed pierced Sabine's ears.

"Who goes there?" A bright blue eye peered through the gap.

Sabine's confusion mixed with relief at the sight of her brother. "Artur," she breathed.

Artur closed the door in her face. Sabine gaped at the wood. Her darkness was right: Her brother *had* held a grudge.

"That's quite the greeting," Elodie muttered.

But after a moment the door opened again, revealing her brother's entire face.

"Artur, I—"

"Where have you been?"

Only a few days had passed, but her brother looked thinner, disheveled. The dregs of the dark blond beard he'd always coveted had finally made an appearance, leaving a shadow on his jaw. But he didn't beam with pride, the way she thought he would. Instead, he glowered down at her.

"I—"

"No, you don't get to talk." A finger pointed at her chest. "Not when Katrynn is on the *Black Rock* because of you. Stuck there, with no way out, save for your magic. And you take that and run? You're even more selfish than I thought."

With a soft clunk, Sabine's mother hobbled over to the doorway, eyes wide as she took in Elodie and Sabine.

"Bet," she breathed. Her eyes were hopeful, but when she caught sight of the darkness on her daughter's skin, her face went white. "You haven't been taking care of yourself." Her mother examined her skin with scrutiny. "You look as though you've been saving up reserves for months."

You've disappointed her. Sabine didn't need her darkness to voice such an obvious truth. Still, it hurt to hear the reinforcement of what she already knew.

"Inside." Her mother yanked on Sabine's arm. "Now."

She's embarrassed, the darkness hissed, as Sabine stumbled over the threshold. *She can't stand to see the sadness scrawled across your skin.*

Inside, the four of them stood, staring at one another. Sabine kept expecting Elodie to shrink away from the grimy windows and the wobbly chairs. But she looked as she always did. Regal. Observant. Kind.

"Who are you?" Artur had turned his attention to Elodie.

"Elodie Marial Warnou." Elodie gave Sabine's brother a half bow. "Velle's first daughter."

Orla gaped at her own daughter. "Bet, what is the meaning of this?"

Sabine, who was distracted by Elodie's middle name, startled.

"Bet?" Elodie looked amusedly at her. "That's adorable."

"Don't you dare," Sabine began, but she was interrupted by her brother, who slapped the table, the sound hollow in the small space.

Elodie, to her credit, did not flinch. But Sabine felt her face flush, anger rising in her chest as she burned with embarrassment. "What are you doing here?" he demanded.

"Artur," their mother chastised, but delicately. Anger simmered beneath her surface, too. "It isn't like you, Sabine, to run off." *To abandon your family, she means.*

"I…"

"It's all right," Elodie said, unshouldering the bag of ingredients for Sabine's fabricated antidote. "We should tell them about the potion."

Sabine's stomach sank as Elodie began to lay the ingredients out on the table. Between the parade and the murderous intentions of the Church, she had nearly forgotten the tangled web of lies she'd woven for herself.

Sabine's mother turned to her daughter. She knew Sabine hadn't the faintest idea how to brew. "What potion?"

Sabine opened her mouth, but Elodie was faster. "We need to wake the Third Daughter."

A frown creased her mother's face. "With this?" She gestured to the strange assortment of ingredients.

Elodie looked to Sabine for confirmation. "This is what we need, isn't it?"

Orla Anders's expression was still twisted with confusion. "For what?"

Sabine thought she might vomit all over the floor.

But Elodie misunderstood the question. "You haven't heard? The Third Daughter is trapped in endless sleep. I meant to give her henbane, but there was a mix-up of the vials." She offered Sabine a small smile. "So we simply need to reverse the effects."

For the first time, Sabine's mother glanced her daughter's way. "We don't know how to reverse the effects of her magic. Even if we did, there's nothing this assortment of ingredients could do."

The hurt that flashed across Elodie's face was sharper than any weapon. Sabine wanted to sink to the floor, but she seemed to be frozen in place.

"Elodie—"

"You told me," the princess interrupted, voice eerily calm, "that you could do this."

"Elodie, I'm sorry." And she was. But the look on Elodie's face confirmed it didn't matter. Her expression was shuttered, her gray eyes like iron.

"You promised," the princess said, and this time, her voice wavered. That tiny glimmer of vulnerability made Sabine's heart twist in her chest.

"I lied." Tears fell from her cheeks—too early, far too early, for the amount of magic she needed. It wasn't time. But she couldn't stop.

"Sabine," her mother said sternly. "Quit that."

"What are you doing, Bet?" Artur glared at her, arms crossed. "We need those for Katrynn."

You wanted to be ruthless, the darkness said. *Now you are. You've shown them what you're capable of.*

"I trusted you," Elodie said, and it was the plainness of her confession that led Sabine to sob harder. She was quickly surrounded, not by comforting hands but polished glass catching the tears where they fell.

Yet as the salt spilled from her eyes, she did not feel the relief that often came from the sweet release of sadness. She felt overwhelmingly hopeless. Rather than leaching from her veins as it ought to, the darkness only seemed to spread. Down, farther into the pit of her stomach, into her ruined heart. She remained at the mercy of this... thing inside her. This thing that took and took and never gave anything but anguish. Left behind nothing but woe.

When finally the tears quelled, the house was quiet, save for the small sounds of evening: mice shuffling behind the baseboards; the groan of the sea slowly eroding the shore. No one would meet her eye.

"Take this." Her mother pressed the half-full vial of tears into Elodie's hand. "For your trouble."

"Ma—" Artur began, but their mother shushed his protests.

"Your sister owes a debt to this girl."

"She owes a debt to Katrynn, too," he insisted.

"We'll make do," her mother said firmly. "Now, I don't know if this will work, but it's worth a try." She moved toward the curio cabinet, the clinking of glass as loud as the sea amidst the silence of the room. She emerged with a bottle of blue glass. A constitutional tonic, for energy and health.

"You'll need to hurry." Orla Anders offered Elodie the bottle. "The magic is most potent when it's fresh. Combine the two. Put a dab behind her ears, on her wrists, and on the soles of her feet. Have her drink the rest."

Elodie nodded. "Thank you." Her voice was dull. "I should go."

If she left, Sabine was certain she would never return.

"Wait!" But it was as though Sabine had not even spoken. Elodie turned on her heel and slipped out the front door without a sound. Sabine begged her body to follow, but it disobeyed. Instead, she remained planted to the floorboards as the wicked gleam of her darkness swirled about triumphantly.

Did you really think this would end any differently? it taunted. *Did you really think that she cared? It was only ever a transaction. But now that she knows the truth, you will never see her again.*

Sabine refused to believe it. Surely Elodie could understand Sabine's impossible position. Would realize her intentions were good, even if, in the moment, her actions appeared deceitful.

I would not be so certain, the darkness tsked. *You lack self-awareness, Sabine.*

She was a gambler. A liar. A thief.

Days ago, she'd told Artur that if he wasn't careful, he would end up like their father. But she'd been wrong. Her brother wasn't the problem. She was.

25

If anger was a fire, Elodie could have set the entirety of Harborside ablaze. She stalked through the streets, kicking at refuse and cursing Sabine's name. She had trusted the apothecary, had genuinely believed Sabine could rectify her mistake. Instead, she had woven pretty stories, spending Elodie's coins on useless ingredients, and wasting her most important resource: time.

Worst of all, Elodie cared for her. She'd been intrigued, then impressed, by the depths of the other girl's emotions, had even begun to open herself up, to pry at the hinges of a heart that had remained carefully closed for years. It was in Elodie's best interest, her mother had insisted, not to let her feelings get in the way of facts.

Well, the fact of the matter was that Elodie had shared pieces of herself with Sabine she'd only ever offered up once before—to Tal. Of course, he had betrayed her, too. The boy who'd known all her secrets and ambitions, who had been her fiercest defender and strongest ally, had shown no remorse when alerting the Loyalists to her presence. Perhaps there was something wrong with her gut, to be given up so easily by those she trusted most.

Luckily, the one person Elodie could always count on was waiting for her at the east gate. She'd sent word ahead to Rob by way of a haphazardly scrawled note pressed into the palm of a young girl, addressed to the viola player, Avery. Elodie knew it would make it to her brother in no time. Still, whether he would show up for her had been a gamble. One she was grateful to win.

"Lady above, I missed you," she whispered once she reached him. "Everyone else is a disappointment."

"You always did have remarkably high expectations." Rob offered her a wry grin. "Come inside before you're seen." Elodie hesitated. "Don't worry," he said, catching the not-quite-closed door to the tower. "I sent Posey to polish his sword. We're alone."

It was just as cold inside, the wind wheezing around the turret with an unsettling, hollow moan.

His hair was shorter, shorn close to the skull, revealing every flicker of expression on his face. His mouth twitched as he leaned against the tower's stone wall. "What are you doing here, Elodie?"

Her smile slipped. "You don't sound happy to see me. I thought you'd be relieved I wasn't all the way in the Sixth Republic."

"Why aren't you?"

"I couldn't leave. Not with all of this."

"Yes," Rob said, eyes narrowing. "Everything's changed, hasn't it?"

Elodie didn't like her brother's terseness. "What's wrong?"

"Nothing." Rob let out a soft laugh. "I'm better than I've been in ages."

Dread simmered in Elodie's stomach. Rob had always been

open and affectionate with her. Talking with him had never been this laborious. "Tal's back, you know."

"I know." Rob's answer was flat.

"He's the one who sounded the alarm on me."

"Well, Tal's always been very by the book." Rob almost laughed. "Tactical. You know."

"How long has he been back?"

Rob's eyes flashed. "He showed up the afternoon you left."

"The whole battalion?" If Rob's father was nearby, that might explain his hardened exterior. General Garvey was a straitlaced man, and in his presence Rob tended to stiffen.

Rob shook his head. "Just Tal."

"Why?"

Her brother shrugged standoffishly. "Couldn't say."

"What is the matter with you?" Trying to keep their conversation going was like pulling teeth.

"Nothing." Rob rolled his eyes. "You treat me like a child sometimes."

"You're my baby brother." She reached to pinch his cheek, but Rob shrank away. Elodie's face fell.

"I'm only thirteen months your junior. Just because our mother gave you more attention while she was alive doesn't mean that you're better than me."

"She was training me to assist Brianne." Elodie frowned. "It wasn't a contest. It wasn't the only measure of her love."

But then Elodie realized that in all her memories where she was sat at her mother's side, Rob was nowhere to be found. In fact, she could hardly remember a time when Tera Warnou had taken much of an interest in Rob or Cleo at all. It made sense then, his bitterness.

"Of course it was," Rob snapped. "She chose you, which told me everything I needed to know. You were always the guiding light, and I was always following in your footsteps. It's cold in the shadows, El. But I've finally found my place."

Elodie caught a glimpse of gold beneath her brother's collar. It made her skin itch, how closely it resembled the clergy's ornaments. It made her uneasy that Rob, the soft, bright boy she'd always known, had dipped his head toward the heavy magnetism of the white-robed clergy folk. Elodie had been preparing to lose her country to the Church. She hadn't expected to lose her brother to them, too.

"Rob, I don't think—"

"He warned me you wouldn't understand," her brother interrupted, voice cold.

Elodie's expression darkened as her suspicions were confirmed. The Chaplain had vied for Rob's loyalty in Elodie's absence. "You've been spending time with him?"

Rob frowned. "Of course."

"You say that like it's obvious."

"You're naive to think it wouldn't be."

Elodie sighed. Perhaps it was her own fault, gallivanting about with Sabine while she left Rob and Cleo in the Chaplain's clutches. The Church was certainly good at indoctrination. The Chaplain had convinced the people of Velle to give him the crown with a single sermon and a macabre procession through the city square. It wasn't surprising that he had turned his attention to Rob, the son of the country's leading military mind. He'd need the support of the soldiers for anything to change on a larger scale. Still, Elodie had believed her brother more discerning.

"Don't worry, sister." He smiled serenely. "There's room for you, too, you know."

"In the Church?" Elodie scoffed. "I'll pass." She shifted, the bottles clinking in her pocket. "Rob, this has all spiraled out of control. I'm here to set things right."

He frowned at her. "How do you mean?"

Elodie bit her lip. "You were right to be suspicious about Brianne's condition." Her stomach churned. "Someone did slip her something."

Rob's eyes widened.

"Me."

He stared at her, stunned.

"I was trying to protect her. The Chaplain, the Church, was going to ruin her, take advantage of her agreeable nature and turn Velle into something sinister and strange. I was going to wake her up when she turned seventeen, when she no longer required a regent."

"And in the interim, you thought *you'd* be queen." He squinted at her. "Lady above, El, I never imagined you so ruthless."

"I didn't do it for *me*." Elodie scowled, frustrated that her brother would willfully misinterpret her intentions. "I did this for Velle. For Brianne."

Rob let out a laugh. "For Brianne. That's rich, El. If you really meant to wake her up, why didn't you do it before you left for Ethliglenn?"

"I tried," she insisted, "with the smelling salts. But there was a mix-up with the potion. That's where I've been. Procuring what I need." She pulled the vial of tears and the blue bottle of tonic from her pocket. "Now I just require your assistance to get to her."

Rob studied the glass containers. "How does it work?"

He sounded more like himself. Elodie's jaw unclenched. "Mix the vial with the bottle," she said, repeating Sabine's mother's instructions. "Dab on her wrists, behind her ears, and on the soles of her feet. Get her to drink the rest. She should wake."

Rob looked up at her. "Will, or should?"

Elodie swallowed thickly. Her tongue felt too large for her mouth. "Should."

"You don't know." It wasn't a question. "And that's good enough for you?"

"Aren't you the one extolling the virtues of faith? This is a good thing, Rob. We can have Brianne back."

Rob cleared his throat. "The Church won't like it."

"The Church should thank me for resurrecting their New Maiden." She wanted to tell her brother about the other third daughters. The ones taken too soon. "Rob, this prophecy—"

Her brother held out a hand to shush her. "You haven't the faintest idea what you're talking about."

"No, *you* don't," she said, raising her voice. "The clergy has murdered girls, Rob."

Rob shook his head. "They have not."

"I saw it," Elodie insisted, wishing she had pocketed one of the Archivist's family trees when she'd had the chance.

"You saw clergy folk with knives in their hands?" Rob asked sardonically.

"I saw the records," Elodie insisted. "In the First Church. The Archivist there—"

"Records can be falsified," Rob snapped. His dismissal was concerning.

"Why don't you believe me?" Elodie was close to pulling out her hair.

"You haven't given me a reason to."

"I'm your sister."

"That's not enough," he shouted, voice reverberating through the tower. "Lady above, El, you have been so wrapped up in this plot of yours, this play for power, that you fail to see what's right in front of you."

"What are you talking about?"

"You're on the wrong side of this."

"What side is that?"

"The side that does not embrace change. Progress. You're narrow-minded."

Elodie raised her eyebrows. "Careful, brother. You're starting to sound like Chaplain René."

Rob folded his arms. "You're too quick to judge."

"And you're too quick to forget your loyalty." They stared at each other, their argument echoing above them.

"You're right." Rob deflated slightly. "I'm sorry. There's so much happening here, it's hard to keep a level head."

"I understand." Elodie eyed him suspiciously but didn't want to spook him. Instead, she tapped a fingernail against the glassware. "Will you take me to our sister?"

Rob held out his hand for the bottles, slipping both the tonic and the vial of tears in his pocket. "Keep your head down."

Elodie followed her brother up the spiral staircase, to the main floor of the east tower. Their footsteps were loud and clunky, graceless as she returned home. The castle smelled differently. The soft, clean scent of cotton and cloud had been replaced with the heavy perfume of bergamot, thick like smoke. The doors to the servants' quarters were flung open wide. The long bunks with cozy comforters had been stripped away. Steel bed frames with thin bed-rolls lined the walls, as cold and unfeeling as the Chaplain's eyes.

"What's happened here?"

"Order," Rob said simply.

It seemed a bit more militant than orderly, but Elodie held her tongue. She didn't want Rob to veer them off course. But in the end, her restraint didn't matter. She realized too late that they were nowhere near Brianne's chambers. Instead, Rob had steered them toward Elodie's room.

"What are we doing here?" She turned to her brother, voice echoing in the empty hall.

"What I promised him I'd do," Rob said darkly, rapping three times on the entrance to Elodie's bedroom. The door swung open to reveal three Loyalist guards dressed in red. As they took in Elodie's presence, their expressions turned bright.

"What are you—?" Elodie asked bewilderedly as Rob shoved her over the threshold into the waiting arms of the Queen's Guard.

"I'm sorry, Elodie."

The vials clinked in her brother's pocket as Rob turned on his heel, taking Elodie's only chance at waking Brianne with him.

26

Sabine had once looked forward to brewing days. After a good cry, the sadness leached from her, the darkness gone from her veins, she would emerge sparkling and bright, her mind clear. But even though she had wept, she was still saddled with guilt, the darkness swirling in her head propelled by her brother's harping and her mother's pointed quiet.

"You're a fool, Bet," Artur spat from the kitchen table, where he sat with his arms crossed. "Sitting in the corner under a blanket while the rest of us scrape and scramble to survive."

"You'd have nothing to scramble with if it wasn't for me." Sabine's voice was loud in the small room, tinged with a darkness she'd only ever heard in her head. The words were hot in her throat, scratching on the way back up like bile. Her insides churned; her blood was cold. And for the first time in a long time, Sabine didn't feel sad. She was angry.

"None of you ever cared what happened to me so long as I could produce my magic," she continued, relishing the words in her mouth as sweet as sugar. "You didn't notice that I sat helpless in the corner, blankets bearing down on me like a weight. Do you think I wanted this?" She pushed up her sleeves, exposing the dark veins running up and down her arms. "Do you think that I like being consumed by my emotions?" She tugged down her collar to reveal the dark veins snaking up her neck. "Do you think I enjoy being sad?" She chuckled darkly. "Maiden above and among us, you have no idea what I have done for you. What I have endured for this family."

Both her mother's and Artur's faces were shocked and full of terror, bitter and burnt like the herbs her mother charred for her brews. It left an acrid taste on her tongue.

"What has happened to you, Sabine?" Her mother's voice wavered. "Where is my sweet girl?"

Sabine glowered. "You're not listening," she said, as the darkness in her head said the same thing. *She isn't listening.* "I was never sweet, I was merely holding it together so we could survive. This sadness, this darkness, is killing me, and yet you turn away, too repulsed by my emotion to see what it's doing to me."

Although she should have been fresh out of tears, Sabine found herself weeping again. *Yes, that's a good girl. Let it out. Let it all go.* For once, it wasn't her mother urging her. It was the darkness.

"Sabine." Her mother's voice was streaked with pain. Sabine hated it and reveled in it in equal measure. She retreated to the corner where her pallet lay, unfolding the quilt and wrapping it around her shoulders. She wanted to lick her wounds in peace. But her actions seemed to have the opposite effect on Artur. Where the sitting calmed Sabine, it infuriated him.

"You shouldn't say things like that," her brother swore. "Flying fish, you're poisonous."

Sabine turned on him. "What did you say?"

"I wish it was you on that ship, not Katrynn."

"I wish it was me there, too," Sabine said, her voice deadly calm. "I wish a lot of things, Artur." *Tell him what you think, what you really believe,* came the voice. "I wish I'd never been born, not here. Not as...this."

"You shut your mouth." Her mother's tone was sharp, cold. "I lost one of my babies. You don't get to wish away your life. How dare you?"

That shut Sabine up. It even gave her darkness some pause.

Your mother's grief should not dictate your choices. But you've let it, for years. Let yourself be a conduit for what she will not feel.

"I don't like this version of you." Artur cleared his throat. "I haven't liked you for a long time."

"Brilliant, Artur. Thanks for that." But Sabine's stomach twisted.

"Children." Their mother looked tired, ragged. "Please." It was only the waver of her voice that offered Sabine and Artur pause. She rested her head in her hands.

"When will you be ready to extract again?" Artur turned back to his sister.

Sabine swallowed. "I don't know if I have anything left to give."

Artur glanced at the black in her veins. "You'd leave Katrynn to rot?"

Sabine pulled the quilt over her head again and curled up into a ball. Why had she come back here? Why was her family so cold?

Why aren't you hurting them back? Why do you take and take and hold it all inside when there is more to you than your tolerance for distress? More to you than what anyone sees?

It was the first time the darkness had ever seemed to affirm her. It was unnerving and disorienting. But it was also empowering. It made her family's little wounds feel lesser.

"Look at her." Artur's voice was not nearly as muffled as Sabine would have liked, even as her head was buried underneath her blanket. "Collapsing again."

You don't need them. Just me. Just us.

Sabine emerged once more from beneath the quilt. "I need some air." She got to her feet. "It's clear I'm not wanted here." Neither her mother nor Artur argued as she closed the door behind her. She sank down onto the steps of their apartment, her skirt sinking into the endless puddles that ran like rivers between the cobblestones.

At first the breeze helped clear her head. It was crisp and cold and dried some of the sweat that had pooled in unspeakable places. She sank her chin in her hands and let her hair whip about like a hurricane. As the dockhands shouted and the seagulls cried, Sabine let herself breathe. In...like the waves lapping against the ships docked in the harbor. Out...like the fury that flowed through her as she recalled the exchange with her family.

She could still hear them, moving about behind the door. The pounding of footsteps and the clanging of cupboards. Sabine hadn't realized that their life had been so loud, that anyone could hear what was happening on the other side of the door. That she'd taken up any space at all.

A tiny laugh tinkled from the mouth of her mother. It made Sabine's stomach sink. All it had taken for her mother to smile was her absence. Maybe Artur had been right: The family *would* do better without Sabine. Without her, they wouldn't have lost their coin at the midnight market. Katrynn wouldn't be trapped on the *Black Rock*. Their family would be whole.

They would be better off without you. The time for the darkness to build her up was clearly over. *But you'd be better off without them, too. You're not powerful enough to hold their attention. This isn't it. You're not fulfilled.*

Sabine pushed open the door, wind at her back. As she reentered, her mother shrieked, and Artur jumped.

"Oh," her brother said, blinking. "It's only you."

Only her. Sabine's feelings had been sacrificed for so long, had been offered up in place of everyone else's needs. A dumping ground for her siblings' fear, her mother's grief, and her father's losses.

"Yes." Sabine's fingers clutched the doorframe.

"You should have stayed outside."

"You should stay quiet."

"Children!" Their mother's voice was sharp as she chastised them again.

Why was Sabine only ever referred to as a child? At seventeen, she was an adult. The other girls her age in Harborside were being married off. Meanwhile she was standing here wringing her hands.

"I am not a child." She could practically hear the darkness swelling in her own voice. It was sharp enough that she saw it reflected upon the kitchen wall, like fire casting shadows.

"What was that?" Her mother was looking fearfully at the spot on the wall where Sabine had noted the darkness moving.

"Probably a mouse." Artur hadn't even looked up from the frown he had directed toward his feet.

"No," their mother's voice wavered. "This was large. Big as a bear."

"On the wall?" Artur raised his blond eyebrows.

"Yes," Sabine said softly, "it was gigantic."

She caught a glimpse of it again. Something dark and looming, too tall and broad and wide. All-encompassing. The way it felt in her head.

Suddenly it was clear that the shadow on the wall was the same one that splayed itself across the corners of her brain. It was larger than she'd expected. No wonder her blood had turned black. Still, it was terrifying to see the space it took up when freed from the confines of her mind.

As Sabine looked at the shadow dancing across the walls, she noticed that the veins in her right pinky finger had faded back to blue. Her heart fluttered. Could she possibly find her way back to feeling balanced? Was some strange exorcism of anger all that it took?

But then the shadow began to winnow its way into the hearth, a gaping mouth forming as though to swallow the ashes.

You do not trust these folk. The words echoed like a bell in church, tolling loud and wide in her mind. The shadow continued to spread, inching forward out of the fire and onto the floor, creeping toward her family. *They do not trust you. I can take care of them, eliminate the threat. You should only be surrounded by those who believe.*

Sabine frowned. The darkness was heading for her brother. The shadow moved swiftly, stalking Artur. Only once did it look back her way, a single hesitation wherein *her* gut, *her* instinct, toyed with allowing the darkness to consume him.

That power felt good enough to make her shout: "Stop!" She feared what she would become if she silently acquiesced.

Artur and her mother jumped, looking at her with concern. The shadow stilled, then seeped slowly back, back, back into her, filling up her veins with the inky-black darkness. It was a part of her again, her family none the wiser.

"Sabine…" Her mother looked desperate and frightened by her daughter.

The apothecary was afraid of herself, too. Afraid of who she had very nearly become. She'd tormented her family enough. She couldn't hurt them anymore.

"It's okay," she whispered. "I'll go." She cleared her throat. "And this time I won't return."

"That isn't what I meant…" Her mother's protest was only half-formed.

But it had been. Sabine didn't need the darkness to tell her that.

27

Elodie's room was ransacked. Lace had been ripped from the hems of dresses she'd left behind, jewels unseated from their strings and cast about the carpet like fallen stars. Gray sheaths had been flung over the portraits that hung on the walls. The room dressed in forest green was glum and drab, save for the pop of red uniforms. The Loyalists were far too pleased to see her.

"Elodie." Maxine's expression was positively feral as she lounged back on the princess's bed, which had been stripped of its silk sheets and finery. Her mud-caked boots rested upon the bare mattress, a hand wrapped delicately around the handle of her sword. Elodie was beginning to regret their last interaction, where she'd pulled on the guard's braid. The girl seemed anxious to retaliate with more than hair tugging.

"Easy, Max," said Toph, a towering boy about Elodie's age, nudging Maxine's boot. "We're here to escort her, not to harm her."

"Not yet, anyway," chimed in Old Fred, a corporal in the guard who had been wearing the red before Elodie was even born. He got up from his place on Elodie's favorite chaise longue, sneezing indelicately and spraying phlegm all over the room.

Elodie shrieked as she was splattered. It was then that Toph made his move, grabbing Elodie's arms behind her back, encircling both her wrists easily with one of his large palms. Maxine grinned as she tugged a rope from her pocket and snapped it in the air before roughly tying Elodie up.

"Always wanted to do that," Maxine grunted as she tugged the final knot tight.

"So you were flirting with me all those years." Elodie winked at her, trying to keep her voice light even as her wrists burned beneath the rope.

Maxine rolled her eyes. "You're so vain. I bet you loved seeing your face plastered about the city."

"Those were wanted posters," said Old Fred, unhelpfully.

"At least someone wants me." Elodie shrugged. "Not that any of you can say the same."

"I wouldn't be so smug, Princess," Toph said softly. "The Church is angry."

Elodie tried not to let her fury show on her face. Toph didn't mean the Church. He meant the Chaplain. She couldn't figure out what René had done to get everyone so devoutly committed in so little time. "He's got you all on quite the tight leash, hasn't he?"

"We have our orders, yes," said Maxine, "but we are happy to obey."

"Well, aren't you a band of docile little house cats," Elodie spat, anger rising so high she could drown in it. First Tal, then Sabine, now Rob. Was she truly so objectionable that her mere presence inspired betrayal?

Maxine smacked the back of Elodie's head. "Let's get a move on. He's expecting her."

She shoved Elodie forward, out the door into the hallway. The guards paraded her down the corridor, where the servants pointed openly, whispers following her with every step. The changes to the castle were more subtle here—the torches that once lined the walls had been replaced with bone-white tapers; the servants' uniforms had been quickly stitched with crooked purple moons to signify they were in the New Maiden's service.

By the time they reached the south tower, Elodie was panicking in earnest. Rob had swept away the vial of Sabine's tears, leaving her empty-handed. She did not know if he would wake Brianne or hand the magic over to the Chaplain. Either way, Elodie had been removed from the equation. She had no say in what happened next.

"Elodie?" At the foot of the stairs, Cleo blinked up at her, brown eyes wide with concern. She threw herself in the Loyalists' path. "What are you doing here? Where are you taking her?"

Elodie nearly wept in relief. Her sister's indignation inspired in her a hope that the Church had not indoctrinated all of her siblings.

"Your sister is a prisoner of the Church," Toph said sternly. "Let us pass."

Cleo folded her arms, frowning. "No."

"It isn't a request, Princess." Maxine glowered down at her.

But Cleo didn't move. "And you are not my commanding officer. You answer to me."

"Not anymore," Old Fred chimed in. "Church's orders."

"The Church does not outrank me." Cleo scowled at the guards. Her neck, Elodie noted gratefully, was not enveloped by a gold chain. "I am a Warnou."

Elodie warmed herself with her middle sister's fire.

"It is unbecoming," Old Fred interjected, voice warbling through the hallway, "to argue in public. We must forge ahead. We have our orders."

"I'm coming with you, then," the middle Warnou sister challenged.

But Elodie shook her head. "You should go back to your rooms." She didn't want Cleo in the middle of all of this. Didn't want to extinguish the burst of Cleo's reverence directed toward her. "I'll find you once this is all settled. Wait for me there." She exhaled deeply. "I'll see you soon."

Cleo bit her lip, then nodded. She hurried up the steps, casting a worried glance over her shoulder before she turned the corner and disappeared.

Toph took the lead, guiding Elodie down the corridor and out into the garden. Outside, the air was heavy with the threat of rain. Thick gray fog enveloped the greenery, making Elodie ill at ease. As they marched past Queen Tera's mausoleum, Elodie's heart clenched.

Every action she had taken had been an attempt to protect her family, but all she had done was tear them apart. Her mother would be so ashamed. Elodie had been trained to be smarter than this. Instead, she had intertwined the Church and crown so closely she did not know if they would ever come untangled.

And if that was the case, what did it mean for Elodie? Who was she, if not a Warnou woman in service of her country? What did she truly have to offer the world if she could not protect her people?

The Loyalists paused before the giant doors of the royal chapel. Old Fred produced a key, which he took his time jiggling in the lock.

"Let her free, Max," Toph chided. Maxine huffed as she used a knife to cut loose Elodie's binds, nicking her skin in the process. "Whoops," the guard said flatly, not an ounce of remorse in her voice. "In you go." She shoved Elodie inside.

"He'll be with you shortly," Toph added, before shutting the door in her face. Old Fred locked it with a loud click.

Shadows pooled through the wide windows of the church, darkness from the gathering storm spilling inside the sanctuary. Elodie stepped forward tentatively, her footsteps muffled in the hollow space. It had been years since she'd been alone in the house of the New Maiden. The silence was overwhelming.

"Hello?"

Her voice echoed in the eaves. Elodie wasn't expecting an answer, but disappointment still swelled. She took a few more hesitant steps down the aisle, the empty pews crowded with the ghosts of the murdered third daughters torn down in the clergy's quest for...what?

"Why didn't they want you to return?" Elodie looked up at the iconography of the New Maiden. "What are they so afraid of?"

The New Maiden looked down upon her mournfully.

Elodie ascended the steps toward the altar.

She had gotten herself trapped in something so much larger than she could even fathom. But one thing was clear: The Church no longer served the New Maiden. Which begged the question: Who *did* it serve?

A copy of the *Book of the New Maiden* rested on the pulpit. Elodie began thumbing through its pages. The Maiden's life had been short but impactful. She had rebuilt Her homeland, had performed miracles, had gathered devoted followers in the form of Her Favoreds.

Ruti had penned the book immortalizing Her work. Sebastien had become the first Archbishop of Her word. He had spoken for the New Maiden when She no longer could. The same thing the Chaplain was doing now.

A clap of thunder echoed through the church, an ominous accompaniment to her speculation. Rain pelted the windows, the hammering drowned out only by the crash of the chapel's doors being thrown open. Elodie jumped, the *Book of the New Maiden* falling to the floor. A bolt of lightning backlit the figure standing in the doorway, the face in shadow.

"You don't belong up there, Elodie Warnou," came a voice. But it wasn't the one she had expected. For when the figure stepped into the light, it wasn't the Chaplain at all.

It was Tal.

28

There was a cemetery on a hill, just before the fork in the road that led to the city's center. It was guarded by towering wrought iron gates, protecting the gray headstones emblazoned with the names of those wealthy enough to own land even in death. Sabine had never been inside, though she made certain to pass by every time she went to market. She had always been fascinated by the tall tombstones carved with the profiles of strangers long gone.

A thin mist clung to the bare tree branches like fingers tangled in the silk of a spider's web. The graveyard was littered with headstones of all shapes and sizes, some wide and made of slate, chiseled with paragraphs of text. Others were crooked and made of wood, leaning drowsily like Loyalist guards on midnight patrol. Some graves boasted no markers at all, in which case the only proof of the dead was overturned earth and shriveled flower petals scattered about like ashes in a cold hearth. The field had not been treated with care. The grass was unkempt, long, brown, and trampled by the footsteps of mourners.

She hadn't known where to go once she'd fled home. The raging din of the gambling halls and the tavern windows frosted over by the breath of patrons had all felt so loud. After her angry outburst, Sabine needed quiet. As she stared at a plot of freshly tilled earth in the cemetery, she tried to shake the darkness from herself, but instead it seemed to take control more fully, clouds rolling in over the afternoon sun and casting a weak pallor onto the cobblestones where she stood. Sabine shivered as rain began to fall, giant drops splattering the top of her head and rolling down her neck.

An omen, perhaps? A sign to move on?

She would not give her darkness the satisfaction. And so she made her way forward, deeper into the lair of the dead as the opaque fog drew closer, wrapping itself tighter, smothering her. Suffocating her. She gasped for air, clawing at the fog, and just when she thought she could bear it no longer, her vision cleared, her lungs expanded, and she drew in a deep breath of crisp autumn air.

The hair on her arms stood up straight. The moment had passed, but Sabine couldn't shake the sensation that this wasn't the first time she'd been buried alive in this cemetery. Dots sparkled across her vision. She shook, teeth chattering.

There, there. Now you know the danger of the water. Of the earth. Of the elements around you.

Sabine hadn't the faintest idea what her darkness was talking about. But she knew she needed to get out of this graveyard. She turned back the way she'd come, ducking down an alleyway, feet leading while her mind wandered. She wasn't certain when she'd come to refer to the darkness as *hers*, but the ownership felt right. It was a part of her as much as she was a part of it.

You thought that about the princess, too, but she's gone and left you alone.

Sabine did her best not to dwell too much on that word: alone. Her mother and brother wanted nothing to do with her. Her sister was imprisoned on a gambling ship. Her father was, well, Maiden knew where. And Elodie's eyes had been filled with such betrayal that Sabine knew she'd never see her again. Sabine's only companion was her darkness.

When she looked up, she found herself in a strange alleyway, one that loosely hinted at familiarity. She kicked aside a broken crate, revealing a trapdoor. *You miss her so much you've retraced her steps to a sewer.*

At least there she would find shelter from the storm. Sabine hauled the door open, ducked down, and closed the door behind her, then deferred to her feet, which seemed to be following a scheme her mind knew nothing about. As she descended, the stench of waste and rot overpowered her, but there was comfort in that familiarity, too. She could almost hear Elodie's footsteps ahead of her, the soft, dismissive click of her tongue as she waited for Sabine to match her pace.

But when Sabine blinked, she was alone. Again. She followed the path until she came out on the other side, the door opening onto the rolling hills, no longer gold but brown. The rain fell here, too, pelting, and sharp as stone. Still, Sabine's feet led her forward, sent her scurrying toward the only structure for miles.

Curious, that this is where you would seek safety, mused her darkness as Sabine reached the front doors of the chapel. Sabine stepped over the threshold, soaked from head to toe. Still, she felt immediate peace, a calm so serene that she nearly slumped to the floor. She reveled in that silence, until it was broken by the careful thump of a cane.

"Who goes there?" The Archivist held up a candle to better see Sabine. "Why do I know your face?"

Sabine's heart stuttered at the sight of the woman. Her mind caught up with her feet, though there were still gaps in her memory from when her darkness had shrieked during the procession. After they had left the chapel, Elodie's face had been plastered about the city. Someone knew she had not gone off to Ethliglenn. Until that point, they had been so careful. Anonymous, until they'd come here.

"Because you've betrayed me."

The Archivist frowned. "I tend to remember the ones I've wronged, and you are not on my list."

Sabine chuckled, despite herself. "Is it a long list?"

"Many pages have been filled." The woman's smile lasted only a second. Then she nodded. "Ah. Now I remember. You were with the princess."

"The one you turned in to the clergy."

The woman frowned. "I did no such thing."

"Then how did they know she was still in Velle?"

The woman shifted uncomfortably. "The Church has eyes everywhere."

"I'm guessing two of them are here?" Sabine stared pointedly at her.

"Whatever trap you're trying to set for me, girl, you best forget it." The old woman's expression hardened. "I serve the New Maiden, not the clergy."

"You do not seek to protect them?"

"I seek to reveal the truth," the Archivist said. "Whatever that may be."

"Why have you kept your records to yourself, then?" Sabine asked. "If other people knew what they were doing, if they were privy to these horrors—"

"It would change nothing," the woman said forlornly. "Besides, there are consequences to the truth."

"What do you mean?"

"I am not the only one who has kept these records, girl from Harborside. But I am the only one still living."

Sabine shivered. As the chill ran through her, the two lit candles in the back of the chapel flickered, then extinguished, as though a strong breeze had blown through. But the tapestries hung from the wall did not stir. It was a strange silence. A telling one.

When finally the Archivist tore her eyes away from the soft plumes of smoke floating up from the empty wicks, she swallowed thickly. "How did you do that?" She took a step toward Sabine, eyes widening as she caught sight of the darkness in her veins. "What is this?" She grabbed Sabine's wrist roughly.

Sabine tried to shrink away from the woman's attention, but her grip was surprisingly strong. "Let me go, please."

"Who are you?" The woman's tone was hoarse.

"My name is Sabine Anders," she said, voice shaking. "I'm just a girl from Harborside."

The Archivist dropped her arm. Her eyes were so wide they threatened to fall out of her face. "Oh, Sabine Anders," she said, her voice reverent and her knuckles white where they clutched her cane, "I can't begin to tell you how wrong you are."

29

Tal took his time approaching the pulpit, his footsteps drowned out by the pattering of rain against the tall windows. The shadows seemed sharper, the darkness more consuming, as he made his way forward.

"What are you doing?" His voice was full of amusement, like Elodie was a child he was humoring. It was the same tone she had often taken with Brianne when her sister forgot basic facts around Velle's import schedule and seasonal trade routes.

Elodie did not move. "I could ask you the same thing."

His presence shook her. She'd been prepared to have another embittered exchange with the Chaplain, to get him to admit what the Church had done to the third daughters, to finally understand the root of their play for power.

Instead, Tal's presence left her with more questions than she had the space for. Still, she knew that she needed to keep her emotions in check, no matter how embittered she was about the betrayal she had suffered at his hand.

"I am a man of mystery, Elodie." He paused at the bottom of the altar, hands folded. A wry smile played about his lips.

"I wouldn't know." She looked him up and down. "Last time we were close, you were only a boy."

"I've changed." He exhaled softly as he took in her appearance. "As have you."

Elodie looked down at her days-old dress, her tangled hair, and the dirt beneath her fingernails. "You're mocking me."

"I'm not. You look good, Lo." He appraised her. "Fierce."

"I've always been fierce." Elodie stuck up her chin.

"You're right," Tal chuckled. "How could I forget?"

Elodie crossed her arms, suddenly self-conscious. "You didn't say goodbye. The least you could have done was write to tell me you were coming back."

Tal rubbed the back of his neck. "I didn't know you cared."

"*I* wrote you." Elodie tried and failed to keep the hurt from her voice. "You're the one who never responded."

Tal's brow furrowed. "You did?"

"Of course I did." The memories of those carefully penned diatribes were as crisp as the parchment she'd written them on.

"I didn't know." Tal looked unbearably sad.

Elodie stared down at him. He was only a head shorter than her even with three steep steps between them. "You thought so little of me?"

He shrugged. "I thought perhaps you'd moved on."

"With what?" Elodie had meant it as a joke, but it came out sounding bitter. She had nothing to depend on, that much was clear. Even her brother had betrayed her.

Tal didn't laugh. "I think you mean with *whom*."

Elodie's heart clenched. He'd seen her with Sabine. But she and Tal had never stepped beyond friendship. He had been her confidant, her best friend. Someone she could not bear to lose. Lovers were always lost.

She didn't bother to deny it. "It's over now." A lump formed in her throat. She'd been a fool, to think things might be different with the apothecary. To believe that Sabine would be the one who lasted.

"I'm sorry." He sounded like he meant it.

Elodie blinked at him. "Are you?"

"Of course." He held out a hand. "Come here, Lo."

She obeyed, letting Tal guide her down the steps and pull her into an embrace. He smelled the same, the metallic whiff of steel and sweet spice. She relaxed into him, grateful that someone was strong enough to hold *her*, for once. "You're all right," he murmured into her hair. "You're safe here."

She stiffened at that word. The same one he'd uttered in the alleyway before sounding his whistle, alerting the Loyalists, the Church, to her presence. "No thanks to you."

Tal pulled back, frowning. "What do you mean?"

"You're the reason my face is plastered on posters throughout the city." She searched his eyes for a glimmer of shame. "You should have let me go."

He looked mournful. "I couldn't. I have a duty, Elodie."

"To the Loyalists?" She shook her head uncomprehendingly, pinching the sleeve of his uniform. "Why did you don the red in the first place?" Tal had never aspired to patrol the city. He wanted to defend it.

"It's a stopgap." He shrugged, as though it were so simple. "I have my orders."

"From whom? The Chaplain?"

They'd once laughed together at the way Chaplain René read from the *Book of the New Maiden*, the way that his voice cracked and his eyes shone with tears as he delivered Her word. She could hardly believe he would so willingly obey the same man he'd once mocked.

"René?" Tal laughed darkly. "I don't answer to him."

Elodie frowned. "But he's the Queen's Regent. He has claimed ownership of the crown." She grimaced. "He has convinced Velle he is the New Maiden's voice."

"Perhaps," Tal acknowledged, "but not for long."

Elodie shook her head uncomprehendingly. "There's a military coup?"

Tal's laughter was bright. "In a way, I suppose that's true."

"Rob's father would never—"

"Oh no." Tal shook his head. "This is bigger than him." He cast a glance at the statue of the New Maiden. "Bigger, even, than Her. That's why I put the call out for you. I needed you here. With me."

Elodie held her breath. She could sense that any interruption might break the spell and cause Tal to rethink his explanation.

He began to pace. "I learned a lot on the front lines." He cast a glance up at the icon of the New Maiden. "It's odd, the way we take Her word at face value."

"Do we? Here at home the Chaplain has begun to put words in Her mouth."

Tal frowned. "He shouldn't be doing such things."

"There are many things the clergy shouldn't be doing. Tal, the Church, it—"

"Are you not faithful, Elodie?" He interrupted, looking intrigued.

She sighed heavily. "I don't know what I am anymore."

"Curious." Tal began to climb the steps to the pulpit, leaving Elodie standing alone in the aisle. "Tell me, Elodie. What did you mean to do with these?" He pulled from his pocket the blue bottle and the vial of tears, the ones Rob had taken from her.

Elodie gaped at him. "How did you—?"

Tal offered her a crooked grin. "My relationships within the palace walls are still strong."

It clicked. Rob hadn't been talking about the Chaplain at all. He'd been operating under Tal's orders.

"Why did you put the Third Daughter to sleep, Elodie?" She squirmed beneath his propulsive stare. "No," he continued, before she could answer, "the better question now is: Why would you wake her up, when there is another way to put a Warnou woman on the throne?"

He employed the same conspiratorial voice that he'd used when they would plan pranks on Rob, when they would steal cheese from the kitchens and climb to the tallest tower to picnic on the turrets.

Elodie hated the thrill that slithered through her. "What in Her name are you talking about?" She followed him up to the altar.

"I need you, Elodie," Tal whispered, and something stuttered in Elodie's chest. "This is my coup, which means the crown is mine for the giving."

He knelt, both knees pressed into the lush carpet of the New Maiden's altar, and stared up at her with dark eyes. Rain pounded on the windows, and the chapel shook with another clap of thunder as he asked: "Will you be Velle's queen?"

30

It was colder now than the last time Sabine had followed the circular staircase down into the Archives of the First Church. The Archivist made no sound, releasing nothing so much as an errant breath. It was as though Sabine was being led to the depths of the afterlife by a ghost.

The quiet unnerved her. The woman's words echoing in her ears unsettled her even more. Sabine kept looking over her shoulder to offer Elodie a conspiratorial glance, but of course the stairwell behind her was empty. Even her darkness made no sound, as though it could sense that its groveling, slithery voice might bring her comfort for once, instead of concern.

When at last they reached the stone floor, the cold leaching up through the cracked soles of Sabine's shoes, the Archivist still did not speak. The air around them bristled, like the strike of a match against a ragged surface, or a flash of lightning. Paper rustled; the wooden shelves groaned.

"Now then." The woman leaned heavily on her cane, looking at Sabine expectantly. "We can speak plainly."

"I…" Sabine glanced upward, as though answers would be written beneath the staircase's circular steps. "I'm afraid I don't know what you mean."

The old woman tsked. "You're sensible to be afraid. But there's no reason to keep pretending. Not down here."

Sabine was so confused that she looked over her shoulder in case the woman was speaking to someone else.

"You, girl," the woman snapped. "I mean you, daughter of Orla Anders."

Sabine gaped at her. "How do you know my mother?"

"You're the one with the…" The woman paused, choosing her words carefully.

"Magic," Sabine whispered as the Archivist settled on "affliction."

Sabine was having trouble breathing. "Who are you?"

"Friend more than foe, even if you don't believe it. While I am, of course, in Her service," the woman said, turning toward the shelves, "I never forget my roots."

Sabine thought she caught a hint of salt in the woman's voice. Her accent wasn't stormy, like the sea, but smooth like a settled harbor. Almost as though she'd once frequented Velle's docks, too. It would make sense, then, how she'd known Sabine was a Harborside girl. The Archivist wasn't a mystic. She was from Harborside, too.

Sabine waited for the sharp hiss of her darkness, prepared for the voice to taunt her for believing in magic over logic. But her mind was quiet. Still.

"Here." The Archivist reappeared, hugging a thin brown volume to her chest. It was far smaller than the *Book of the New Maiden* resting on the desk, but the woman clutched it even tighter than Her holy word. "If you will not listen, maybe you will see."

"What is that?" Sabine reached for the book, but the woman held it even tighter.

"What had to be done." The woman adjusted her glasses, pushing them up her nose with a plump finger. "This is the official ledger, the one that holds all of Velle's family trees. This is where my life's work began. It's also where it ends."

Sabine stepped forward, taking in the dizzying maze of black inked lines connecting names and dates, parents and children, partners and lovers, and every type of family in between. The Archivist turned the pages slowly, and Sabine took in name after name, line after line, death date after death date.

None of the third daughters' deaths were emphasized there. Dates were penned, but in such an innocuous way that they simply bled into the background of other losses. It was impossible to see the pattern unless a person knew it was there. Unless a person made copies of family trees and struck out every dead daughter until the truth was unmistakable.

"You're the one who realized what the Church was doing." Sabine looked up from the page in awe.

The Archivist's eyes blazed bright. "My mother held the suspicion. I'm merely the one who proved it: Not a single third daughter's third daughter lived longer than five days on this earth.

"The first one born after the prophecy, Mina, was brought joyfully to the altar. But instead of being celebrated, she was slaughtered, her blood staining the stones of the church's floor. When her mother tried to sound the alarm, the Archbishop turned the congregation against her. She was committed. No one believed her"—the woman swallowed—"until it was too late."

Sabine had seen that level of mania, that ferocity in the eyes of the Chaplain as he stood on the pulpit of the bell tower, staring out at the Queen's City. She believed the clergy were capable of what the Archivist claimed they had done, and surely of much more.

Sabine shuddered. "That's horrible. But I still don't understand. What does that have to do with me?"

The Archivist continued to flip the pages, showcasing familiar surnames. Sabine traced the family trees of her neighbors, people she had grown up with, had sold her magic to. She followed the lines from father to son, mother to daughter. She turned again to the Archivist. "What am I looking for?"

The woman flipped the page and paused at Sabine's family name. She cleared her throat. "A lie."

Sabine looked up from the lines of her family—taking in the inky names of Katrynn, Artur, her mother, her father, and herself. "You're not a very good record keeper, are you?"

The woman squinted at her. "How do you mean?"

"There was another child," Sabine said softly. "A baby between Katrynn and me."

The woman merely stared at her. After a long pause, she dipped her head slightly. "As I said. You are looking for a lie."

"Your riddles make no sense." There was no lie in mourning the loss of a sibling, even if it was one she'd never known.

"That's because you're too focused on the present. Look up the line." She nudged Sabine's finger upward to her mother's family.

Sabine didn't know much about her mother's side. Most of them had died young, and Orla Anders didn't speak of them. That was confirmed on the page, in the swiftly penned death dates. As Sabine ran her finger across the line, she took in the names of her mother's mother, her mother's father, her two sisters, and her three brothers.

"I didn't know my mother was the youngest." Sabine smiled softly. She'd always pictured her mother with the strength and surety of Katrynn rather than the spoiled bravado of Artur.

"Yes." The woman dipped her head quickly. "Which makes her—"

"Wait." Sabine ran her finger back over it again. Counting. Three sons. Three daughters.

But surely she would have known. Her mother would have mentioned it. "How strange." But then, her mother never spoke much of her losses. So perhaps it wasn't so surprising. "I see. You kept a close watch over our family in case there were three daughters. That's why you know so much about me."

The woman nodded her head once. It didn't feel like a gesture with any sort of finality.

"Well...that's nice." It seemed the woman wanted something from her. Something she did not know how to deliver. "Thank you for your diligence. Even if it was wasted."

The old woman sighed. "I had hoped I would not have to spell it out, but I can see that you are distressed." She made her way over to the desk chair, lowering herself into it with a soft grunt. "I am a record keeper, Sabine. Which means I can also make records disappear."

"And...?"

For the first time, Sabine missed her darkness. She missed the validation offered by that hollow voice, the safety it allowed her to judge or fear or shrink away from anything that felt too big. Too much.

"You're asking the wrong questions, girl."

"Fine," Sabine snapped. "Tell me what I should be asking."

"You should be asking me what I made disappear." She shifted in her chair. "*Who* I made disappear."

Sabine shook her head to clear it. "But..." She glanced down at her family tree once more. There was a little too much space between her name and Katrynn's. As though someone had not been forgotten but erased. "You removed the baby. The one who died."

The woman steepled her fingers. "Yes."

Sabine thought she'd finally uncovered the question the Archivist was begging her to ask: "Why?"

"Because her life, however brief, was a danger to you if recorded."

Sabine paused. "*Her* life?" The woman nodded. The baby was a girl. And suddenly it all made sense. The riddles, the secrets, the moments she caught the old woman looking at her with something akin to pride.

"So you see now," the Archivist said, "what I did for Harborside. I kept its secret. I kept you alive." Her eyes gleamed with tears. "The New Maiden was not born a princess. She is a girl made of sea and salt and sadness, come to save us all."

Brianne

All Brianne felt was relief.

Her entire life had been constructed around her title, around the future commanded by her father and expected by her mother. But knowing she was not the New Maiden, that she was just a person...Brianne wanted to weep in release.

What other things could she endeavor, once her life was her own?

The other girl mistook Brianne's tears of relief for anger. "It's all right to cry," she said, her fingers curled into a fist. "The Church took so much from us. Took our lives. Took your future."

The other girl was right. Brianne's change of fate didn't avenge the Church's murders. Murders to which her father was complicit.

"Why am I here, then?" She was still afloat in this strange, liminal space and did not know why. She could not wake. She could not leave. Though she had tried, Brianne could not seem to exit the room's threshold.

"The New Maiden is in danger," the girl said solemnly.

"Who are you, to care?" Brianne asked.

She now understood that the shadows were lives lost in pursuit of the prophecy. Slain third daughters whose company she might have kept were it not for the privilege of her parentage. But the girl with the strongest outline, the one who had entered the room first, still had not revealed her identity.

"My name is Mina," she said, pursing her lips. "I was the New Maiden once. Briefly. Before."

Brianne's eyes widened. "You…?" This was not what she had expected. The girl laughed softly. "Before what?"

"Before He took it all away from me."

Brianne stepped forward. "He, who?"

The shadows in the room began to shout, a ripple of hurt running through the souls of the murdered third daughters like a stone dropped in a still pond.

Mina smiled sadly. "The one who betrayed me."

Part Five

The New Maiden came from nothing. A girl born from dirt,
made of silt and wood, gritty and sure and strong. "I will
disappoint you," She admitted to Her Favoreds, days before
Her death. "Soon, I will leave you, and you will wonder
why. But I have tried my best to provide what you needed. I
hope I have succeeded."

"Beyond our boldest dreams, Maiden," said Mol, kneeling
at Her feet.

"You certainly have, Maiden," echoed Beck, then Petra,
then Theo, then Hera.

"Without question, Maiden," murmured Ruti, eyes cast to
the ground.

Sebastien was the last to speak. "You have changed the
world, Maiden. You have opened it wide to make way for all
that is to come. Rejoice! Your work here is complete."

She smiled at him then, eyes sparkling like the stars above.
"I am destined to return, Sebastien. Each of us shall, one
day. Until we meet again, I hope the work you do is good."

—Book of the New Maiden,
verse 212

31

I *would make a better queen.* Elodie had whispered her deepest desire into the ear of her best friend four days before he went off to war. It had been a relief back then to admit what she'd always felt—that her position as the first daughter had been wasted by a prophecy. That she was better prepared for the tides of change, the fight for her people, than Brianne ever would be.

She could have been a good queen.

Of course, that had simply been the emotion-fueled, loose-tongued confession that came when a friendship was running out of time. She had never expected anything to come from that confession. Certainly not that it would plant the seeds for a proposal more valuable than any offer of marriage.

"Are you serious?" She stared down at Tal, shadows pooling all around him.

"Entirely." Tal's eyes blazed. "Elodie, you were born to rule."

Elodie's first instinct was to laugh. Her second, to faint. In the end, her weak knees won out and she sank to the floor, staring up at Tal, who had risen to his feet. He descended the steps from the altar, again offering her a hand.

"You're out of your mind," she said, even as she let Tal pull her upright.

"I'm not." He smiled down at her. "I finally see. More clearly than I knew was possible."

The chapel doors banged open again, raindrops spilling onto the threshold, soaking the corners of the carpet that led down the aisle. "What is the meaning of this?" Chaplain René stalked forward, eyes fixed on Elodie and Tal's intertwined hands.

"This is none of your concern, René."

Elodie was flummoxed by the calculated familiarity with which Tal addressed the Chaplain. They were not peers. Tal was younger than the Chaplain by thirty-odd years, yet he spoke as though he was the Chaplain's commanding officer. Dismissed him as easily as if he was a servant.

The Chaplain seemed similarly surprised by Tal's boldness. "I beg to differ. I am the acting regent. You cannot make decisions without my consent."

Elodie thought that was rich, the Chaplain suddenly being a stalwart of consent. He was the one funneling the Church's tithes into the pockets of Velle's allies while Harborside's house of worship remained padlocked.

"We both know that isn't true." Tal chuckled softly. "You've been so narrow-minded, so focused on your own power, you've forgotten the greater cause."

The Chaplain sniffed. "Who are you to appraise the decisions I have made in Her service?"

"There's your first mistake, Chaplain," Tal said, tightening his hold on Elodie's hand. "You seem to have forgotten who you truly serve."

His words sent a chill up Elodie's spine. Even without context, it was clear there was something fundamentally changed about the Tal who stood in front of her in contrast to the boy she had known years ago. It wasn't just the way he held himself, spine straighter than she remembered, eyes sharper. It was the strength of his grip. The certainty in his voice.

The way he seemed to serve a singular purpose.

"I think it is you who forgets yourself," the Chaplain muttered, casting another glance at Elodie. "What is she doing here?"

"Elodie is here at my invitation," Tal said, as though the chapel was his domain. "You would do well not to sneer at my guest."

"She blatantly disobeyed orders. She's supposed to be in Ethliglenn."

"You will not marry me off to some failed despot's half-wit son." Elodie shook her head. "I would be wasted in Ethliglenn, which I imagine was the point of your arrangement."

Tal's expression darkened. "Elodie is not your pawn, Chaplain."

"Oh, but I am yours?" The Chaplain glowered at him.

"You have plenty to answer for, René. Elodie here was just filling me in on what happened while I was away. I believe she has some questions for you."

Elodie reclaimed her hand from Tal, crossing her arms in front of her chest, and turned toward the Chaplain. "Why have you been twisting Her word?"

"Yes, René," Tal said, eyeing him wolfishly, "I am curious about that myself."

The Chaplain swallowed, visibly perturbed. "I merely sought to reinforce the spirit of Her vision."

"Those weren't your orders, Chaplain." Tal stared at him. "You are not a commander in this fight. You are simply another soldier."

"You cannot classify me so blithely," the Chaplain snapped. "I have executed to perfection. The throne was cleared. The position of Queen's Regent secured. I even removed the Third Daughter from consciousness."

Elodie opened her mouth to protest, but Tal shot her a warning glance. She stayed silent.

"*You* did?" Tal raised his eyebrows. "You are the reason the Third Daughter remains trapped in sleep?"

The Chaplain cleared his throat. "The night of Brianne's coronation, I prayed for a smooth transition. I prayed for the New Maiden to step aside. And, as always"—he smirked—"She listened. The next morning, Brianne would not wake. The path was cleared, thanks to my faith."

Tal laughed outright. "You overestimate your importance, René. As you did when you fathered the Third Daughter. As you did when you assumed the crown. Perhaps the old guard didn't mind fixing your mistakes, but there is a new order now. What's more: Elodie is the reason the New Maiden is trapped in sleep, not you. She rectified your mistake. 'Do not claim false order, for the kingdom will fall.'"

Tal seemed to be quoting something, but the source material was unknown to Elodie.

"*You* did this?" The Chaplain rounded on her, eyes bright with fury. "How did you—?"

"Strange, that you'd be bothered by my actions when your

Church has been murdering third daughters for centuries," Elodie interrupted, growing more frustrated with every new retort left unexplained. She turned to Tal. "I cannot accept your offer until I understand what is at stake. Who exactly, do you serve?"

The Chaplain laughed darkly. "You haven't told her?"

Tal shot the Chaplain an unreadable look.

"Tal?" She was starting to get nervous. "What is he talking about?" There was another clap of thunder. Elodie shivered as the darkness seemed to creep closer still.

Tal settled himself on the steps to the altar. He tapped the carpet beside him, gesturing for Elodie to come closer. She did, sinking to the ground, their closeness familiar and foreign all at once. It was like old times.

It was like nothing they'd shared before.

"The truth of the New Maiden is not the easy, tidy tale you have been fed, Elodie," Tal said, his voice low. Steady. "She was magnificent, yes. But terrible, too. By the end of Her life, She carried a darkness. A fearsome, volatile vengeance powerful enough to end the world. The Church has been working to preserve humanity by preventing Her return. Hence the"—he cleared his throat—"removal of third daughters. We could not risk the prophecy fulfilled. Until, of course, it was." He cast a sour glance at the Chaplain.

Elodie frowned. "The New Maiden held power enough to end the world? How do you know?"

Tal turned to face her. "He watched Her darkness bloom. Watched it consume the woman he had worshipped once. He sought only to preserve Her legacy. To keep Her memory pure and true. And so he spread the warning. We have been following his orders ever since."

"We?" Elodie searched her best friend's face. Tal had never been captivated by religion. Had attended mass irregularly and with skepticism. But he spoke with a reverence that Elodie had never before heard pass through his lips.

"Those of us on the righteous side of history," he whispered, eyes blazing. His excitement was infectious. His devotion true. "And so I ask again, Elodie: Will you join us?"

Warmth flushed down Elodie's spine, but never without suspicion. "Why do you need me? Why would you have me rule?"

"A Warnou woman belongs on the throne." Tal smiled. "You know that. I know it, too. It's what Velle needs." He appraised her carefully before continuing. "And it will make the conversion easier."

Elodie's skin prickled. "What conversion?"

"To His word from Hers."

Elodie's mind was as tempestuous as the sky outside the chapel's windows. "Why would the Church seek to change the word they worship? Why His? Why now?"

"The New Maiden passed from Third Daughter to Third Daughter," Tal explained patiently. "Eliminating them wasn't enough. After one death, another girl was born, another vessel created for Her spirit. But because Brianne is trapped in sleep, so, too, is the New Maiden's soul. She cannot escape the body She is housed in. Now that She lies dormant, He is free to claim His rightful place in power.

"So now you see, Elodie," Tal continued, looking at her as though she was the reason the stars shone above, "why you must wear the crown. It was you who opened the door for Him. It is *you* who cleared a path for the Second Son."

32

Sabine was sinking. She'd thought, once, that she knew what it meant to drown in the dark and the deep. But this was new—the tightening of her lungs, the gasp caught in her throat. She could not move. She could not speak. She could only fall.

"Are you all right, dear?" The woman's face was far too close to Sabine's.

"But...my mother never told me." Sabine shook her head, trying to clear it, like water stuck in her ear. "She never said. She spoke only of the baby."

The Archivist nodded her head once. "She was protecting you. As was I."

Sabine almost missed her darkness, how it tapped into the corners of her heart. "Why?"

"You're the second coming of the New Maiden. You are Her."

"I'm no such thing. I'm just a girl from Harborside."

"Exactly." The Archivist's eyes were too bright. "The crown has never understood the importance of the New Maiden. Of you."

"I can't… I don't…" Sabine took a step back, nearly tumbling over the Archivist's desk. Her hand landed on the thin, leather-bound volume she'd flipped idly through the last time she stood in this basement. She'd felt no connection, then, to the New Maiden's words.

"Take it." The Archivist's eyes landed where Sabine's attention was focused. "It's yours, after all."

"It really isn't." But she curled her fingers protectively around the book nonetheless. She pushed herself back to her feet, tome pressed to her chest.

"I see your heart and your head are not yet aligned. But as She always said, what matters most is the soul."

"Did She?" Sabine asked weakly. She was still struggling to surface from beneath the tidal wave of shock, tossed and rocked like a ship in a storm.

"*You* did."

She hated that knowing glance. It made her itchy. Made the collar of her dress feel too tight—the suffocating pressure of expectations taking shape.

"This is ridiculous." Sabine wanted to weep, but she'd been wrung dry. "It can't be true. I can't be…" She held the book of the New Maiden in front of her face and screamed. The dusty leather cover smelled like home.

"Or are you exactly where you're supposed to be?" The woman's words sent a chill up her spine.

"How do you even know I'm the New Maiden? There were nearly twenty daughters murdered by your Church. There's a Third Daughter comatose in the palace now. How would anyone know who the true Maiden is?" Sabine wanted to absolve herself of the responsibility, wanted to pin the power, the promise, onto someone else. Sure, there was a time she had hoped that a girl from Harborside might be special enough to fulfill the prophecy, but she hadn't meant *herself.*

"She wrote it in Her journals. She spelled out the signs." The Archivist moved behind her desk and riffled through the top drawer, emerging with a small book with a blue cover. She flipped to a page filled with cramped words. "Do you ever feel a stirring within?" she read eagerly. "Could you weep one million tears to bring the water back to the Lower Banks?" She looked up from the journal to examine Sabine. "Does power run through your veins?"

Sabine's stomach dropped to her feet. Her tears had not been a weakness. The darkness had not been trying to control her.

It had been trying to wake her up.

"I'm so sorry." Sabine pulled away, out of the woman's silk-soft grip. "I just need a moment." She took the circular staircase up two steps at a time, the laces of her boots smacking the stone, but she didn't care, didn't worry about tripping, she merely needed to reach the surface, needed to emerge from beneath these sunken depths. At the top of the staircase, past the pews, out in the falling rain, Sabine finally took a breath.

So, now you know my origin, the darkness returned. *Know why I sit and fester. Why your sadness calls to me. It is the placeholder for my anger. Our anger.*

Sabine felt a rush of relief. The voice that coiled around her head and her heart felt familiar, like opening the door to a messy room, one lived in, one inhabited by a loving family. At the heart of the mess was good. Sabine needed to believe there was some good amidst all of this, somewhere.

"What are you?" She whispered, rain pooling in her boots. "What am *I*?"

Powerful. Special. Sacred.

But if that were true, why did the darkness harass and harangue her so? Her every thought, every decision, had been haunted by its presence. Was it the voice of the original Maiden, judging her as the second coming?

She wasn't the second coming of anyone. She was hardly even Sabine these days—wasn't a good daughter, sister, friend. She wasn't anything but a miserable wretch at the mercy of her darkness.

I am only trying to prepare you. With power comes responsibility. You need to be ready.

Sabine leaned back against the church doors, exhaustion slumping her shoulders and souring her stomach. She could hardly fulfill the responsibility of providing her family's only valuable resource. How could she bear the power of being a deity? How could she possibly live up to those expectations, when her family was already ashamed of her? When she had pushed away the only person who had ever seemed to value her up close?

Now is not the time to feel sorry for yourself, Sabine, the darkness hissed. *Now is the time to prepare. To discover who you really are.*

Sabine's first instinct was to argue, to fight against the voice the way she once had. But her darkness's guidance was certainly necessary, considering that she hadn't even known she was a third daughter—*the* Third Daughter—until now.

Shouldn't you have known? It wasn't her darkness this time, but her heart. *If this is truly who you are, wouldn't you have seen the signs?*

Maybe if her mother hadn't lied. Sabine had questions, and not just for her darkness. Outside, rain had stopped falling but that swirling haze was waiting for her, a thin, cloudlike mist, somber as midnight.

You're ready, then? For answers. Sabine shrugged her shoulders back, trying to block out the voice. She didn't appreciate that her deepest insecurities also came from the ancient voice of her country's savior.

As she shuffled through the sewers on her way back to Harborside, every step took on new meaning. What Sabine carried with her was the potential of power with absolutely no idea how to harness it or how to use it.

And why should you? Her darkness wasn't helping.

The *plink, plink, plink* of dripping water scraped at her nerves like a scrubbing brush against a floor. Despite it all, she kept a tight grip on the *Book of the New Maiden*, the leather slick beneath her sweaty fingers.

Once she finally reemerged amidst the salt and the sea, she went straight for the narrow alley that housed her apartment. But she paused at the front door, the black mist of her darkness still lingering around her. She had fled once already to protect her family when her darkness pooled beyond the confines of her own head.

Yet now she had returned without a second thought. She wasn't responsible enough to be a leader, to use her magic for anything but household brews and tonics. As she worked up the courage to turn the door handle, she begged her darkness to behave. They were both in pursuit of the same thing, after all: the truth. The wind sighed, and Sabine took it as a sign. She pushed her way indoors.

The house was quiet, the lanterns extinguished, the sweeping half done. But there were still embers cooling in the hearth. Sabine took a chair down from the wall and settled herself in it. Mercifully, her darkness was no longer visible. It swirled about only in her head.

She settled the *Book of the New Maiden* on the table and began to flip through it. As the house creaked and groaned around her, she read of the New Maiden's miracles, read of Her exploits and Her failures. Warmth spread through her as she discovered stories she had never heard in the stark pews of their neighborhood church.

The Maiden captured between these pages was a dreamer, a bright-eyed girl filled with hope and good intentions. She was the kind of person Sabine aspired to be. The kind of person she might still become.

She didn't look up when the front door opened. She could tell by the shuffling of footsteps, by the sweet, sweaty scent of dried herbs, that it was her mother.

"Bet?" Sabine hated the uncertainty in her mother's voice. "What are you doing here?"

Sabine swallowed, then slowly lifted the book she was reading to show her mother its cover. As Orla Anders's eyes swept across the title, her expression flickered from confusion to concern, before finally settling on fear.

"Why are you reading the scripture?"

"You and I both know this is more than scripture." Sabine kept her voice quiet. "This is history. *My* history."

Her mother swayed in the doorway. "Who told you?"

"A woman. She works in the Archives of the First Church of the New Maiden. Older than you. Black eyes."

"Genevar." Her mother's voice was grave. "She kept my secret longer than I deserved."

"Why did you keep it from me?" Sabine blinked back the burning in the corner of her eyes. "Don't you think I deserved to know?"

Her mother's eyes were glassy with tears. "I thought you deserved to live. I couldn't lose another one of my babies."

"You made me feel as though my sadness was a stain," Sabine said. "You were so quick to dismiss my emotions, to urge me not to feel." She'd been deprived of understanding her very nature. Instead, Sabine had been left to drown in her own feelings. Isolated. Alone.

"My girl." Her mother hobbled over to the table, wincing as her knee popped. "I only wanted to protect you." She brushed a lock of hair behind Sabine's ear.

"It wasn't fair," Sabine said sharply, "for your fear to dictate my existence."

"You're right," her mother whispered. "I should have prepared you. You had a right to know who you are. What you are."

"I did. I do." Her life would have been so different if she'd been allowed to interpret the emotion she felt not as weakness, but power. "Other people's lives could have been different, too."

Had Sabine known who she was, she would have had no reason to lie to Elodie, would have been able to free their country from the corrupt Chaplain. Would have been able to helm the Church. To reroute funds back to Harborside. To give her neighborhood what it deserved.

You say this like it's too late, her darkness said. *You say this like you still do not know what you are.*

The darkness, which billowed behind her like a shroud, had less bite than usual. Now that Sabine could name it, it wasn't threatening in the same way. The shadows running through her veins felt more like streams of power than something to hide beneath her sleeves.

She wanted to share that strength. Wanted to prove that power to the world.

So, go, the darkness goaded. *Stop scheming, Sabine, and do.*

This time, when the voice gave her instruction, Sabine did not resist. When her darkness urged her to go, she did.

33

The Second Son. Elodie very nearly laughed despite her discomfort. It was a title designed for one-upping. It was telling that the Second Son had worshipped the New Maiden before setting a course to undermine Her word. That shift felt personal, vindictive.

Elodie looked at Tal, a sliver of uncertainty glimmering in her stomach. She knew this story too well: faithfulness, *until.*

Tal, Sabine, Rob—each had followed that same pattern, building her up and then bringing her down. Just like the New Maiden, Elodie had been certain she possessed their unwavering devotion. *Until.*

That familiarity gave her pause. How could she know His was the right word to follow? How could she pledge to someone who had ultimately betrayed the New Maiden, when she, Elodie, had so freshly been betrayed?

"Elodie?" Tal searched her face. "Are you all right?"

"I don't know," she whispered. "This is a lot to take in."

"It's not very complex, really. You said it yourself." Tal nudged her. "You're not so faithful these days."

The Chaplain glowered from where he stood in the aisle.

"What is it about His word, Tal?" She searched her best friend's face. "What about Him made you a convert?" Before she could agree to Tal's proposal, she needed to understand.

Tal beamed at her. "You always knew the right questions to ask." He got to his feet, ascending the pulpit so that Elodie had to crane her neck to see him. "His word is grounded in the truth of men, rooted in the earth, rather than the stars above." Tal's voice rumbled through the chapel, low and daunting, like the thunder outside. "There are no unknowns, no mysticism. Every edict He has offered has come to pass. In fact, He foretold that the Third Daughter would be eliminated this very season, and that whoever so vanquished her would reign by His side." Tal gestured for Elodie to join him. "Of course," he said conspiratorially, "René here thought it would be him..."

Elodie stared down at the Chaplain, who didn't bother to disguise his scowl. It was a delightful role reversal. Where once Elodie had watched sourly from the balcony as the Chaplain claimed the position of Queen's Regent, now she was the one stood at the altar. She would be queen.

"She hasn't agreed yet," the Chaplain said, but he sounded resigned.

"Elodie?" Tal turned toward her, eyes wide. "Will you stand with Him?"

The rain pummeled even harder still as a small voice whispered a warning in her ear. Her mother had been working to separate Church and crown. If Elodie agreed, she would bind the two even more closely, this time on purpose.

It wasn't the same, she argued with herself. As queen, she would be able to keep everyone in line. She would be fully in control.

She turned to Tal, a flutter in her chest. "What do you need from me?"

Tal pulled her into an embrace. "Get changed," he urged. "Find Rob and Cleo." His eyes were bright. "Then, we're going to tell the world."

Elodie raced down the aisle and flung open the chapel doors, much to the bewilderment of the Loyalist guards.

"Where are you—?" Maxine began, but Elodie was gone before she could finish her sentence. She ran, dodging raindrops, dress billowing behind her as she sought shelter inside. But even once she was safely indoors, she did not stop running. She ducked and weaved, whizzing past servants and courtiers going about their business. If anyone cursed her, she did not hear them.

Instead of turning toward her own ransacked rooms, she headed up a set of stairs, toward her middle sister's chambers. She wanted to make right on her promise to Cleo. Her sister also had a better collection of gowns for such an occasion. Elodie didn't stop moving until she burst into Cleo's room, where her middle sister was sipping tea.

"Elodie?" She recovered from her surprise, managing to not spill a single drop. "What's going on?"

"Told you I'd be back," she panted, as she tried to catch her breath. "Now I need you to help me pick out a dress."

"For what?" Rob raised an eyebrow from his place on a chaise longue. "Your trial?"

"No." Elodie couldn't help the giggle that burst from her lips. "My coronation."

Cleo dropped her teacup.

"Your what?" Rob looked incredulous.

"You were just in Loyalist custody." Cleo dabbed liquid from her corset. "What happened?"

"You aren't nearly as excited as you should be." Elodie pouted. "This is a good thing."

"You colluding with the Church is a good thing?" Cleo raised an eyebrow. "Sounds suspicious to me."

"Everything sounds suspicious to you," Elodie shot back.

"What's going to happen to Brianne?" Rob interjected. His expression was unreadable.

"You're both missing the most important piece of this," Elodie said, waving away their concerns. "This unseats the Chaplain. This keeps the throne in our hands. The crown will once again belong to a Warnou woman."

"You mean Tal will tell you what to do?" Cleo said flatly.

Elodie shot her sister a sharp look. "I know what I'm doing."

Rob took a loud sip of his tea. His silence was pointed.

Elodie rounded on him. "I'm the one who should be angry here, Rob. You pushed me into the arms of the Loyalists and didn't tell me that you were working with Tal. I thought the Chaplain was going to imprison me in a tower and leave me to rot." She glowered at him. "What was all your scheming for if you didn't want me to join forces with Tal?"

Rob's hands began to shake. He clenched them into fists. "Forgive me for caring about Brianne."

"There's no need to be sanctimonious, Rob." Elodie hated the way she was speaking to her brother, hated the anger he was inspiring in her. They'd always been of one mind, had always been close. They'd never had cause to fight this way. But then, she supposed, that was why her brother had finally boiled over.

Cleo was watching her older siblings guardedly.

"Fine," Elodie sniffed, trying to tamp down the unease bubbling in her stomach, "I'll get dressed myself."

She made for Cleo's closet, an entire room draped in lace and satin and silk. She riffled through gowns of midnight blue and sunrise orange, pausing as she examined a soft pink gown she'd been missing for months.

"Thief!"

Cleo, who had followed Elodie into the closet, hardly blinked. "It looks better on me."

"Just for that," Elodie said, beginning to unhook the dress's never-ending trail of buttons, "this will be my coronation gown. Everyone will see me wearing it, and you'll never be able to steal it again."

She shrugged off her stained gray dress and pulled the pink garment on over her head, mussing up her hair even further in the process.

"Lady above." Cleo rolled her eyes. "You look awful. Come here." She moved toward the vanity and motioned for Elodie to sit on the velvet stool. Cleo reached for a brush and began to run it through Elodie's tangles.

"Have you really thought about this?" Cleo caught Elodie's eyes in the mirror. They were bright with worry.

"No," Elodie admitted. "But sometimes bold decisions are the best ones." She winced as the bristles caught a particularly nasty tangle. "Why's Rob pouting, anyway? Was he like that before I got here?"

Cleo sighed. "He'll be fine. He's just jealous."

"Jealous?"

"Everything always favors Elodie." Cleo started brushing faster. "Plus, Tal's back, which of course has him reeling."

Elodie frowned. "What are you talking about?"

Cleo stared incredulously at her sister, her wide eyes reflected in the mirror. "You're joking, right?" Elodie shook her head uncomprehendingly. "Rob's been in love with Tal since he was a child," Cleo said, extracting the bristles from her sister's hair. "You had to have known. He was always mooning over him; it was all he ever talked about." She rolled her eyes. "When Tal left, Rob locked himself in his room for weeks. I had to convince him not to enlist."

Elodie blanched. "You're lying."

Cleo raised her eyebrows. "I'm not. It's your own fault you didn't notice."

"What about Avery?" Elodie was completely nonplussed.

"A person can have more than one crush, Elodie," Cleo said flatly. "Besides, it's been two years." Cleo's fingers moved quickly as she braided a pink ribbon into Elodie's hair. "Just be careful, okay? When it comes to the Warnous, Tal seems to have a gift for getting under our skin. Be sure you know what you're doing."

"I do," Elodie said, sounding more certain than she truly felt.

"All right," Cleo said warily. "I trust you." She gave Elodie's hair a final once-over. "But I don't trust Tal. You're done."

"Thanks, Cleo." Elodie reached for her sister's hand.

"Any time, Your Majesty." Cleo gave her sister a dramatic curtsy before sashaying back into the sitting room.

Elodie followed, brain buzzing. She had thought she and her brother were close. But for Rob to have been harboring romantic feelings for their best friend, surely Elodie would have noticed. Surely Rob would have confided in her.

Their brother sat, glowering on the chaise longue, exactly as they'd left him.

"Rob, I—" Elodie wanted to make amends, needed to see her brother's easy smile. But before she could launch into a full apology, there was a knock on Cleo's door.

She expected Loyalists. But it was Tal. The moment he entered the room, Rob stiffened. It was suddenly clear, exactly as Cleo had said. Elodie simply hadn't been paying close enough attention.

Tal grinned as he took in Elodie's appearance. "You clean up nice, Lo."

"You're welcome," Cleo muttered. Rob continued to frown.

Tal turned to him. "You can't attend a coronation with sugar on your shirt."

Rob jolted to attention, nervously swiping at his shirt. "I didn't think you needed me."

"Of course I need you," Tal said easily, and Rob's expression softened. "Get up. Cleo, you too," he added as an afterthought.

They were a strange parade, the three Warnou siblings led by Tal and trailed by a band of Loyalists. Several clergy folk, including a begrudging Chaplain, made up the rear. They moved swiftly through the castle into the courtyard and loaded themselves into waiting carriages. Tal pulled Elodie to sit beside him. She avoided eye contact with both Rob and Cleo.

"Now here's how this will go." Tal spoke in hushed tones. "We sent word ahead to gather citizens from the Iron, Garden, and Commerce Districts. We have allies there."

"How will we explain away the Chaplain's edict?" Elodie could not shake the roar of the crowd during the last public outing. The people of Velle had embraced the Church so easily. She could hardly imagine this change in leadership being announced as smoothly.

"Shouldn't be too difficult." Tal shrugged. "We simply let them know the Third Daughter has passed on."

"What?" Elodie's blood ran cold. "Is she—?"

"No, of course not," Tal said quickly, putting a hand on Elodie's in reassurance. "This will simply eliminate any confusion over royal hierarchy. It also removes any threat of someone trying to wake her up." He laughed softly. "She'll be safer this way. I swear it."

Elodie's stomach churned, but she chalked it up to nerves. This was what she had wanted, after all. The only difference was that she had to let go of Brianne. Leave her asleep for good.

But sleep wasn't so awful as death, Elodie rationalized. And perhaps, after some time—once she better understood the Second Son and the conversion was complete—she could plead for her sister's mortal being. Elodie was certain she could find a way to convince the powers at play to bring back her sister, one day.

Elodie would be Queen of Velle, after all. Surely that mattered. Surely that meant she would have a say.

Although it had stopped raining, the cobblestones were slick beneath the clattering hooves of horses. The driver directed their carriage the long way to the church, ensuring that the royal seal would be spotted by as many people as possible en route. And indeed, it worked. A battalion of merchants, shopkeepers, and citizens followed in the caravan's wake.

At the church, they exited the carriage and Tal led Elodie up the stairs to the bell tower. With every step he looked back at her with a reassuring smile.

"He is so grateful," Tal said, squeezing her hand. "He couldn't have done this without you. *I* couldn't do this without you."

Elodie exhaled, trying to calm her nerves.

"Are you ready?" Tal gestured to a Loyalist who carried the chest that housed the crown. The guard opened the box. Tal flung the doors to the balcony open. "Let's change the world."

34

The air bit at Sabine's face as she made her way down Harborside's main thoroughfare. After the rain, the neighborhood felt fresh, the cobblestones were clear and the windows glistened in the fading daylight.

Faster, her darkness urged, but Sabine didn't know where it wanted her to go. She needed to find Elodie, needed to reach Castle Warnou, but she did not know the way.

At first she thought to reenter the sewers, even though abandoning the crisp post-rain air felt like a crime. If the sewers were an escape route from the castle, then surely they also provided a way *in*.

But before Sabine could turn in to the alleyway that led to the trapdoor, she stumbled upon a commotion, a crowd of Harborside residents shouting wildly at a battalion of red-clad guards. The Loyalists stood side by side, creating a human barricade, keeping those from Harborside behind their line.

"What's happening?" Sabine turned to the person next to her, a woman called Breta who grew potatoes in her cellar to sell at the morning market. "What's going on?"

"Something's afoot, dear," Breta said, her forehead furrowed. "Tom the errand boy caught word from a town crier in the Iron District that there's an announcement from the Church. Something about the Third Daughter."

Sabine gasped. "Has she woken up?"

If Elodie had been able to accomplish what she'd so desperately wanted, perhaps she would be more likely to grant Sabine an audience with her. Perhaps Sabine even had a true chance at forgiveness.

"Don't know, Sabine." Breta shook her head. "They won't let us through." She jerked a thumb at the Loyalists' grim faces.

"Why not?"

"Says we're not *worthy*," said a man in front of them. "We're too poor and dirty to look upon the queen."

"That's not what they said," snapped a woman to his left. The man raised his eyebrows. "But it's what they implied," she acquiesced.

"That's ridiculous." Sabine had spent her entire life being discounted, called names and easily dismissed, because of where she was born and who she had come from. "That's not a good enough reason."

Why don't you do something about it? her darkness goaded.

Sabine didn't give herself a chance to hesitate. "Excuse me," she said, squirming between the throng of bodies, making her way forward even as her heart pounded in her throat.

For so long she had been made to feel like nothing, like no one, someone impossible for even her family to love. But now she held a truth no one could take from her. She was a third daughter. *The* Third Daughter. And she would show the world what that meant.

Face-to-face with the guards, however, Sabine balked.

"Get back," one spat, spittle flying precariously close to her cheek.

"Why won't you let us through?" Sabine had meant to sound commanding, but her voice cracked, ending her question with a squeak.

"Ooooh, fearsome, this one," said the guard beside the first, his laughter as shrill as a hawk's screech. "Might have to detain her." His eyes were predatory.

"Leave it, Winn," said the first. His gaze was fixed on the ground. "Don't want to get mixed up with the likes of them, or you'll be exiled next."

"Exiled?" Sabine blanched. "But we're Velle citizens."

"Not for long." The first guard shrugged. "The New Maiden does not smile on you. And so the crown is building a new border."

"Leaving us on the outside," Sabine finished for him.

The first guard nodded. "Go on, then," he said, waving her away. "There's no way past us. It's not just our jobs on the line. It's our faith." He glanced up at her quickly, then down to the ground again.

Seems like the faithful are falling away from you, her darkness said. *Call them back.*

But it wasn't so simple. The guards had their orders. They believed they knew who they served. Sabine could not simply blurt out the truth. She would be skewered for blasphemy. And Katrynn's jokes aside, those Loyalist swords *were* sharp.

That night at the midnight market felt so far away now. Sabine had left her sister on that ship for days, Katrynn's resentment allowed to ferment like the beer brewed in bathtubs in some of Harborside's dirtier taverns. If she did not rescue her sister soon, Katrynn would never deign to look upon Sabine again, reincarnated deity or not. Katrynn could hold a grudge.

Speaking of grudges... Sabine scoured the crowd, searching for Artur's blond head, but the throng of frustrated people was too dense. When she was jostled forward, ramming into the wolfish guard, she extricated herself quickly, then ducked back the way she came. She needed a new route. Perhaps the sewers would do, after all.

She kept to the edges of the crowd, soaking in her neighbors' frustration and anger. These were good people, worthwhile folks who had done everything expected of them and still ended up cast aside by the Church. Harborside didn't deserve this. Not when the New Maiden had emerged as one of them.

A girl made of sea and salt and sadness, the Archivist had told her. *Come to save us all.*

Sabine had backtracked enough that she was at the cemetery, the tall iron gates more intimidating when shut. The fencing was too tall to climb, the bars too close together to slip through. Though, just for good measure, the Loyalists had chained and locked the gates, too.

Sabine exhaled sharply. It was the same kind of padlock that had appeared on the door of Harborside's church. The same padlock that had sparked Harborside's decline. The same one that threatened this new tentative way of life her neighborhood had built for themselves.

First they took your faith, her darkness whispered. *Next they'll sequester you, and let you eliminate yourselves.*

Sabine couldn't allow it. Especially not as her neighbors began to deplete, their anger turning to defeat. Elodie had told her once that she was brave, to do what she did. To give up so much for the people she loved. She needed that sort of conviction now more than ever. She rattled the gates desperately. Unsurprisingly, the chain did not budge.

You look ridiculous.

"I don't care." It was the first time she'd purposefully engaged with her darkness aloud. It made her feel safer, releasing her words into the evening air. She began to smack the padlock against the iron of the gate. It clanged dully but did not dent.

That isn't how you pick a lock.

"How do you know?"

Because unlike you, I am everywhere. Which means I know all things.

"So go on, then," Sabine said, frustrated. "Help me."

It wasn't a question. It was a command. And to Sabine's shock and utter delight, the darkness listened. Although she couldn't see it, she could feel it dispelling from around her and slithering through the keyhole, twisting, turning, and picking the lock until it released a soft click and the chain clattered to the ground.

"Oh." That one syllable held more weight than she could carry. Sabine reveled in that single breath of power. It was the first time she had truly felt like magic.

"This way," she called, her voice catching as she struggled to understand what she had done. But even more surprising was that when she called, her people answered. As her neighbors streamed through the cemetery toward the square, Sabine nearly wept a new kind of tear.

Once, it seemed as though she would only ever whisper. But her screams held power, too. She followed the flood of people flocking to the city square. A giant crowd had gathered, much larger than the procession the Chaplain had organized. But instead of lingering near the back, the way she always had before, Sabine pushed her way to the front. She needed to know the news.

A man stood at the balcony of the bell tower: not the Chaplain, but someone much younger. He was tall and tanned, his face boasting a sharp nose and wide jaw, his hair a mess of dark curls that glinted almost blue in the light. Unease stirred within Sabine as she recognized him as the Loyalist who had set her darkness screaming. To the stranger's right was the Chaplain, who had taken off the ridiculous crown and instead stared at the young man with murder in his eyes.

To the man's left was Elodie. Sabine nearly called to her. The princess's eyes were wide, her lip bitten between her teeth as she listened to the man speak.

"It is a new dawn for Velle," he shouted, shoulders back and eyes blazing. "We welcome in a new age. A new era. A new ruler." He turned to Elodie. "I introduce to you now the first daughter, Elodie Warnou." He lifted a gold crown from a wooden box and set it upon Elodie's head. "Your queen."

Whispers spread through the crowd like wildfire.

"But what of the New Maiden?" called someone.

"Where is the Third Daughter?" asked another.

"The New Maiden is no longer able to serve," said the man, voice clanging like a bell through the assembled crowd. "But a War-nou woman still wears the crown." He put a hand on Elodie's back. Sabine watched the princess hesitate.

Lies spread quick from false prophets, the darkness hissed. *Set them straight. Show them the truth.*

Sabine glanced up at the bell tower, so tall that her voice would not reach the ears of those standing above. "They won't be able to hear me," she whispered, frustrated. Tears began to prickle at the corners of her eyes. "They will not listen."

Then make them.

Sabine's throat began to burn, as though she had consumed hot coals. She gasped, barely able to swallow through the pain.

Speak, the darkness urged her. *Before it is too late.*

Sabine took a step forward. "You claim the New Maiden cannot serve," she said, startled as her voice thundered through the city square, at ten times its usual volume, "yet here I stand before you." Her words were clear as a whistle, drowning out the clamoring of the gathered audience. Those around her fell silent and began to back away, offering her a wide berth. The shift in the crowd alerted those in the bell tower to Sabine's location.

Elodie was the first to spot her. Her eyes widened, first with shock, then concern. But the man beside the princess only looked angry.

"Who, pray tell, are you?" he called down to her coldly.

"My name is Sabine Anders," she said, throat still burning as her words echoed around her. "From Harborside. And I am the prophesied Third Daughter."

The man began to laugh, a twisted, cruel thing. "Harborside has fallen out of Her favor," he snapped. "You cannot expect me to believe that She would return to such a place. Besides, we set up barricades. No one from Harborside could make it through."

"'You cannot contain light,'" Sabine said plainly, quoting the words of her forebearer. "'I have always been, as I always will be.'"

"You are a liar," the man spat. "Do not blaspheme Her name with your nonsense."

They are so far from the light that they cannot recognize their own wrongs.

Sabine's darkness began to twist and turn, snaking out around her like it had at her family home. Only this time, Sabine didn't want it to stop. In fact, she urged it forward, her frustration mounting as those on the balcony continued to stare, eyes wide as the darkness reached for them.

Or perhaps they do not recognize their own deity.

"What are you doing?" The grim-faced young man watched Sabine with fascination bordering on obsession. He reached for something that hung around his neck. Sabine caught a glint of gold as his fist clenched around a small medallion.

Or that their faith has changed.

The darkness paused at Elodie's feet. She looked down at Sabine with confusion. Concern. There was tenderness there. It bridged the gap between them, the space Sabine had filled with doubt.

"Not her," Sabine begged. The rest of them, but not her.

Sentiment doesn't suit you, Sabine, her darkness said, but it obeyed, circling Elodie's feet and offering her a small radius of safety. Sabine exhaled sharply with equal parts relief and surprise. It seemed she could now control the darkness as once it had controlled her. She wanted to test it just a little, to see what she could really do.

"Go," Sabine whispered, and the darkness rose like the tide. It burst forward, spilled over the heads of those who would deny her, who would murder daughters like her in pursuit of power. Those who would subject her to senseless sadness, would reduce her to feelings of helplessness when she should have known strength.

The city square was black as night, filled with the sound of drowning. The magic Sabine had once contained leached from her, every ounce of black in her veins pouring forth. A release. Leaving her new. Letting the light in.

It started from her fingertips, spreading through the square like the morning sun through a crack in the curtain. It did not overshadow the darkness but rather, embraced it. The light was just as much a part of her, the only match for her sadness. Not better or worse but *also.*

Sabine was more than just her sorrow. She was dark and light and everything that existed in between.

And then the darkness dissipated, and the crowd fell to its knees.

35

Elodie remained standing. As the people of Velle fell to their knees, hers locked. She swayed but did not fall. Her reticence wasn't because she didn't believe Sabine. It was because she did.

Sabine held power in her darkened veins. She carried so much, all in secret, even when it threatened to burst forth. To see it now, in its purest form, left Elodie both awed and furious. It was another betrayal by omission, this one of far greater magnitude.

Beside Elodie, Tal had gone rigid. He clenched the balcony railing so tightly his knuckles were white. "I don't believe this," he whispered, shaking his head, jaw clenched. "How could you let this happen?" He rounded on René. "You oversee the Church. It was your duty to keep a close eye on the lineage."

The Chaplain shrugged. "It seems as though something was overlooked." He wasn't nearly as remorseful as Tal wanted him to be.

"What are we supposed to do?" Tal's voice took on a sharp, high pitch. "There are too many witnesses not to address it."

"We must take a step back, my son," the Chaplain said. "Wait until the moment is right."

Tal pursed his lips. "Find a way to eliminate *that one*, you mean."

Elodie looked back down at Sabine, who had transfixed the crowd, a sea of believers cementing into worshippers. The princess couldn't shake the feeling that she ought to have known. She'd seen Sabine's magic at work, had felt the girl's magnetic sadness, that well of emotion so much bigger than herself. She had simply not realized how all-encompassing the girl's power was. But what did that mean for Velle?

If Sabine was the New Maiden, Brianne couldn't be. Elodie's youngest sister was just a girl, a casualty trapped between sleep and consciousness for no reason. If Brianne wasn't the New Maiden, then the Chaplain had no claim to the crown. By the word of Velle, the throne would revert to the first daughter, Elodie's right to govern inalienable once and for all.

Tal turned his attention to Elodie. "You are more important than ever, Lo. You'll be essential to His work." He nodded, as though steeling himself, desperately working to pivot without compromising his allegiances. "You will take the crown. Befriend this New Maiden. Share with us her weaknesses." His eyes brightened. "Our time will come. Yes," Tal said, nodding again, looking far more sure of himself than he had moments ago, "all will be righted"—he grabbed Elodie's shoulders—"so long as you are willing to stay by our side."

His intensity was unsettling. As was his assumption that Elodie would be so willing to undermine the New Maiden. Of course, he knew nothing of her relationship with Sabine, nor of the New Maiden's role in Brianne's condition.

Based on Tal's hostility, it was best not to mention their existing connection. If he had noticed that the girl below was the same one he had spotted retching in an alleyway, he was careful not to air his suspicions.

Elodie nodded, reassuring her oldest friend. She had already agreed to partner with Tal and the Second Son, and Tal's sense of loyalty had surely been intensified by his service on the front lines. She couldn't abandon their alliance…not yet, anyway. Not until she truly understood what the Second Son stood for and what it was He wanted. What He meant for Velle.

Still, there was one thing she needed in return. Something to reunite her family and perhaps earn Rob's forgiveness. She addressed Tal: "Can I have my potions back?"

Tal blinked at her, as though returning from somewhere very far away. "What?"

"To wake Brianne," Elodie said, loud enough for Rob to hear. "Now that we know she is not the New Maiden, there is no reason to keep her sleeping."

Tal frowned. His hesitation slipped around Elodie's heart, threatening to squeeze until it burst.

"Tal, come on," Rob insisted.

Tal acquiesced. "Of course."

But as he handed over the vial to Elodie, he grabbed the hand that met his. "Find me the elixir you used on Brianne. We'll need it again." He leaned down over the balcony to stare at Sabine.

The apothecary looked up, eyes snagging Elodie's. She jerked her head, signaling for Elodie to join her. Elodie found herself oddly nervous. The betrayal she'd felt based on Sabine's lies was insignificant compared to what was happening now.

Tal accompanied Elodie down the steps of the bell tower. She wanted him to leave her alone, let her approach Sabine privately, but she didn't know the best way to ask. So instead, she let him follow.

She was grateful for him when she reached the ground, the crowd pushing roughly against them as they flooded toward Sabine. "Make way for your queen," Tal called roughly, keeping the people from jostling Elodie.

The crowd parted, clearing the way for Elodie to hurry toward Sabine. When finally they were face-to-face, the girls simply took each other in.

"You're a third daughter." Elodie examined the apothecary's eyes for another trace of betrayal. She'd revealed it once before, guilt scrawled across her face when her mother had laid bare the truth of her deceit. Now, though, Elodie could excavate nothing from Sabine's expression. If she didn't know any better, she would have trusted her.

"I didn't know until I went back to the Archives." Sabine offered Elodie a hesitant smile. "I missed you, and I wanted to—"

"You missed our appointment, yes," Elodie interjected, casting a glance over her shoulder at Tal, who was watching her like a vulture. "You *are* the girl who was supposed to deliver the vial, are you not?"

Sabine frowned. "I—"

"No matter. I procured it from your brother instead." Elodie rolled her eyes. "Be sure not to waste my time again."

"Where did you source that vial?" Tal asked, at the same moment Sabine asked: "Did you wake Brianne?"

"Not yet." Elodie responded to Sabine, casting another glance at Tal. "But now there is no reason to hesitate."

Tal begrudgingly nodded his head.

"Who are you?" Sabine eyed him suspiciously.

"This is Tal," Elodie said quickly. She feared the escalation that might come from a conversation between Tal and Sabine. "We grew up together. He's my best friend."

Sabine appraised him. "Funny. You never mentioned him."

Tal's eyes widened with recognition. Elodie swore silently. She had hoped to keep her relationship with Sabine quiet for much longer. "You were the girl slumped in the alley." He turned his attention to Elodie, eyes curious. Questioning. Angry.

"That doesn't sound like me," Sabine sniffed, even as she searched Elodie's eyes.

Elodie wanted to sink into the earth's core. It was as though they expected her to choose, to declare her loyalty to one in front of the other. But she no longer knew where her dedication belonged.

"This is Sabine," Elodie finally said. "It appears she is the New Maiden." The words felt false on her tongue.

"Yes," Tal said, eyeing Sabine up and down, "so it seems."

"What of it?" Sabine challenged him with her eyes.

Elodie felt as though she was outside her body. She didn't know how to keep Sabine safe when Tal and the Second Son wanted the New Maiden incapacitated. She didn't know how to appease her best friend, whose entire sense of purpose seemed entwined in eliminating the New Maiden.

"I suppose that's a question for our queen," Tal said, putting a hand on Elodie's shoulder. "Although her coronation was interrupted, I doubt anyone will protest her claim to the crown."

"We need to discuss what comes next," Elodie agreed, casting an uncertain glance at Tal. What she truly needed was to speak with Sabine alone. "We must align on the directions of Church and crown."

"I don't know if I'm qualified to make those decisions." Sabine tugged on her fingers nervously.

"On the contrary," Tal said tersely, "it seems that you are uniquely qualified."

He was angry. Elodie could see the vein pulse in his tense jaw.

"Shall we away, then?" Elodie desperately wanted to get out of the city square. She needed a moment to regroup.

But Sabine hesitated. "I can't go with you." She shook her head. "Not yet."

Elodie frowned. She didn't believe that the apothecary was in any position to refuse her. "Whyever not?"

"You have the chance to free your sister from sleep, Your Majesty," Sabine said, dipping her head and offering a smile that was half-reverent, half-playful. "And so before I go with you, I need the chance to free mine."

36

Sabine was still shaken by the way darkness had dispelled from her. She felt empty without the constant whispering in her ear and the warm, heavy comfort of its embrace. But it hadn't left her empty-handed. She knew now what that voice had been trying to accomplish, what it needed her to see—how much she would be able to do for Harborside.

She had opened the gates for her neighbors. Had offered them entry into the city square. And when the crowd had fallen to their knees, it had been more than just the people from Harborside. Every citizen of Velle had looked at her with awe. Everyone, that is, except for Tal.

Sabine instantly mistrusted him. Although Elodie claimed they were childhood friends, there was something strange and forceful about him. The princess—no, queen—almost seemed to defer to him. That sort of submission from Elodie was something Sabine would hardly have believed possible had she not witnessed it for herself.

Tal made her uneasy. Put her on high alert. So she was disappointed when Elodie offered to accompany her to the *Black Rock* and Tal followed.

"They won't take kindly to a Loyalist on board," Sabine warned sharply.

"Precisely why I've decided to accompany you," he said. "If you want your sister back, my presence will assist."

Sabine raised her eyebrows but said nothing. She very nearly missed her darkness and the way it had validated her snide judgments.

"Bet!" A blond head bobbed through the crowd and pushed its way past Tal. Artur's eyes were wide, his expression hesitant. "How did you…I mean, are you okay?"

Sabine felt her cheeks warm. "Did you see…?"

Artur nodded. "Why didn't you tell me?"

"I didn't know," Sabine admitted. "I thought I was broken. That sadness…"

Artur rubbed his neck nervously. "I'm sorry if I made you feel worse. You were just so sunken and I was afraid. Da's gone. We can't afford to lose anyone else."

"I'm sorry, too." Sabine shook her head. "For the cruel things I said to you. It can't have been easy to witness my dark days without understanding what was happening. I didn't even understand it myself."

Tal cleared his throat pointedly.

"Oh, right," Sabine said, looping her arm through her brother's. "Come, then."

Artur frowned. "Where are we going?"

Sabine smiled. "To free Katrynn."

"You have money, now?" Artur appraised her with more interest, Sabine noted, than when he had learned she was the New Maiden reincarnate moments ago.

"No," Sabine admitted. "But apparently our new Loyalist friend is going to help me."

Artur wrinkled his nose. "A Loyalist? Help you?"

"I can be quite persuasive," Tal chimed in.

Sabine's brother examined the guard skeptically. "Sure." He turned to Sabine with a bemused expression.

Sabine rolled her eyes, which seemed to be enough of an answer.

As they made their way out of the city square, the barricade of Loyalists was still in place.

Sabine turned to Tal. "Call off your guards." She gestured to the line of uniformed people still standing in the street. "Harborside is just as much a part of Velle as any other district. They deserve the same information, the same service, the same right to worship as anyone else."

Tal glared at her, the vein in his jaw throbbing slightly.

"Tal." Elodie's voice was gentle as she put a hand on his arm. Sabine tried to stop herself from seething. It didn't quite work.

"Fine," he snapped, waving off the Loyalists. "Back to patrol. Your work is done here."

The guards frowned at his order but obeyed. Most wandered away, splitting off into pairs and turning down corners.

One guard approached Sabine, eyes wide. It was the man she had spoken to, who had kept his eyes low. The guard who viewed his order as proof of his faith.

"Lady above and among us," he said, falling to his knees, "forgive my trespasses. I did not know it was you."

"Gentry," Tal snapped. "What are you doing?"

"We saw the entire thing. The square went black. The New Maiden is present, among us." The guard looked up at Sabine. "I live to serve you."

Sabine blinked at him. "I...thank you?"

Receiving accolades would take some adjustment. She was hardly used to being liked, let alone worshipped. Behind her, Elodie laughed softly.

"Strange, isn't it?" she asked, falling into step with Sabine and Artur. "Being revered? Hello, Artur."

Sabine's brother nodded warily.

"I'm not going to compromise your family this time," Elodie promised. "I'm here to give you something back."

At the *Black Rock*'s port, they were met with their first obstacle. A bruiser, different than the one Katrynn had sweet-talked, stood watch, his hulking frame larger than the queen, the guard, the New Maiden, and her brother, all put together.

"Halt," grunted the man.

In the blink of an eye Tal's sword was bared. "This is Velle's queen, and this, the New Maiden," he said sharply. "You will let them pass."

"The ocean has no queen," the bruiser shot back. "We are subject to no jurisdiction. Not even the New Maiden's." He offered Sabine a polite head nod, although he did not let her pass.

"Then you leave me no choice." The Loyalist moved so quickly that Sabine missed the motion. One moment, the sword was by his side. The next, the tip of it was pressed delicately to the hulking man's throat. A thin trail of blood dripped down his neck.

Beside her, Artur uttered a soft, awestruck gasp.

"Go on, then," Tal called, ushering the rest of them forward. "I've got this handled."

"*This* is the plan?" Sabine raised her eyebrows. "It's barbaric."

"Do you have a better idea?" Tal snapped.

"No, but—"

"Go on." Elodie nodded for Artur and Sabine to lead the way up the gangplank.

At the bottom of the steps from the deck they entered the familiar hallway, loud with the echoing shouts of men. Sound swelled through the cabins, hollering and chaos. And bursting through it all, a sweet, high-pitched giggle Sabine knew far too well.

"Katrynn!" Artur hurried forward, Sabine at his heels.

They found her in the canteen, six tables of men slurping soup and listening to their older sister spin a tale about a girl with wings who flew to the stars. She held the gamblers' rapt attention. When she looked up at the commotion in the doorway, she stopped her story, causing grumbles and groans from her audience.

"You came." Her eyes were bright as she rushed toward them, pulling Artur and Sabine into a tight embrace.

"Of course we came," said Artur fiercely.

"I'm sorry it took so long." Sabine bit her lip as she examined her sister's face. Katrynn looked the same, no worse for wear save for some split ends. "There were some, ah, mishaps along the way."

"Ooh, and who are you?" Katrynn had caught sight of Elodie.

"A friend." Elodie offered Sabine's sister a little smile. "Here to repay a debt." She glanced at Sabine. "Here to rescue you."

"Can't save what isn't for rescuing," piped up a man at the table nearest them. He was grizzled and gray. A chunk of gristle was stuck in his beard.

"But we can free what isn't yours for the keeping," Elodie sniffed. This was a new side of her, one Sabine had never seen. She sounded regal. "Katrynn is coming with us."

The gamblers at the table stopped to stare. "You can't take Rynn," a man with an eye patch called from the farthest table.

"She tells the best stories. No one spins tales quite so nice," said another.

"I've built a legacy," Katrynn laughed, squeezing Artur's shoulder.

"Do you...not want to leave?" Sabine examined her sister curiously.

"Lady above and among us, of course I want to leave, Bet," her sister whispered. "Please get me out of here."

"Funny you should say that," Artur began, but Sabine quieted him with a shake of her head.

"Not here."

"Not anywhere, unless you've brought me twelve thousand kelbers," a new man grumbled. Sabine recognized him as the person Katrynn had made her original promise to.

"Or consider," said Elodie, who hadn't even flinched, "that my guard has your bruiser held at sword-point at the end of the gangplank. Bruisers of that size are difficult to come by. So I propose a trade. Let Katrynn go, I'll let your man go."

"Liar," the man said, even as Katrynn looked at Sabine with something like fear. "No one could best Oleg."

"Are you really willing to take that risk?" Elodie asked. The silence in the room was charged. "You run a gambling den. You're the house, which tends to have the cards stacked in its favor. You've grown complacent. Overconfident. Which is when you mistake a loaded hand for a bluff. So again, I ask: Are you willing to make that bet?"

The man's exhalation whistled through his missing front teeth.

"I'll take that as a no. Don't make me watch you as we walk away." Elodie turned toward the Anders siblings, a coy smile playing at her lips. "Go ahead."

Katrynn hooked an arm through each of her siblings', and then they were running. Back above deck, Sabine flung her arms around her sister. "Rynn, I missed you."

"Missed you, too, Bet." Katrynn ruffled her hair. "Thanks for coming back for me."

"Let's go." The queen shot past them, a blur of white hair and limbs as she ran down to the dock, where Tal maintained his upper hand over Oleg the bruiser.

Sabine pulled Artur and Katrynn along with her, and they made it off the ship and away from the swaying dock to the solid hold of land, Tal and Elodie at their heels.

"We did it," Sabine laughed, joy bubbling up through her. She felt invincible.

Until she didn't. Elodie's expectant eyes fell upon her. She had been avoiding what came next.

"Shall we?" Tal held out a hand to Elodie, who glanced back at Sabine.

"Go home," Sabine urged Katrynn and Artur. "Ma will be so pleased to see you." She gave her sister one more embrace.

"But where are you going?" Katrynn frowned at her. "Bet, what's going on?"

"Tell her, will you?" she asked Artur.

"Tell me what?" Katrynn looked warily between her siblings.

"That your sister is the Third Daughter—the New Maiden incarnate," Elodie said, unable to tamp down her smile. "And I am Velle's queen. Which means we have quite a lot of planning to do. Speaking of..." Elodie dropped Tal's hand to offer hers to Sabine. "We ought to be going."

Katrynn stared bewilderedly at Sabine. "Bet—what?"

"It's true," she said softly. "That's why I have to go. I need to figure out what this means for me. For us. For Harborside."

Tal rolled his eyes but did not say anything. Sabine clenched her fingers into a fist.

"I'll see you soon," she told her siblings. "And now you know I make good on my promises." She glanced guiltily at Elodie. "Most of them, anyway."

The new queen very nearly laughed. "Come now." Elodie and Tal turned away.

Sabine offered her siblings one final embrace before she followed.

37

Elodie returned to Castle Warnou with the crown perched upon her head. It was heavier than she'd expected, which made balancing it as she walked rather difficult. Her steps were stilted, and she was cognizant of every move, every eye on her as she passed.

Despite her newfound self-consciousness, the bustle of the castle was a welcome change from the strained silence of their carriage ride—Tal and Sabine had spent the entire trip studying each other with guarded expressions. Elodie's opinion was solicited no fewer than six times as soon as she entered the castle's keep, the topics in question ranging from menus to ladies-in-waiting.

She had not taken the appropriate time to consider what being Velle's queen meant. The footsteps she would have to fill. The endless demands of her opinion, on her time, of her presence. But the day-to-day decisions would have to wait. Elodie had more pressing matters to attend to.

She sequestered the three of them in the queen's study, a wide, round room in the east tower. Elodie had not crossed the threshold since her mother's passing, and as she settled into the cushioned chair behind the long wooden desk, she had a moment of nearly unfathomable grief.

She missed her mother. She had barely even begun to grieve the loss of the woman she had idolized. After Tera's passing, Elodie had been thrown into competition with the Chaplain and had put her youngest sister into an enchanted sleep, all for the sake of preserving Tera's legacy, to ensure the separation of Church and crown.

Now, though, as she looked at Sabine and Tal sitting across from her, it was clear her efforts had been in vain. She'd thought she was doing right by her mother. Tera Warnou had been a calculating woman—she'd needed to be. But Elodie didn't know if her mother would be proud or horrified by the lengths her firstborn had taken in the service of their country.

Elodie didn't know if she was proud or horrified of herself.

She adjusted her position behind the desk. She could not afford to get too sentimental. Not while there were so many decisions to be made. Her mother had sat behind this desk, doing her best to maintain Velle's everlasting reputation as a vibrant, powerful nation. Now Elodie would sit here and continue her work.

It was strange to consider the permanence of this newfound appointment. When she had imagined ruling in Brianne's stead, that dream had always come with an expiration date.

But then, everything was different than Elodie had expected. She'd imagined fighting with the head of the Church, not kissing her. She'd imagined consulting strategy with Tal, not becoming a pawn in his coup.

"Now then." Elodie folded her hands on top of the desk, hoping neither Tal nor Sabine could see how far out of her depth she felt. "We have much to discuss."

Sabine glanced at Tal. "What role does he play here?"

"I am a man of all seasons, Sabine." Tal offered her a wry smile.

The apothecary pursed her lips, eyes searching Elodie's. Sabine's posture was stiff, her expression guarded. It was clear she did not trust Tal.

Well, Elodie didn't entirely trust him, either, which was why she needed to keep him close.

"Tal." She cast a glance at her best friend. "Could you watch the door?" Tal turned his chair slightly, so that he could keep the door in view. "*Tal.*"

He shrugged. "Merely following orders." He winked, his cheekiness rubbing her the wrong way.

"Tal," Elodie snapped, offering her best impression of her mother. "I am not asking you. I am commanding you, as your queen. Go out and watch the door."

His playfulness disappeared in an instant. Tal rose to his feet, eyes dark, the energy between them so combustible that Elodie nearly expected him to come around the desk and grab her by the throat. But in the end, Tal merely nodded. "As you wish." He left the room, slamming the door behind him.

"He seems…" Sabine didn't bother to finish her sentence.

"Don't worry about him." Elodie rolled her eyes, hoping her dramatics masked her uncertainty. Sabine had every reason to worry about Tal. "How are *you*?"

Sabine laughed softly. "Unsettled. You?"

Elodie reached up to remove the crown from her head and set

it on her desk. She instantly felt more like herself. "Overwhelmed," she admitted.

There was something about Sabine's vulnerability that allowed Elodie to be honest. It was a relief not to have to pretend, not to have to consider every possible manipulation in the mind of the other person. It offered her safety.

"I'm sorry." Sabine sat forward in her seat.

"It isn't your fault." Elodie leaned back in her own chair.

"I meant for lying to you." Sabine looked down at her hands. "I didn't mean to deceive you. I only wanted to free Katrynn." She swallowed. "I was desperate."

"I know." And Elodie did. She had seen the reunion between the Anders siblings. The love they shared was clear. Much deeper than whatever tenuous relationship she now seemed to have with Rob. "Now that you're the New Maiden, you can make it up to me by reviving Brianne." She eyed the other girl, who shifted in her chair. "You really had no idea?"

"I thought the darkness was something to be ashamed of," she whispered. "You're the first person who never made me feel wrong. The first person who saw *me*, not just my sadness."

Warmth spread through Elodie's chest. "I'm so glad you're here." She meant it. Sabine was comfort in a space that had only ever been calculating.

"I'm not sure how much use I'll be to you," Sabine said. "I don't know the first thing about fulfilling prophecies."

"Your existence is fulfillment," Elodie said. "The rest is just instinct."

"In that case, I'll need to meet with the clergy." Sabine

nodded. "And the chapel in Harborside will need to be reopened, of course."

Elodie bit back a smile. "Seems to me like you know what to do."

"Does that interfere with your agenda, Your Majesty?" Sabine bit her lip playfully. Elodie's stomach fluttered.

With Sabine by her side, they could enact true change—bring money back to Harborside, dismiss corrupt clergy, build true alliances. With Church and crown in step, there would be no need for one to usurp the other. They could finally coexist.

"I think we might be able to find a few ways to work together," she said, leaning forward.

Across the desk, Sabine beamed.

Elodie did her best to ignore the unease settling in her bones. No matter how much she wanted to pretend it wasn't true, Sabine was in danger. The Second Son, whoever He was, had plans of His own, plans to eliminate the New Maiden. She ought to warn her.

But Elodie couldn't bring herself to wipe the smile from Sabine's face. Not now. Not yet.

There would be plenty of time for reality to squeeze the joy from them. Just for a moment, Elodie wanted to linger with Sabine, while anything they dreamed was possible.

Besides, she would keep Tal close. She would stay attuned to his plans, ensure she was always one step ahead. She would make him believe she was on his side in order to keep Sabine safe.

The study doors burst open, startling them both.

"Not a very good guard, is he?" Sabine said quietly.

Cleo hurried in, panicked. "We need you." She paused, gasping for breath.

"What's happened?" Elodie was on high alert.

But Cleo shook her head. "Not you, Ellie." She turned to Sabine. "You."

Sabine raised her eyebrows. "Me?"

"Rob's on his way to the east tower with the bottles you gave to Elodie. I want to make sure he doesn't make a mistake."

Sabine's confusion was evident in her expression. Elodie got to her feet, offering Sabine a hand. "It's time for your next miracle," she explained, intertwining her fingers with the New Maiden's.

It was time to wake Brianne.

38

They had kept the Third Daughter in a room with the curtains pulled tightly shut, a room that smelled of incense and candles at the end of their wicks. She was displayed carefully, eyes closed, hair brushed, hands folded on her chest. She looked like a doll.

Elodie and her siblings, Rob and Cleo, stood in a line on the opposite side of the bed. They all looked expectantly at Sabine. After what they had witnessed in the city square, Sabine couldn't blame them. She had made that magic look so easy, but it had been her darkness—her anger at the Church, at the country, at her helplessness amidst it all. She had lost all sense of her own control.

But now she was expected to perform a miracle—not as a girl from Harborside, but as the New Maiden. That added a considerable amount of pressure. She was grateful the audience was small, despite the tension between Elodie and her brother. Sabine knew what it was like to fight with siblings, but she could never imagine Artur turning her over to Loyalists, or Katrynn turning her back on the family.

Lady above, she was nervous. Sabine reached for the vial that held her tears. There was no lady above. There was merely the Maiden among them: her.

That did nothing to steel her nerves. She couldn't afford to make a mistake. Worst of all was the hollow space where her darkness used to live. Without it, Sabine hardly knew who she was. She had only the faintest outline of who the New Maiden had been. Was it Sabine's role to re-create the past, or to build upon and adapt Her legacy? For a deity whose life had been meticulously recorded, Sabine could not believe that her predecessor hadn't left more detailed instructions. She would need to return to the Archives of the First Church and convince Genevar to let her read the New Maiden's journals. She had so many questions that could only be answered by the New Maiden Herself.

Sabine uncapped the vial with a soft pop of the wax. The viscous liquid inside jostled lightly as she added the contents of the vial to the blue tonic bottle. With shaking hands, Sabine leaned down, her long hair falling over her shoulder to surround herself and Brianne like a cloak. First she dabbed the elixir on the young girl's wrists, behind her ears, and on the soles of her feet in a gentle, circular motion. Then she pried open Brianne's mouth and carefully tipped the remaining contents of the bottle down the girl's throat.

Sabine stepped back and waited. The whole room held its breath. But Brianne did not stir. Sabine sighed, stomach sinking. She had failed. Just as she'd feared she would. Across the bed, Cleo shifted. Rob squeezed his sister's hand. "Have faith," he whispered. His choice in words gave Sabine pause. That was what she'd been missing, the one thing the New Maiden always had: faith.

Sabine swallowed, looking up at Elodie. Those gray eyes met

hers with an unexpected ferocity. She exhaled. Elodie had not only accepted her apology but had offered her partnership. She was not alone in this. The Queen of Velle was on her side.

Sabine knelt beside the bed, taking Brianne's delicate hand between both of her own. She closed her eyes. And she did her best to believe.

It won't work, came the instant reflex, her doubt loud. Yet this voice was different from her darkness. This voice sounded like Sabine, which meant she could shut it up.

She cleared her mind. She focused. She breathed. And she hoped.

That light, the warm glow that she'd pulled out alongside her darkness, returned. She could feel it rising inside her. Spreading from her fingertips toward Brianne. This time, something took hold.

When the spark faded, Sabine stepped back. Elodie was still staring at her with that same expression of awe mixed with something darker. The room was stiflingly hot, the incense overpowering. Still, they waited. Sabine hoped. And then...

Brianne murmured softly—a moan, then a groan as she stretched and writhed on the wrinkled sheets. Her hair stuck to her sweaty forehead. She rubbed at her eyes crusted with sleep before batting her lashes awake. The middle sister, Cleo, burst into tears. Brianne blinked to clear her vision in the dim room. She tried to push herself up into a seated position. She caught sight of her brother and brightened. "Rob?" Her voice was hoarse, her lips chapped.

"I'm here, Bri." He knelt to her level and clasped her hand. "I'm here."

Brianne's eyes were bleary. She blinked again, glancing at the crowd assembled. Her eyes glazed past Elodie and Cleo before landing on Sabine. The girl gasped. "You're the New Maiden."

Sabine frowned. Brianne could not possibly know that. The collective response of bewilderment in the room confirmed her confusion.

"How do you know that, Bri?" Rob glanced up at Sabine with concern.

"I saw things." Brianne rubbed her eyes. "I met people and they told me about her."

Elodie cocked an eyebrow. "While you were sleeping?"

"No, Ellie." Brianne shook her head, looking exasperated. "While I was there."

Her siblings exchanged worried glances. "While you were... *where*, Bri?" Rob asked.

"They didn't have a name for it," Brianne said, "but it wasn't like here." She shook her head. "It was... everything and nothing all at once."

Sabine shivered. Was it possible that her magic had led Brianne through a curtain to another world? Some strange in-between?

"I have a message for her from the others," Brianne continued, her voice strangely calm. She turned toward Sabine. "A warning."

"What others?" Sabine tried to keep her voice light, despite the nerves creeping through her. There was something profoundly ominous about the girl's insistence. Elodie, too, seemed unsettled. She came around to join Sabine on the other side of the bed.

"They were like us," Brianne said, her eyes terribly sad, "but they were lost."

"Like us?" Sabine exchanged a glance with Elodie. She and Brianne did not seem to share many similarities.

Elodie's mind worked faster. "Do you mean third daughters?"

Brianne's eyes lit up. "Yes."

The hair on the back of Sabine's neck stood straight up. Every third daughter before her had been murdered at the hands of the Church. The Church that she now helmed. Was their warning meant to protect Sabine? Or did they target her for revenge?

She reached for Elodie's hand. The queen held tight, her fingers like ice.

"What was their warning?" Sabine whispered. The room had gone very quiet. On the other side of the bed, Rob was still clutching Brianne's hand. Cleo's eyes were trained on Elodie's and Sabine's intertwined fingers.

"They warned that 'your time will be short and the fall will be far,'" Brianne said, and Sabine's blood ran cold. That certainly did not sound like it was meant to protect. "It seems that He has found a new prophet to spread His word," Brianne continued, her use of pronoun confusing Sabine even further. Could she mean the Chaplain? "This prophet walks among you now and will infiltrate your heart and mind if you let him. When the prophet finishes the work, He will hold the faithful in his iron grip, and Velle will fall at His feet."

Sabine's unease turned into full-blown distress. The room was too hot, the incense too cloying, and Brianne's words too cryptic. Worse, even, was that Elodie's hand had gone stiff in her own.

More likely than not, the queen was reevaluating her partnership with such an obvious liability. Sabine had taken on this new role, and already there was someone out to unseat her. Someone working against her. An unnamed "he."

"Who is this person?" she asked Brianne gently, afraid to spook the young girl who held the answers she so desperately needed. "What is His name?"

Brianne's eyes were bright. "His name was Sebastien." Sabine's mind snagged on the name, struggling to place it.

"The New Maiden's Favored?" Cleo whispered.

It couldn't be. Sebastien had served beside the New Maiden, had followed Her faithfully. He was the first Archbishop of Her Church, had kept Her word alive after death. Surely someone so faithful could not abandon their loyalty so quickly.

Brianne nodded, and Sabine's heart sank. "Yes," the young girl confirmed, "but that's not what they call Him."

"What do they call Him?" Sabine's voice was so quiet she could hardly hear herself ask.

Brianne swallowed thickly. Emitted one tiny cough. And then she answered, eyes dark, hair glinting gold in the candlelight. "They call Him the Second Son."

ACKNOWLEDGMENTS

While writing can often feel like a solitary experience, this book is proof that an author cannot do everything on their own. I owe many thanks to the following folks:

The Third Daughter would not exist without the belief of Jim McCarthy, who never loses the forest for the trees and who always bets on his authors. I've said it before, and I'll say it again: I'm so grateful to have you in my corner.

To Jessica Anderson, who saw potential in paragraphs and asked, *Is there more?* From the moment I answered the phone, I knew this book belonged in your hands. Thank you for your thoughtful partnership, your keen eye, and your championship not only of Elodie and Sabine but of me. I appreciate you endlessly.

To everyone working tirelessly (and sometimes thanklessly) behind the scenes, please know how appreciated you are. To the team at Christy Ottaviano Books, the folks at LBYR/Hachette, including Jen Graham, Logan Hill, Richard Slovak, Janelle De-Luise, and Hannah Koerner; to Molly Powell and the team at Hodderscape; and to the cover artist Gemma O'Brien and the art director Karina Granda for a perfect package.

To Emma Warner (who let me borrow their last name), Jen St. Jude, Kelly Quindlen, Rebecca Mix, Allison Saft, Courtney Gould, Mary Roach, Meryl Wilsner, Lyndall Clipstone, Kiana Nguyen,

Ashley Shuttleworth, Leslie Vedder, Morgan Rhodes, Tehlor Kay Mejia, and Rachel Kellis: Thank you, friends, for your eyes and ears and words and hearts.

To the readers, booksellers, and bloggers who have shown up for my books time and time again. Without you, there is no me. A special shoutout to: Anna and Charlotte (readsrainbow), Taryn (girlinread_), Dilly (justforqueerbooks), Lili (Utopia State of Mind), Chloe (theelvenqueen), Kailey Stewart, Cody Roecker, Mike Lasagna, Ally Scott, Hailey Harlow, Layla Noor, and a special thanks to Kay Frost for *Sofi*'s gorgeous Kids' Indie Next blurb.

To the best enablement team in the business: FJB, KP, CJ, and MG, thank you for offering me balance.

To Mom, Dad, Grandma, Dylan, Rosa, and Pat B: Thank you for everything all the time.

Finally, as always, to Kate—sometimes I still can't believe we get to do life together. Thanks for wrangling the puppy when I "just need to finish this chapter, just a few more words, I swear." It's never just a few, but I did promise you all my words forever, so you'll have to make do. Anyway, I love you.

ADRIENNE TOOLEY grew up in Southern California, majored in musical theater in Pittsburgh, and now lives in Brooklyn with her wife; their dog, Biscuit; eight guitars; and a banjo. She's the author of *The Third Daughter*, the Indie Next List selection *Sofi and the Bone Song*, and *Sweet & Bitter Magic*. In addition to writing books, she is a singer-songwriter and has released several EPs, which are available on Spotify and other streaming sites. She invites you to visit her online at adriennetooley.com and on social media @adriennetooley.